The House of Girls

'Though expatriates have lived in Arab lands for decades in pursuit of livelihood, meaningful cultural exchanges between them and the local people remain rare. Communication often happens from opposite sides of an invisible wall shaped by historical, social, and linguistic barriers. Consequently, Malayalam literature has only a handful of works authentically exploring Arab lives.

'Sonia Rafeek's novel bridges this cultural gap with remarkable sensitivity and depth. Through precise and unique observations, the novel vividly focuses on Emirati life, offering a rare and intimate portrayal. Infused with Arab folklore, astute life reflections, and a keen appreciation of nature, this novel stands out as a significant literary achievement. It not only narrates a story but also opens a window into a world seldom explored in Malayalam literature.'

—Benyamin, winner of JCB Prize for Literature, 2018, Vayalar Award, 2021, and Kerala Sahitya Akademi Award, 2009

'The stories of love, loss, suffering, helplessness and courage of three Arab girls shape this novel, which stands apart due to its striking theme and narrative style. It surprises us that in 1950 Arab world, along with the Emirati women, parallel narratives of Indians and Zanzibarians existed. This novel by Sonia Rafeek speaks about the agonies of women and the enslaved in a patriarchal society, which rings true beyond the divisions of tribes, languages and national borders. Along with the history and culture of the Arab world, the stories of women across the world have been seamlessly merged in the script. Undoubtedly, *The House of Girls* is one of the most powerful novels created in diasporic literature.'

—S. Hareesh, winner of JCB Prize for Literature, 2020, and Kerala Sahitya Akademi Award, 2019

The House of Girls

Sonia Rafeek

Translated by **Ministhy S.**

Published by
Rupa Publications India Pvt. Ltd 2025
7/16, Ansari Road, Daryaganj
New Delhi 110002

Sales centres:
Bengaluru Chennai
Hyderabad Jaipur Kathmandu
Kolkata Mumbai Prayagraj

Originally published in Malayalam as *Penkuttikalude Veedu* by DC Books

Copyright © Sonia Rafeek 2025

Translation copyright © Ministhy S. 2025

This is a work of fiction. Names, characters, places and incidents are either the product of the author's imagination or are used fictitiously and any resemblance to any actual person, living or dead, events or locales is entirely coincidental.

All rights reserved.

No part of this publication may be reproduced, transmitted, or stored in a retrieval system, in any form or by any means, electronic, mechanical, photocopying, recording or otherwise, without the prior permission of the publisher.

P-ISBN: 978-93-7003-032-9
E-ISBN: 978-93-7003-956-8

First impression 2025

10 9 8 7 6 5 4 3 2 1

The moral right of the author has been asserted.

Printed in India

This book is sold subject to the condition that it shall not, by way of trade or otherwise, be lent, resold, hired out, or otherwise circulated, without the publisher's prior consent, in any form of binding or cover other than that in which it is published.

'Your house is your larger body.
It grows in the sun and sleeps in the stillness of the night; and it is not dreamless.
Does not your house dream?
and dreaming, leave the city for a grove or hilltop?'

—Khalil Gibran, *The Prophet*

Writer's Foreword

That extraordinarily strong missive which pushed me out of my home was like a command, an appeal or even a revelation. It was the time of abject restlessness; I was tossed about by thoughts on what to write after *Herbarium*.

Those days, I used to go for walks in the districts of Dubai, places that were cradling ancient lore. Possibly because I was inspired by historical tomes, or had nothing better to do, and was lured by the enchanting climate. I would meander through the Deira, Bur Dubai and Al Shindagha districts. I adore such places. It was during such a wandering that I entered the Women's Museum in the Gold Souk. Never had I heard of such a museum. Except for the doddering old Filipino lady who handed over the tickets, the place was devoid of visitors. I was in the thrall of a new discovery. The museum called Bait Al Banat was originally a house belonging to three women. They were three 'girls' who had defied any manly succour all their lives and lived by themselves. Emiratis, natives of the United Arab Emirates (UAE), refer to all unmarried women, regardless of age, as 'girls'.

From the moment I entered that house, the impact on my creative life was ineffable. Because from that moment, the three girls made me part of their house, or made me their own. In other words, my body became their house and it became clear to me that unless I scripted their story, they would not let me be in peace.

However, after that first visit, my life diverged into many paths: translations happened, another novel took life, and many stories were born. Yet those women continued to love me. They were willing to wait for me patiently.

Meanwhile, the time of COVID crept in and the world became

confined to one's house. And the houses started bursting at their seams. My house assumed multiple roles—of office, school, hospital, restaurant, cinema, theatre, et al.—and kept away the external world safely from within. The house turned into a prison, determined to kill off introverted characters like me. I started contemplating many ways of escape and even indulged in some listless cooking experiments!

It was then that the girls inside me started chattering relentlessly: 'Let us free now, we want to live, sing songs, narrate stories, fall in love, dance around, fight our battles.' I became discomfited by that noise, but slowly started enjoying that chaos. It dawned on me that I could relish a solitary existence with them on a psychological plane.

I shared my ideas with some friends but even those who knew of my writing intimately ended up dismissing them. 'How do you think the Malayali reader is going to appreciate the lives of Emirati women living in 1950s? Why don't you reconsider?' Such queries were raised by many.

My girls and I slipped into abject depression. Dark days followed. Totally helpless, watching and listening about COVID-related deaths, I found myself anticipating such an end for myself.

But neither am I used to such hopeless waiting, nor do I believe in such morbid brooding.

I started reading as much as possible, and scoured libraries for books on the history of the UAE. This was the time that I started conversing with Arab women. Reading history has always been my passion: it wounds me and also stimulates me. In my perspective, history is an awakening of human beings to a great story which has been written. As my research into the UAE's history traversed many stages, my girls started dancing in joy, circling me while clapping their hands.

My writing began—about three ordinary women, glossed over by history. However, the flow wasn't there, and I started worrying about my audacity in attempting such an adventure. Innumerable

Writer's Foreword

anxieties pushed me into darkness again. My father passed away unexpectedly. Owing to COVID, I could not attend his last rites. Since I haven't seen his face in death, I am yet to believe that I have lost him. Waking to reality is not the trait of a writer and for me, my father's death continues to be fiction. I firmly believe that in my ability to visualize it in that manner lies my true strength.

My writing slipped into a lethargic phase. When COVID protocols were eased up a bit, I travelled to my native land. The forced quarantine period shoved me back into writing. But I found myself unhappy with the structure of the novel; indeed, it was not a happy time for my words. My own voice was accusing me from within, 'You are not like this when you write!' I returned to Dubai after a month and light started creeping back into life in general. Filling my novel with another novel, I started strewing stories within it aplenty.

The Arabian Nights are not just the legendary *1001 Nights*, but also the umpteen stories told by Arab women. They skillfully wove in many folk tales to make their children sleep, to teach moral lessons to their growing sons and wayward husbands, to keep lascivious predators at bay, to handle their inner turmoil, and to turn their own fears to cinders. A bunch of Arabic folk tales, collected assiduously from many sources, have become part of the narrative. There were apprehensions that the flow of the novel would be affected by their inclusion. But the youngest of my girls, Shamsa, is a true-blooded storyteller. Her very existence revolves around stories. She cannot help telling stories!

So many characters became part of my book: those who have lost their houses, those who left their houses behind, those trapped within houses, those fighting to retain their houses... The music of love started percolating into the house of my girls. The flame kindling inside me during the entire duration of creating this novel was of love. The unique 'I' split up into many women, including those who had abandoned me long ago. And in their lives, both my dreams and imagination merged spellbindingly.

Meanwhile, the much-awaited guest dropped in—COVID-19 knocked at my door—and gifting me well, returned amiably. My house lay wreathed in pain, feverish and nauseated, and utterly insecure. My girls prayed for me. They had known by now that their freedom lay in my resurrection. The guest departed without causing much damage. COVID taught me about the sheer uncertainty of life, making me realize that 'tomorrow' was a hazy dream. The new life truth happens to be: *So long as it is, may it be.*

I vowed to finish the novel in three months' time and turned my writing into a sacred ritual. My girls welcomed me with a sumptuous fare—they danced, creating melodies in the strings of Oudh. They seated me lovingly in their swing, and swung me high.

As my writing progressed, I noticed the changing expressions of the Buddha statue inside my home. The figurine, which had granted me serenity in every inner mayhem, unanimously raised a question, 'Why did you subject me to house imprisonment again? You very well know that I had long renounced home.'

'The world is another home, isn't it?' I replied.

The Buddha smiled at my temerity.

Then my girls spoke to the Buddha: 'We have struggled a lot not to be pushed out of our home. Dear Buddha, it is very easy to renounce your home, but very challenging to reclaim it.'

My Buddha sighed on hearing that, and so did I.

Sonia Rafeek, Dubai, 2025

Nazia Hassan

I AM NOT A WRITER, AND my reading is rather limited. Indeed, I have hardly any literary friends or a library membership.

I don't read books; books end up reading me. As each page flips, I become more and more revealed to the author and her characters. When my privacy gets severely encroached upon, I usually shut the book. If I were to read a three-hundred-page novel, imagine the thousands of eyes which would be swooping down on me! No, it's better not to read; let some peace prevail.

And into such hands as mine, the courier delivers a book!

It was a Saturday—a busy day in hospital. After completing the formalities, I received the parcel and hastily put it under the desk. While I was hurriedly tucking it away, the crystal vase holding the red Gerbera flowers toppled over and water spilt on the desk. As I mopped the drops with a tissue paper, the administration officer started glaring at me loathingly. Apparently, he was peevish yesterday about how the receptionist dared to be late by five minutes after lunch! After the latest 'watery' escapade, would he proclaim that 'my cup of sins runneth over'?

When the winding queue to take the out-patient token was done with, I tore one end of the parcel and took a surreptitious look. The book had a blue cover. Poking my forefinger inside the parcel and opening it wider, I caught a glimpse of the last few letters of the author's name: '*...ssan*'.

I hid it under my desk even as my heart beat wildly. As I cracked my knuckles anxiously, the ENT department called me, enquiring about a patient's insurance papers. Retrieving the file, I moved forward. Then retracing my steps with double speed, I pulled out the parcel beneath the desk and slipped it in my handbag.

An object of that proportion was being fitted into my bag for the first time. The bag's zip refused to cooperate and turned recalcitrant. The edge of the book sort of burgeoned from the partially open parcel. As I walked away with the bag, the other receptionist, Matilda the Filipina girl, gestured 'what's happening?' The Bengali lad who was busy cleaning the floor wondered loudly where Nazia Didi was rushing off with her bag! Not answering anyone, I scurried to the pantry. Hiding the bag in an empty rack, I raced to the ENT department with the insurance file.

I hardly saw Lizzy the nurse, whom I call 'Lizzy Chechi', coming towards me with a plastic cup filled with tea. We collided and half the tea ended up on my blue coat.

'What on earth is the matter with you? Are you driving the metro rail?' Lizzy Chechi was annoyed.

Handing over the insurance file to her, I murmured apologetically, 'Chechi, trust me, I am having a horrible day! Everything has gone crazy since morning…'

'Do join me for lunch, Nazia! It is tapioca and fish curry today…leftovers from Friday's cooking!' Lizzy Chechi smiled at me. Giving her a thumbs-up, I continued to walk. Not displaying any lethargy associated with her pregnancy, Lizzy Chechi stepped inside the doctor's room.

Until the lunch hour, my mind was filled with the book cover and the alphabets which I had glimpsed on it. When Matilda asked me to join her, I pretended to be busy. I ignored Lizzy Chechi's message reminding me of our lunch session. When everyone reported back to work after their lunch, I sidled up to the hideout, grabbed the book and rushed into a washroom. Wiping my perspiring hand on the trousers, I dumped the wrapping in a bin and seated on the toilet seat, stared at the book as if gazing at a mirror.

The novel's name was *Bait Al Banat*.

The sky shone from the book cover's upper part and the deep blue of the ocean, from below. The yellow of the sand dunes was in the middle. With a pang, I touched the name of the author: Nazia Hassan! My finger stilled on my name, and my palm became sweaty again. I feared that my pinkie, shivering dreadfully like the tail of a lizard, would detach itself. To convince the woman in the next cabin, I pressed the flush button and emerged tremblingly. Then I walked back to the reception with that book protruding from my bag.

'Nazia, why didn't you come for lunch? That Tina gobbled up everything in seconds! Now she is happily snoring away in the examination room!' Lizzy Chechi griped.

'I will binge on your tapioca and fish another day, Chechi.'

'Are you not feeling well? Issues related to periods, eh?'

'No, no… I am still reeling from the sins accrued because of yesterday's late arrival. Let me get back to work, Chechi.'

With what utter ease Lizzy Chechi saunters into every room with her bulging tummy, greeting everyone so cheerfully! The book which landed in my hands seemed to be heavier than that eight-month-heavy stomach.

I saw many 'sea-sights' in the faces at the hospital queue. Young men, dowagers and girls, who brought to mind sea shells and coral reefs… Though I continued working till the evening, my only companions were a tremulous voice and darkness-filled sights.

As usual, when I was leaving work, I knocked at the door of Dr Anees Sayyid Amin. He was examining a patient. As I waved goodbye and gently shut the door, he hailed me, 'Hey, just a second, Naz!' When I opened the door again, he asked, 'Anything wrong?' I winked to allay his worry and retraced my steps. I had known that he would raise a red flag. Dr Amin could discern the minutest change in my facial muscles. When I asked him once about that special acuity, he resorted to Da Vinci for elucidation. Apparently, Da Vinci, who had mastered human anatomy, knew the structure of the nerves and muscles controlling the lips. That was why Mona Lisa's smile created so much perplexity! He convinced me that such minutiae contributed to his deductive capabilities.

Possibly there was some truth in it.

Dr Amin was from Egypt. Aged around sixty, he has wide eyes, a sharp nose and a bald head. I call him 'Peace Amin'. He is always so peaceful and serene. There were many tumultuous events which unfurled in the hospital. Never has a small wave of disturbance risen on his face. He was born smiling perhaps? What other nickname for somebody so peaceful, a connoisseur of music and food, possessing a fine sense of humour, and always surrounded by friends?

As I sat in the Dubai metro train, clutching the novel which I hadn't written, I peeked at the photograph of the author on the back cover. In it, I was gazing at an approaching ship at the Jumeirah Beach and the sun's orange hues were reflected on my cheeks. My hair was waving in the wind and the singular sparkle in my eyes was caused by the artist behind the camera. Before I could read the description beneath, the train reached the station. Settling myself in an empty chair in the waiting area of the station, I turned the first page. As if possessing a legally banned object, I covered the book with my bag, and furtively started reading it.

Bait Al Banat: Foreword

For me, the city of Dubai has been a place of curiosities. Especially the creek and the humming of lives around it. The creek at Deira does to Dubai what the Nile does to Egypt and the Thames to London. Though the commercial centres created by waterways have always enamoured historians and travellers, my perspective has been different.

That day, I had gone to that place with a very beloved person. As we wandered in the Gold Souk market in that small port city, unexpectedly the signboard of 'Women's Museum' struck me. If at all there was a museum for women, we were not going anywhere without visiting it first. When we stepped in, hand in hand, never did I imagine that it would be the beginning of a novel like this one! The locals referred to that building, which was built in 1950s, as 'Bait Al Banat'. This house, where three unmarried women resided, was turned into a women's museum in 2012.

'Bait Al Banat' means 'The house of girls'. When I became obsessed with that house and its surroundings in my thoughts and dreams, I had to write their story. Let me share with you the love, passions and rebellions of those three Arab women...

Nazia Hassan

1959, July 10, 11 p.m.

Mariam was not asleep. Eight years ago, on a night similar to this one, when both the sky and the sea were swollen with heat, her Baba had left home. She retrieved a red silk bag from the almirah carved from sandalwood. Shamsa and Soraiyya were in deep slumber. Ahmad Manzuri had shipped the almirah from Bombay when the house was being constructed. The panels had carvings of tuskers, and the edges had intricate designs of flowers, leaves and creepers. The inmates of the house had seen the long-tusked elephant only in the woodwork and in clothes shipped from Bombay. 'Baba, is an elephant larger than a camel?' The girls would wonder aloud. Ahmad Manzuri would laugh. Maybe he himself was unaware of the colour and size of an elephant!

Spreading the Haseer mat woven from date palm leaves, Mariam sat cross-legged with the red silk bag in hand. She was apprehensive about Soraiyya waking up. Soraiyya disliked bringing ancient relics to life by caressing them. That too, vestiges of Baba's memory.

Mariam was the eldest of the three sisters. She looked older than her age of forty-five years. Soraiyya was nearly forty-one. Shamsa, the youngest, was in her thirties. In that coast, no one ever marked their ages accurately. Tantamount to assessing the time by looking at the sun's movements, people judged how old anybody was by looking at their bodies. The house where the unmarried trio lived got its moniker, 'Bait Al Banat', years back. In the Deira shore, any Arab woman who was unmarried remained a 'girl'.

Mariam was rather short, with a curvaceous body. When she let down her curly hair, it covered her posterior. Neither Soraiyya nor Shamsa had such beautiful hair. Both would grieve that their late mother, their Ummi, had gifted exclusively Mariam the tresses. Soraiyya was stubborn by nature. She was slender and tall. Between her two sisters, she stood majestically like the flagmast of a ship. Soraiyya wasn't given to much laughter or tears but she was loquacious. She would stride through the souk and the streets without batting an eyelid. Mariam tended to be deferential.

She could not haggle with the traders like Soraiyya. She was interested only in embroidery. In Shamsa, one could see the amalgamation of both her older sisters. She laughed delightfully and was skilful with words, narrating anything with the finesse of a story. There was another world inside Shamsa, a secret world without the sand dunes, sky and sea. Her face was oval shaped, and anyone would cast a second look at her long eyelashes. Lush, joint eyebrows was her unique feature, which her sisters did not have.

■

Mariam gathered the white pearls in the red bag close to her heart. When she dipped her face into their shiny, round surfaces, the warm waters of the Persian Gulf spread their saltiness on her blooming cheeks. She popped a pearl in her mouth. Swishing it against her teeth, she checked its quality. A real pearl would be rough, and the fake one smooth. Had Soraiyya seen her, she would have questioned the need for remembering such trivia.

True, the world no longer viewed pearls from the Persian Gulf as the finest of their ilk. Yet, it was not easy to forget the splendour of those times when Ahmad Manzuri had ventured into the seas in his big ship full of workers to collect pearls. When the business died down, most of the families in the coast had been driven to penury. But her Baba had overcome those adversities by discovering other business avenues. As a result, when neighbours lived in *barastis* made of woven palm leaves, or hovels crafted from sand and lime of sea shells, he could build a concrete house like Bait Al Banat.

Mariam curled up on the Haseer mat until the *subhi* or call for dawn prayer arose from the Omar Ali Bin Haider Mosque. In the sweltering month of July, the sun woke up before five in the morning. In the four-roomed house, there was only one window. In the room where all the three sisters slept, there was a small square window with two iron bars, beyond the reach of their hands.

Mariam opened the front door wide. Putting water to boil, she sat on the doorsteps and pounded the coffee to make *kahwa*. The children asleep in the barastis had awoken due to the din created by the souk's sellers. They raced through the narrow streets, chattering one to a dozen. Very few of them went to school. In the single school in Deira, a teacher had recently arrived from Palestine to teach mathematics and the Quran. His predecessor from Bahrain had left the shores barely a month after his arrival. There was no decent place to stay, no income to eat three meals a day, and the students could not afford to pay any fees. He had left, a sickly man, griping about the inconveniences. Flies had been buzzing near his eyes which had been dreadfully infected and his legs had been swollen as if by filariasis. The children who had gone to bid him goodbye had wept all the way back home.

Mariam felt a twinge of jealousy watching young girls, dressed in white tops and blue skirts, troop to Fatima Al Sahar, the new school in Al Rigga Street. Kuwait government was providing them with free food, books and even footwear. And they had excellent teachers from Egypt. In the morning, there were classes for unmarried girls, while the afternoon sessions were for married women.

A little boy thrust a clay bowl at Mariam. His Ummi had asked him to borrow some coffee beans from Bait Al Banat. Mariam dropped a fistful of beans into that bowl. The boy made a sound resembling the siren of a ship and whooshed through the souk's shops, back to his house. Mariam dropped the powdered coffee into the boiling water and covered it with a lid. After a while, she added two cardamom pods and a few threads of saffron to the concoction and poured the kahwa into the old Dallah flagon. That particular brass container belonged to Nafisa, Ahmad Manzuri's Ummi.

Nafisa stayed in the barasti—-with the palm leaf thatch—-in close proximity to Bait Al Banat. They had all been staying in that small hovel before shifting into the new house. Nafisa had refused to stay with her grandchildren in the concrete house because the four walls seemed to suffocate her. Her barasti let the breeze blow inside, in every season. Besides, she could hardly step on the concrete floor which would burn her feet. She could stand firm only on the sand floor inside her own hut. Khadeeja, the slave woman, was her bosom companion. Nafisa and Khadeeja brought up the girls after their mother died during the third childbirth.

Though Ahmad Manzuri was proud to own one of the first concrete houses in the Deira region, he did not live there long. After marrying a second time, he shifted to Jumeirah. Nafisa consoled her granddaughters saying that when a man became rich, he often behaved in such ways. Why would he live the rest of his life remembering Yasmin who surrendered to death without even giving him a son? She placated the girls by justifying that their father had no reason to stay single when he could afford to offer *maher*—pre-nuptial marriage gift given to the bride—and get a wife for himself. In reality, Nafisa had freed her son by taking over the responsibilities of her three granddaughters.

Shihab Manzuri, Ahmad's father, had been a deep-sea pearl diver. Thousands of people had dived into the comparatively shallow depths of the Arabian Bay, seeking the precious secrets hidden in the oyster shells. In the daytime, the sea was aquamarine in hue, while it tended to shimmer at the slightest turbulence at night.

It was his father who showed the young Ahmad the sight of the variegated pearl-like drops of water which scattered as the oars of the boats swooped and rose rhythmically. Ahmad accompanied his father from the tender age of six, in order to learn the work. He would be astounded to watch the sea snakes swimming on their backs. Ahmad Manzuri had narrated the story to his daughters about the snakes wriggling and lashing their way through the surface of the sea, exposing their shiny, yellow-coloured undersides. These creatures were utterly terrified of the sharks under the water. The twelve-year-old Soraiyya had querulously asked why her baba hadn't captured one for them to play with! Though younger than Mariam, she was skeptical of what she heard. She never trusted anyone. Indeed, a sharp-witted trader was inside her even at that young age.

Ahmad Manzuri had his own explanation for the pearl inside the shell. 'An oyster shell yearning for a pearl lay waiting inside the sea for the rain. When the sky changed hues, the sea responded tumultuously. Then the shell would rise to the surface with an undying wish for a pearl. Ingesting a small raindrop, it would descend to the depths happily. The mother shell would carefully drape the raindrop with her multiple layers and keep it safe in her heart. It would recline there like an unknown precious secret.'

When Soraiyya would vociferously argue that the teacher at Al Ahmadaiyya madrasa had given a different explanation, little Shamsa would start narrating the secret of the pearl's origin as a story. Her discovery was that oyster shells swallowed the raindrops filled with moonbeams. Shamsa's gift for stories flowed strong even now; children from Shindagha, much beyond the souk, dropped in to listen to her fantabulous tales.

'Soraiyya... Soraiyya, wake up! The kahwa has gone cold. What sort of a sleep is this? Look, Chhota Kishan is waiting outside!' Mariam almost tossed her sister out of the bed.

Chhota Kishan was the grandson of Kishan Lala who had migrated from India to the Arabian coast as early as 1850. No one knew his real name. Lala was a big-time moneylender. Everybody in Deira borrowed money from him. Most of the traders in the souk were indebted to Lala, who fleeced them with exorbitant rates of interest. Though Lala's family was very well off with their trading and moneylending, Chhota Kishan wasn't a part of them, and lived by himself. His family would occasionally board the British steamers to visit India. It was a journey of ten days. Often, they returned after many months at a stretch. Chhota Kishan was rumoured to have broken into his grandfather's shop during such a visit, and having robbed enough money, set the place on fire! After that incident, he became an outcast in the family. Though he indulged in many business ventures, nothing succeeded. After he became a taxi driver, he started doing well. The taxi, which ran between Dubai and Sharjah, belonged to Soraiyya. Apart from the taxi, she also owned a perfume shop at the souk.

'*Sabah-al-khair!* Didi, the taxi needs some repair work and cannot run today,' Chhota Kishan said. Before the taxis started plying, the only way of travelling to Dubai from Sharjah was through boats crossing the Khan creek.

'How come the taxi is always having some problem or the other?' Soraiyya sleepily approached the door. She was clad in a kaftan with red flowers embroidered around the neck. Around her head, she had carelessly wrapped a black *shayla*, a headscarf. Chhota Kishan wasn't as tall as Soraiyya. His attire comprised a loose kurta and pyjama. Soraiyya felt queasy on seeing his long hair, which was oiled and combed flat.

Though women conducted different kinds of businesses in the souk, Soraiyya was the only one to own a taxi. Chhota Kishan cribbed about manoeuvring the vehicle through the *sabkha* saline terrain, where mud and clay fused inexplicably. In utter dread of sinking, he had apparently resorted to following the tyre marks of the vehicles that had gone ahead. Whenever the tyres became mired in slush, he would disembark and curse profusely, with his hand on the head: 'Go and see Apollo Road in Bombay! This wile place shall never see such roads!'

Counting all the vehicles in the Deira, Bur Dubai and Shindagha regions, the total number of taxis turned out to be thirty or so. These belonged either to the sheikhs or to British officers. Petrol was not available sufficiently either. 'Yet I drive this taxi and manage to give you money every day, Didi!' Chhota Kishan would argue vociferously. Soraiyya had long realized the gift of the gab of the bania traders from India.

She hurled the taxi key towards Chhota Kishan. However, he tarried, as if wanting to say something. 'Do you need some money?' To Mariam's whispered question, he nodded anxiously in reply. Retrieving five *ek rupaiyya* notes—one-rupee notes—with the imprint of the Ashoka pillar from her thread box, Mariam tucked it into his hand. When Chhota Kishan reverentially touched the notes to his eyes before depositing them in his kurta pocket, the Ashoka pillars from across the sea experienced the warmth of the breeze. Chhota Kishan had never noticed any hesitation on the part of the natives in carrying out commerce in a foreign currency or any sense of lacking because they did not have any currency of their own. The waves carried multiple things into their land, and they seemed to take this aspect too in their stride. 'Don't tell Soraiyya Didi about the money,' he requested Mariam before taking his leave.

Mariam went back to her embroidery. Over the round *Khajoojah* pillow—round cushion that craftswomen used to spread cloth— on her lap, she spread the sleeve of Shamsa's dress and started embroidering it with silver threads. In most of Mariam's creations, one could perceive the remnant of a lost love. The *thawb*, the traditional costume that she had stitched for Safeera, who lived in the street beyond the souk, was evidence of the poignance within her. The dress was awash with weeping doves. Many tittered later that the bride abhorred wearing it for her wedding.

In every one of Mariam's handiworks, the signs of Farhad's lost love would be present. Soraiyya used to remind her intermittently that he was leading a good life in Germany with his wife and kids. Farhad was their cousin, the son of their Ummi's brother. They had grown up playing together. Girls were never married off to strangers in those parts. Mariam had been betrothed to Farhad at a young age. She safeguarded the memories of her passion for Farhad deep in her heart.

Mariam remembered a day of her youth. Every full moon night, the women would troop to the Khor region, near the creek. Though they did not know how to swim, the ladies would gleefully play, splashing water on one another. Fully dressed, they would submerge themselves in water till dawn broke. It was the night of women and no man dared walk that way! But Farhad used to hide behind the *abra*s, the wooden boats, on the shore, waiting for her.

Leaning against one of the fishing boats, Farhad would hum the song of the famous Egyptian singer Umm Kulthum for her. He adored the song that the lady, eulogized as the 'Star of the East', sang while launching Radio Cairo. That was the only medium which connected young men like Farhad to the world outside. It was through Radio Cairo that the twenty thousand-odd population got to hear of the political developments of the Arab region and the fluctuations in the price of crude oil, while living in their thatched hovels on the small coastal town.

Farhad always had big dreams. He was unlike those lads who stopped their education after learning some mathematics, the Quran, and the classification of different types of pearls at the Al Ahmadiya madrasa. Though girls could go to school, they were allowed only to learn the Quran. Knowing fully well that writing was allowed only to boys, Farhad taught Mariam the letters. While holding her hand and teaching her, he would murmur, 'Learn well. I shall take you to the land of the English speakers.'

Farhad occasionally sang Umm Kulthum's famous song, 'Al Awela Fel Gharam'.

First, he entangled me in his love,
Second, he commanded me to wait patiently.
Third, he vanished without any warning.
The one who blazed a fire in me with a mere look,
Where is he now?
Where shall I find that love again?
The promise of a return is like a goodbye;
I bid farewell to myself, my hand on my heart.
The only solace are my eyes—
They weep generously even now...

Shamsa caught a glimpse of Mariam's tearful eyes. Fondling her hair affectionately, she sat beside her. The younger woman gave her patient company until Mariam regained her poise, and then she left silently. Shamsa's language of emotions worked that way. Hers was an indescribable presence; sometimes, it was as if she spread her fragrance in the whole house like an incense.

After sipping the kahwa that had been prepared, Shamsa donned her *abaya* and stepped out to meet Yakub. She expected him to be in front of the customs office at the Khor. Yakub's work was to unload the merchandise from ships. Yakub was the son of Khadeeja, the child of a slave woman. When Ahmad Manzuri returned from Zanzibar in the summer of 1909 after purchasing timber to make boats, there were two petrified travellers in his ship. A reed-thin woman purchased as Nafisa's handmaiden from the slave market of Zanzibar, accompanied by her four-year-old daughter. His wife had scolded Ahmad Manzuri, wondering why he had got another girl to the house instead of a boy. The young girl with the stricken look in her eyes, who had held on to her mother's hands for dear life, slowly became part of Nafisa's own life. Her name was Khadeeja. Her mother died after a year or two due to an unknown disease. Nafisa tried to save her, as she lay writhing in severe stomach ache, by trying all the herbal medicines including 'Halol'. She even brought a Sayyid from Deira to tie an amulet with verses from the Quran around the woman's neck. But she died soon, leaving the little girl behind. Khadeeja grew up to be part of Nafisa's family.

When Khadeeja grew up to become Mariam's and Soraiyya's companion, Nafisa arranged her marriage with another slave called Hilal. The couple continued to live with the family even afterwards. Of their offspring, three died before reaching the age of ten due to multiple sicknesses. In 1930, very late in the marriage, Yakub was born. Khadeeja was around twenty-five then. Yakub was one-and-a-half years younger than Shamsa.

Today, Shamsa was carrying a piece of kunafa, semolina-based dessert soaked in melted sugar, for Yakub. The sun was scorching. The indigo colour from the burqas hiding the women fish sellers of the souk seemed to leak and paint blue stripes on their faces. Shamsa did not wear the burqa which covered the eyebrows, nose and lips because it was not mandatory for unmarried women to don those.

Sandra, Varun

AFTER REACHING THE FLAT, I showered and changed my dress. The tea stain on the uniform resembled an unknown continent. Should I soak it in soap? No, I was not in a mood for that!

I stretched on the cot with my book. The last book I had read was almost four months back. *My Autobiography* by Charlie Chaplin.

I had jotted down a few lines on my notepad:

'Like everyone else, I am what I am. An individual, unique and different, with a lineal history of ancestral promptings and urgings; a history of dreams, desires, and of special experiences, all of which I am the sum total.'

The book which I purchased at the previous year's Sharjah Book Fair had been kept aside for a while. For the first time, here was a book—*Bait Al Banat*—which could not be relegated to the side with the assurance of reading it sometime later!

As I started the second chapter, the doorbell rang shrilly. I raced around the room in a frenzy, trying to hide the book. First, I nestled it under the pillow, then pulling it out, I tucked it away at one corner of the bookshelf, then finally settled it in the drawer where I kept my lingerie. There is no other owner of those, except me. In my schooldays, I used to keep Samad's love letters safely in my sanitary napkin packet. There was no one to wage war over that in my home! After all, it was an 'untouchable' object whose mere presence was embarrassing for others.

When the door opened, Varun walked in. He works in a designing firm at Jebel Ali. By the way, he is awfully proud of his thick, curly hair, usually tied in a pony tail. Asking whether Sandra hadn't returned yet, he slumped into the sofa. Hurling his shoes to one corner, he loosened his necktie and then gazed at his phone. Usually, I tend to have tea with him, chatting about all and sundry, but today, I found myself trying to escape him. Indeed, I had the feeling of indulging in something sneaky.

It has been a while since I have pitched camp with Sandra and Varun. They were conducting a 'living together' experiment. Sandra told me just yesterday that it might culminate in marriage, but that she wasn't ready to bet on it. Sandra and I go back a long way—we studied in the same school in our native place. We weren't childhood friends or anything close. It was during a school alumni meet in Dubai that we had met again. This city connects people so fast! Except for a few changes brought about by Dubai city, she remains essentially the same girl. The branded clothes, the tattoo on her arms, coloured hair, the occasional binge of beer and the English which she spouted often…well, these were Dubai's contributions.

'Why are you so flustered?'

Sandra fished out my discomfort the moment she stepped into the house. She stopped me when I tried to wriggle away from her questioning. With an intense cross-examination, she unearthed my secrets. Finally, I untangled the book from the hooks of the brassiere and showed her. I stood sheepishly, as if exposing a naked body.

'Oh, fuck! *Bait Al Banat*, written by Nazia Hassan!'

I narrated the whole story: the courier who descended like a bolt from the blue, the accompanying panic…

'Stop, did you check the address from which it was sent?'

'Some Mumbai address… I don't know anyone there.'

'Even if you have nobody in Mumbai, someone managed to write a book for you… Great!'

Sandra looked at me knowingly, scratching at her tattooed arm. I was left speechless.

'It is he, undoubtedly! See, I had warned you so early not to fall in love with these crazy writers! Now, we will have to see what more he shall publish under your name… If you end up seeing some porno snippet in your name, don't get shocked, okay?'

'Why do you imagine such extreme complications? He'll never do such a thing!" I replied.

Sandra hadn't bothered about any warnings when she started living with Varun, did she? That too at a time when it wasn't legal in this country! Varun, who was snoozing, woke at the sound of Sandra's voice and asked whether coffee was ready. When he did not get any response, Varun walked into our room.

'Girls, what's the matter?'

'Nothing, I'll get your coffee.'

Probably Sandra took the easy way to mollify me. But she would definitely discuss the issue with Varun. There were no walls between them. When I had started living here, I was worried about intruding into their privacy. As the days went by, I realized that even if ten people lived with them, their invisible network would continue as strong as ever.

In this flat, which has two balconies giving on to the Shaikh Zayed Road's glittering show lights, the smaller bedroom is mine. When I came seeking refuge at their door on a December night, with nary a purse in my hand, Sandra had promptly given me shelter. Except for the receptionist job at Al Zahara Hospital, I had nothing to depend on in the city. The way I had ventured out that bone-chilling December night without even a jacket! My pyjamas and top had been drenched in the drizzle; my fingers had frozen due to the cold wind. It was an unbelievably horrible experience!

It was my legally wedded husband who had pushed me out of the door that night. Viewed in that perspective, one cannot find fault with Sandra's unconditional trust in Varun, her sweetheart. Their relationship has neither the backing of relatives nor of law. I had all of those in my marriage.

'Nazia, have you dozed off already?'

When I opened the door, Sandra was standing clutching two wine glasses in her hands. She wore a sleeveless top and shorts and her face was glistening with the night cream she had applied. I always feel that she looks prettier at night than in the day. After darkness falls, her face becomes radiant in the yellow light of the room. When I mentioned it, she countered by questioning whether I was the reincarnation of an owl.

'Look, the work of art which can be ingested!' Handing over the bottle of wine, she clambered into bed and sat with a pillow on her lap.

'Miss Nazia Hassan, what's your plan now?'

'What plan? I shall go to work tomorrow, return and go to sleep as usual.'

'You mean to say that this book has caused no change in your life?'

'I got it just today and I have read only one chapter till now.'

'Nazia, you are acting way too cool. You are tense!'

'So what? What if I am tense?' One wine goblet slipped from my hand and shattered into bits. Sandra got up wordlessly and moved out of the room. Pretending that I had not intentionally let it slip, and that it had fallen accidentally, I started gathering the splinters. Sandra was rummaging through my almirah for the book. I rushed towards her, shoved her out of the room and latched the door. I could hear her lambasting me as she spoke to Varun.

'That brat! She did not even let me touch that book... We have heard of serpents guarding treasures inside groves and caves, haven't we? She has turned into a snake herself! Will spit out venom if anyone touches her book.'

Varun was murmuring something conciliatory. I did not bother to call her back or listen to their talk further.

'Are you okay?'

I ignored Varun's WhatsApp message.

Pouring some wine into the goblet which had lost its partner, I sat down to read.

∞

Shamsa uttered Bismillah and inserted a delectable chunk of kunafa into Yakub's mouth. The solidified milk melted in his tongue, along with the sweetness of her fingers. A long sliver of semolina hung from Yakub's thick, dark lips. In the moist breeze, it kept rhythm with the lip's movement. Like testimony to a lifetime of unhesitatingly obeying orders, springs of Yakub's hair always stood alert and ramrod-erect. Shamsa felt that each lock of his hair was an eye, keeping watch over her with tenderness and care.

She would always bring him a keepsake whenever she visited. Yakub loved desserts. Sometimes, Shamsa would gift him bottles of *ittar*, perfume purchased from the souk. When she would dab drops of perfume behind his ears, Yakub would protest lovingly, 'This is meant for beauties like you, Shamsa. Not for the likes of me!'

Every Friday, Yakub would visit Khadeeja at home after partaking in the Jumu'ah Namaz. During those times, Shamsa would stay afar. Khadeeja knew of the snags in their relationship.

'There is a camel race at Jumeirah this Friday. Why don't you come along?' Yakub cajoled her.

'*Habibi*, my love, would you haul me up on your shoulders like the merchandise from a ship?' Shamsa giggled.

'*Habibti*, my beloved, I shall stitch the sails of ships to your beautiful eyelashes, and you shall come floating in the wind…'

'Hush, hush…think you are a great poet, don't you?' Shamsa teased and flicking the thread of semolina from his lips, put it in her mouth.

'Why? Can't I recite poems like Mubarak Al Oqaili? Aren't the children of slaves allowed poetry or songs?' He playfully scattered dust over her.

'Ha, here comes a poet! Have you seen Al Oqaili's house? Apparently, it cost around 18,000 rupaiyya! It is so mammoth in size. The doors and windows are of teak wood and the roof of sandalwood! A double-storeyed house with an inner courtyard. Nowhere in Deira would you find another like that.'

Yakub looked crestfallen. With eyes bereft of smiles, he stared at her. 'Shamsa, never will I be able to offer you a home like that.

Ya Allah, O God! Why did I have to be someone who can never fulfil your wishes?'

'Yakub, I desire nothing but you. You are everything to me!'

'Shamsa, I am a slave. My Ummi works in your home even now.'

'Why do you keep saying that? Don't I know it?'

'Our wedding...will it ever take place?'

'What if it doesn't happen? You and I are soulmates. We shall continue loving each other like this till death,' Shamsa argued.

'What about our children?'

Shamsa sat with downcast eyes. When a faraway ship hooted its siren, she lifted her head and said, 'Do you see the mast of that ship? Where is it from?'

'*Habibti*, I do not know.'

'I do not know either. What if we were to escape in it? Yakub, we cannot live together in this land. Let us go away somewhere else...' Clutching his hand, Shamsa walked forward.

'Crazy girl! Who shall ever come to my aid? A slave is a slave in any land!'

Wiping her tearful eyes, Shamsa said, 'You shall never abandon me...leave me desolate like Farhad did to Mariam... That is enough for me, Yakub.'

She leaned against his chest. A few lads driving donkeys laden with vessels brimming with drinking water from the well at Al Hudaiba, shambled past them. The animals were straining due to the heavy barrels dangling on either side of their bodies. The lads were hitting them mercilessly. Seeing the embracing couple, the boys started whistling lasciviously and spouting filthy abuses. With their unshod feet, torn and callused, they kicked sand on the lovers. Vexed by the disruption, Shamsa and Yakub got up and started strolling on the shore.

Ahmad Manzuri had been persistently calling Yakub to work in his new house. But the young man knew that if he did so, Shamsa would become inaccessible like Rub' al Khali Desert to him. Even when he toiled in the scorching sun, his back bent over like a labouring donkey, Yakub did not wish to leave Deira.

'Shamsa, will you come for the camel race?'

'Yes *Habibi*, I shall be there to see the winning camel smeared all over with saffron!'

That answer did not emerge from Shamsa, but from an unseen male hiding behind them, mimicking a woman's voice. Yakub sprang up and peered around.

'Beloved, I shall come along to see the camel smelling of saffron...'

The same falsetto mimicry rang out again.

From behind the lumps of Sisal ropes meant for building boats, a head popped up. Yakub hauled him up by the hair.

'Ibrahim, you wretch, get up!'

Ibrahim, the ship worker, was eavesdropping on the lovers' conversation. He was all of nineteen, and a rogue. Being a handyman on a ship was a job just for the heck of it; Ibrahim's main interest was smuggling. He was involved in the racket of smuggling gold to India. It had been two years since Ibrahim and his gang had renounced the small skiffs used for pearl diving and started building huge boats which moved fast—those being rigged with engines made in Pakistan.

'What are you busy poking your nose into? Are you hell-bent on leading astray every youngster of Deira? Everybody wishes to accompany you to the sea... You rascal, can't you earn your living honestly?'

Yakub gave him a hard knock on his head. Ibrahim rubbed his scraggly hair and muttered, 'It is gold, not liquor or drugs. And gold is not banned here by the way...the sale is forbidden only in India.'

'Yes, and you sell it in India stealthily, don't you?'

'You ask Indians to stop salivating after gold first! They are never satiated with the yellow blocks!'

'Who said only Indians love gold? We Arab women adore it too! Only, we do not have enough wherewithal to buy it,' Shamsa became chatty.

'*Subhan Allah*, glory be to Allah, it is a lucrative business! But one should keep everything surreptitious, that's all. I attach the engine in six hours and the gold is shifted in a jiffy. Then, it is a furious take-off! No one should know when the stuff was shifted and when it will be unloaded. Usually, we aim for the festival days when both the coast guards and police are busy. When we near the shore, we strap the gold blocks around our waists, using belts. On seeing the light of our Dubai boat, a fishing boat will approach from the Indian shore. A secret code is exchanged and the material is handed over. Simple!'

When Ibrahim stood preening, with his hand inside the *kandura* long dress's pocket, Shamsa raised a question.

'What if the fishing boat does not come on days of storm and rain?'

'We wait for a few days and return with the gold.' The lad was leering at Shamsa's smooth, shiny cheeks. Yakub slapped him on his shoulder.

'You better scram! Your Ummi must be waiting for you with *kuboos* flatbread,' he snarled.

When Ibrahim hitched up his soiled kandura and started to move, Yakub held him back by the ear.

'By the way, remember that the date palms are our Ummi and the sea, our baba. The origin of all earnings should be from these.'

'As if you belong here! You are a slave from some foreign land. How can the date palm and the sea be your mother and father? Huh!'

Yakub freed him on hearing those words. Untying the *keffiyeh* scarf on his head and holding it aloft in the breeze, Ibrahim raced away like a ship unleashed from the port. When he reached the customs office, Ibrahim held the pillar and swayed mockingly.

He heckled loudly, 'I heard you begging a few moments ago… *Habibti, Habibti*, let us go watch the camel race! Is the camel your uncle by any chance?'

Yakub ignored him since he was beyond the reach of his hands.

Shamsa and Yakub watched the Louha bird, with black wings, dive in and gulp down fishes. A British steamer named *Bandra* was nearing the coast. Ahmad Manzuri used to board the same ship to visit Bombay annually. The Indian jewellers crafted exquisite necklaces using pearls. Ahmad Manzuri purchased those and brought them to Deira. He would then export them to Paris, from where they travelled to the jewellery boxes of rich American women. The stevedores thronged the port seeing the ship. Yakub bid *Ma'a Salama* goodbye to Shamsa.

She walked through the narrow gullies of the souk towards her home. Beads of perspiration dripped from the edges of the shayla, down her face. Vendors were hailing buyers from either side of the street with tempting offers. There was a bustling crowd around. Bedouins could be sighted among them, with their fiery, tough faces. Shamsa loathed the sight of the guns strapped on their shoulders and the *khanjar*s daggers tucked into their waistbands.

In the olden days, going by Nafisa Jadda's accounts, in the street called Sikkat Al Khail, filthy rich men like Sheikh Dalmukh used to canter by on horseback. That was how it got the moniker 'Horse Street'. Jadda used to babble to her grandchildren that there were no gold or sapphires then; just a few Omani silver tradesmen and dagger sellers!

It was an Indian called Hari Lal arriving from Bahrain who had established the first gold shop in the souk. Shamsa reached the front of Hari Lal's shop and caught sight of Chhota Kishan, who was following her slyly.

'What's the matter, *bhai* (brother)?' Shamsa asked querulously. When he stood stunned, she turned her back contemptuously.

'Shamsa *behan* (sister), I need to tell you something! Would you like to have a samosa?'

The delectable fragrance of fried samosas wafted all over the street from the Bombayite Ram Charanji's shop.

'Samosa is good enough, but I don't feel like having it now.'

It was out of the ordinary even to be seen chatting with strange men in public places, let alone acquiescing to such strange requests! Shamsa wondered what had possessed Chhota Kishan and walked on. But he persisted in accompanying her.

'Shamsa *behan*, Soraiyya Didi is a very fine woman. I really like her a lot.'

Shamsa glared at him.

'Don't be mistaken in my intentions, *behan*. I plan to take Soraiyya Didi to India with me.'

'At least it is clear that you are troubling me because you did not have the guts to speak about the matter to Soraiyya. Am I a five-year-old that you could bait with a stupid samosa? If I were to divulge this at home, you shall be fired from your job!'

'*Behan*, I really mean it...please don't misunderstand me...'

'Better stop now! The women of these shores never marry out of Islam. You know that, don't you?'

'I mean, I'll marry Soraiyya in India and she'll live like a queen...'

'Any idea how old she is, compared to you? Move out of my way...'

By the time Shamsa reached Bait Al Banat, the call for the *dhuhr* prayer—one of the five mandatory prayers—rang out loud. Removing the shayla and rolling up the sleeves of her abaya, Shamsa sipped water from the earthen pot. Soraiyya was nowhere to be seen. She could hear the sounds of Mariam taking a bath in the small bathroom attached to their house. Rice and fish were kept in the kitchen, covered with the *mikab* cover woven from date palm leaves. A salwar suit, newly stitched, was folded and kept on the cot.

Mariam had prepared Safi fish for lunch. Nafisa Jadda adored that fish. The cold water with low salinity, and thriving with a rich biotic life, flowed from the Indian Ocean through the Hormuz Canal and Ras Al-Khaimah and merged with the waters near Deira. That was the time Indian mackerel, anchovies, and tuna fishes swam near the Deira shore. Jadda would send Shamsa to purchase the mackerel, since she loved roasting those. Shamsa packed some Safi fish and moved towards the barasti. Jadda was counting the prayer beads.

'How cool it is inside this hut even in the blistering heat, Jadda!' Shamsa exclaimed. Khadeeja would often pour water on the four square walls of the hut. Shamsa experienced the moist breeze squiggling its way through the gaps of the woven date palm leaves. As Shamsa lay her head in Jadda's lap, Jadda caressed her hair.

'Would I have lain on your lap like this had my Ummi been alive?'

'Why do you ask that? Would all mother-daughter relationships be the same?'

'Jadda! Aren't all mothers very loving towards their daughters?'

'There are those who are different, my child…'

'True… I have heard of such a story too. A folklore from the remote village Giza in south-southwest of Cairo. Zaira, the girl who studied with me in the madrasa, told me this story.'

'This girl never forgets a story even from her childhood days. What a sharp memory you have! *Masha Allah,* Allah has willed it! Tell me, let me listen to it.'

Shamsa wrapped her arms around Jadda, and hiding her face in Jadda's lap started narrating the tale.

The name of the story was 'Fatima and the Pickled Fish Head'.

A man and wife had a daughter named Fatima. Her father died early in her childhood. The poor widow would beg around from morning with a bowl. One day she got two kuboos *and a pickled fish head. She raced to her house and entrusted the fare to her daughter.*

'Fatima, keep the kuboos and pickled fish head safe. I shall return soon.'

Then she set off to beg some more.

After Ummi left, a weary dog came inside their hovel. Fatima's heart welled up with pity and she thought of feeding the dog a bit of kuboos. The dog eagerly gobbled it down. Fatima kept feeding it with more tidbits until there was no kuboos left. The dog became a bit perked up, though it still had a famished look about it. What if the pickled fish head made a difference? When Fatima extended the fish head towards the pitiable creature, it swallowed the delicious offering in one gulp.

After some time, Fatima's Ummi returned.

'Fatima, fetch me the kuboos and pickled fish head. Time for us to relish the feast.'

'Ummi, I gave the food to a sickly dog,' Fatima said.

'Damn you! You are fibbing, must have eaten it all by yourself!'

'No Ummi, I did not. God is my witness.'

'You ate the two pieces of kuboos and pickled fish head by yourself.' Ummi raged and riled. 'You prefer a dog to your own hungry mother, don't you?'

She hit Fatima and sent her packing from the house.

Fatima laboured on until she reached the precincts of a large palace with a beautiful garden. There was a dustbin nearby. She rummaged through the dustbin hoping to find something to eat and ended up salvaging two dry crusts of bread. The maid of the prince saw Fatima and informed her master. He saw her through the window and ordered that she be given refuge in his palace. Thus, Fatima ended up as a maid in the kitchen. After a while, with proper food and care, Fatima blossomed into a lovely young woman.

One day, the prince saw Fatima and fell in love with her. He asked the Queen Mother to get her married to him. Though his mother protested against his desire, mentioning that nobody knew Fatima's whereabouts or her origin, she finally succumbed to the prince's insistence. Fatima ended up leading a luxurious life in the palace. And one day, she saw her old Ummi wearing tattered clothes, scavenging for bread near the dustbin.

Fatima ordered the maids, 'Bring the old woman to the palace immediately! Bathe her, clothe her well and feed her.'

The next day, she went to visit her Ummi. The woman could not make out that the stunning young lady before her was her own daughter, Fatima. When she introduced herself, her Ummi protested vociferously: 'You? Aren't you the selfish girl who ate two kuboos and one pickled fish head, all by herself?'

'No Ummi, I gave it to a hungry dog, I swear!'

The old woman went on griping endlessly. Fatima stepped out of the room after instructing the maids to take good care of her mother. The old woman lived in the palace in utmost comfort but whenever she would see Fatima, she would say, 'You ate the pickled fish head and two kuboos.'

Finally, when Fatima was fed up, she said to the servant, 'Take this woman, kill her and bury her in the garden.' They seized the woman, killed her, buried her where her daughter had said. On that spot where they buried her, a sapling sprouted.

One day, when Fatima was relaxing with the prince on the balcony, she heard a high-pitched voice: 'Aren't you the selfish girl who ate two kuboos and a pickled fish head all by herself?'

When a befuddled Fatima gazed in the direction of the voice, she saw some dwarf women, hardly a finger's length in size, swinging their feet from the branch of that tree which had grown huge over the years. They were repeating her Ummi's unfounded accusation in unison! Fatima burst into hearty laughter at the sight of the ridiculously tiny women singing that line, from the peculiar seating place.

The prince wished to know why Fatima had laughed. She tried to evade giving an answer. However, he persisted that she was mocking him. 'Either tell me why you laughed or leave the palace immediately!' Fatima was struck by a bright idea. She said, 'O Prince! On seeing your magnificent beard, I was remembering my baba's royal palace. He has a pearl-strung fishing rod and my Ummi, the queen, has a golden broom!' The prince was impressed and stated that he wanted to visit his in-laws. Now, Fatima was at her wit's end. She packed a few things and surreptitiously left the royal palace.

She walked until it was night. Then, she rested awhile and started eating some food. A dog came near to her. Generously, Fatima shared half of her dinner with the creature. Recollecting the events of her life, Fatima burst into helpless tears. 'Why are you crying?' the dog asked. When Fatima recounted her sad tale to the dog, it warmly reassured her. 'Go back to the prince. Tell him that you shall show him the pearl-strung fishing rod and golden broom tomorrow. I shall show you the way.'

Fatima followed the dog's instructions. The next day, the dog showed the way as the prince's chariot rolled on the royal pathways. Soon, they arrived at a magnificent palace. It was twice as splendiferous as the prince's own palace. Inside, there was a fishing rod studded with pearls as large as eggs! And there was a golden broom. The prince was immensely pleased. The dog whispered to Fatima, 'I am the same dog whom you fed the two pieces of kuboos and the pickled fish head.'

The first thing Fatima did on her return to the prince's palace was to issue a royal command. The tree on which the dwarf women sat swinging their tiny feet and singing that hideous song should be immediately chopped down!

When the story was over, Shamsa sat up, tied her hair and asked Jadda, 'Was our Ummi like Fatima's? A scary harridan who scolded Mariam and Soraiyya?'

'Yasmin was a gentle soul. Always busy with some work! In the morning, she would be making *agwa*—paste made of boiled dates—and in the afternoon, she would be busy weaving Sarood mats. Mind you, by the evening, she would hurry to fill vessels with water from the well at Sattwa. She would stay up late embroidering and stitching clothes. Yasmin made all the abayas and kanduras for all of us. The delicacies which she prepared for Ramadan, those were extraordinary in flavour! Shamsa, she gave birth to you on a full moon night. I took her to the wooden pillar behind the barasti and made her sit on her haunches. All the women in the family delivered babies there. Well, I did not see what transpired afterwards. Khadeeja was the one who received you in her hands. Your Ummi lay bleeding for two days in the barasti. After my Yasmin's death, Khadeeja became my only refuge.'

'Jadda, if the Makhtoum Hospital had been there in those times, Ummi would not have died, would she?'

'Death shall transpire when Allah wishes, *binti* (daughter). If she were alive, all of you girls would have been married by now.

Your baba thinks only of making money! *Astaghfirullah,* I seek forgiveness from Allah!'

If mothers were responsible for getting their sons married, the marriage of daughters was the exclusive responsibility of fathers. When their compatriots were wedded at sixteen and seventeen, the three sisters had spent time creating dresses, telling stories and selling perfumes in the souk.

Shamsa tried to imagine Ummi again. Her face changed along with the stories. In the whole world, maybe she alone had an Ummi who could not be pinned into an exact picture! Shamsa decided to keep aside the pickled fish head's tale for the Friday storytelling session with the local children.

∞

When Shamsa was bidding farewell to Jadda, Khadeeja came racing in, yelling, 'Engleesi, Engleesi...!' Stepping out, Shamsa saw a plump foreign woman walking into Bait Al Banat along with Soraiyya. She was dressed in a knee-length skirt, sleeveless top, and wore a hat. Soraiyya was carrying the white woman's footwear. Unable to handle the scorching floor, the woman was almost hopping around. When she had got helplessly stuck in the sand while walking in her stilettoes, it was Soraiyya who had asked the woman to remove them.

The woman was a British journalist who had come to see Dubai. She wished to take some photographs, study Arab customs, and see the desert... Chhota Kishan had enticed the unsuspecting victim from an airline's hotel at Bur Dubai. After showing her around for ten days, he wished to amass some handsome Maria Theresa thalers. The Deira residents were familiar with the wives of British officers who lived in Oman and other adjoining regions. But it was for the first time that the women were seeing an independent woman who had crossed the seas by herself.

Nafisa Jadda wondered aloud, 'What does she want to discover in the desert?'

She asked Khadeeja, 'Is she planning to study our lives and imitate that in her own country?'

'I guess so. What else?'

'Does she get dates there? Does their sea have Hamour fish? Surely they have abayas there?'

'No...'

'Then what is the use of studying all these?'

Khadeeja shrugged and rolled her eyes. Then she sighed, *'Allah Ya Alam.'* Only Allah knows.

Chhota Kishan had battled with all the English words he knew during the trip from the hotel. But on seeing Soraiyya, the foreign woman burst forth into a series of *'As-salamu alaykum, Kaif halak, Ma Ismi...'* (Peace be upon you, how are you? My name is...), and he gaped idiotically. And soon, the lady started conversing with Soraiyya in Arabic without any inhibitions.

Though the foreigner's name was Rosa, Soraiyya addressed her as Ummu William, William's mother. Rosa's son William was in England. Soraiyya was used to calling people the traditional way, as mothers of their progeny.

Apparently, Rosa created an uproar in the taxi during the trip from the hotel, protesting about the insufferable heat. Chhota Kishan had moistened a few pieces of cloth and spread them on the glass panes. Yet, Rosa sweated profusely. She had spread a kerchief across her lap and rested her perspiring hands on it to avoid contact with her dress.

Soraiyya invited Rosa to the *majlis*, the visitor's room, and dusted the red-seated armchair. Rosa struggled to fit herself into the chair, which was very low-slung. Removing her hat, she fanned herself with it and started making small talk.

When Nafisa opined that Rosa's hair reminded her of a Persian cat's mane, Soraiyya shushed her hastily. Soon Mariam stepped in with *sulaimani*, spiced black tea, enriched with saffron threads. Rosa stroked the delicate embroidery on Mariam's dress and wondered aloud, 'How about stitching an abaya for me?'

'Listen, how beautifully Ummu William speaks Arabic!' Soraiyya preened as if Rosa was her rare possession. When Rosa enquired whether Soraiyya and her sisters would accompany her during the desert trip, Nafisa demurred.

'These girls have never moved out of Deira. The only place they have visited is my sister Ayesha's home in Ras Al-Khaimah!'

'That's not true! Did we not go to Abu Dhabi for Ramsina's wedding? We stayed in a green, nice *wadi*—the bed or valley of a stream that is usually dry except during rainy season—during the journey. I haven't forgotten the trip to Al Ain either! What a dust storm that was! Jadda, your memory is very poor,' Shamsa teased.

Nafisa couldn't come to terms with her granddaughters staying with the English woman in tents made of *bait al sha'ar*, goat skin, like Bedouins! She tried to argue that Khadeeja and Chhota Kishan were more than good company for the foreign woman. Finally, Mariam tactfully lured her recalcitrant grandmother away from the room, murmuring that it was time for the next prayer.

Rosa's husband Mark Brighton had died in Dubai. All the emirates, along with Oman, had once jointly been known as the Trucial Coast. In 1936, Brighton had been a young engineer in the PCL Company, which was into oil exploration. Rosa and William were informed that Brighton had died of malaria, but the real cause remained unexplained. While sharing her husband's story, Rosa's anguish was visible; her eyes welled up with tears.

'Do not cry, Ummu William! Teardrops are sacrilegious over here…tears are pearls hidden in the eyes. Keep them safe!' Soraiyya spoke softly.

As she stepped out to leave for the hotel, Rosa peeped into the well in front of the house. It was full of maggots! As she turned away in revulsion, Khadeeja soothed her, 'We use the well water only for washing clothes and cleaning vessels.' She elaborated on how they collected fresh rainwater during the cold season by spreading clothes in the yard and attic.

Soon after, the women started preparing for their ten-day

journey. Even travelling to Shindagha, adjoining Deira, was an adventure! So this trip to Abu Dhabi was not frivolous. Khadeeja helped in packing food and water for the long trip. When she asked them to take Yakub along to ensure safety, Soraiyya was averse to the idea. 'You add Chhota Kishan, the camel keeper, we three girls and Ummu William...that's quite a lot of people already!'

The next week, Chhota Kishan, the three sisters and Rosa set off for the desert on two camels. There was a mule to carry their luggage. Shamsa remembered Yakub then. Carrying the relentless burdens, the man's spine had started curving in. Yet his arms were strong, and his heart was compassionate.

The camel owner's name was Zahran. During a small break, when they rested in the shades, the man fed dates to his camels as if they were toddlers. He would first give the creatures water before taking a sip himself. The hard dates from Iran were first immersed in water to soften them. Zahran would carefully grind them and form balls of date-paste before feeding his camels.

One camel's name was Anoud. The other was her offspring. His hump was yet to develop fully. Zahran dipped his leather bucket into the well, and sniffed suspiciously. Only after ensuring the purity of the water did he offer it to Anoud. During certain trips, clean water was hard to come by. Then Zahran would pinch Anoud's nostrils shut, while helplessly giving her the foul-smelling water.

Mariam took out the sweet dish *batheeth*, made of dates, wheat flour, spices and nuts. Rosa refused, citing diabetes. 'Don't worry about it,' Zahran said and walked away purposefully. His aim was the patch of green behind a far-off sand dune. Soon, he returned with some plants. Giving them to Rosa, he sagaciously suggested, 'These are *hansalan* creepers, real medicine! Even if the plant happens to be very bitter, make a paste of it and drink it.' It was a creeper like pumpkin, with a spiky stem and round fruits, snaking over the sand.

When Rosa was busy wrapping the creepers, Chhota Kishan piped up, 'Memsahib! Why go through three tiring days' journey? In my Toyota, I can get you to Dubai in just a day!'

'We have Toyotas in England too!' Rosa cast a scathing look at Chhota Kishan.

Ever since the stone pathway connecting Abu Dhabi Isle with Dubai was built in 1950, very few resorted to camels for the journey. In the olden days, one had to wait on the shore with the entourage of camels until the tides ebbed. A soldier was on duty at the border post, for keeping records of those who crossed the frontiers. Khan Sahib, the merchant who got the stone pathway constructed, had put up a signboard which said 'SLOW'. Rosa recollected reading somewhere that it was the first traffic signal of the Trucial Coast. Zahran interrupted her thoughts by opining that the locals were clueless about the purpose of that enigmatic signboard!

Zahran quickly milked Anoud and offered it to Rosa. The rest of the milk, he stored in a bag made of goat skin. He was busy calculating that when the milk fermented into *leban*, he would offer to Rosa again and she would delightedly give him a Maria Theresa thaler! Those were thoughts that naturally sprang up in the minds of the residents of Deira on sighting white-skinned foreigners. Mariam had heard the gossip that Farhad's migration to Bahrain and later to Germany had begun likewise when he went currying favours from a Britisher.

Anoud sank into the sandy depths. She sat facing the sun, her vast posterior hidden from the scalding heat. Meanwhile, Rosa dozed off, leaning against a date palm tree. Mariam and Shamsa whispered among themselves. They were out of Soraiyya's hearing, and were chatting about Chhota Kishan's desire. Women were never married off to a stranger's house, let alone a new country across the seas!

'Mariam, help, help!' Rosa shouted unexpectedly.

Mariam raced to her side only to see Abu Jalla beetles rolling Anoud's manure. One of the beetles had climbed onto Rosa's toes and was contemplating a way upwards when Rosa had woken up and screamed.

'Ummu William, do not be scared! Abu Jalla beetles are

collecting the balls of camel manure for their offspring. They will dig holes in the sand and save this treasure before laying their eggs. Their little ones will feast on these manure-balls when they emerge from the eggs.' Rosa flicked her toes with revulsion and ran to Anoud's side. Zahran grinned widely, his long teeth resembling date palm seeds.

'Ummu William, this is nothing... There is a camel spider under the sands! You should see his speed! When he bites, it stings like hell, but it is not venomous, okay?' Mariam neared Rosa and whispered into her ears, 'But he is a smart aleck! The females are larger than the males. During mating, the males caress the females with their forelimbs, making them shudder and shiver for a few moments. In that time, the male completes the mating ritual. Then he runs away for dear life because the female will surely consume him after she gets up!'

Rosa started giggling, clapping her hands like a little child.

'Would you have shown me all these in the Toyota, my lad?' Rosa slapped Chhota Kishan on his back playfully.

Though Rosa tried to capture the photographs of the bugs and spiders during the journey, the creatures could not be sighted again. When *hamad* creepers with high saline content became visible, Zahran let Anoud free for grazing. Anoud had a weakness for the yellow flowering *arfaj* shrubs too. Chhota Kishan suggested that they set camp for the night considering the eventide. The tent was erected and everyone settled in for the night. The Persian carpet was spread on the sand, and the hurricane lamps were lit up. Chhota Kishan and Zahran stayed with Anoud and the donkeys, lying on the furry cloth which covered Anoud's hump during the journey. It was a moonless night, with only sand and wind for company. The hooting of a bird, similar to that of an owl, could be heard from afar.

'Are there any djinns in the desert, Shamsa?'

'Ummu William, djinns dare not come close where there is fire, salt, iron or the Holy Quran. There are both black and white djinns. Some are helpful while others are troublesome. Sometimes they appear from the trees, sometimes from animals… Some control human beings, and during those times, people commit strange acts and attain superhuman powers!'

'Do you know that the word "djinn" or "genie" came from the English word "genius"?'

'Genius? What does it mean, Ummu William?'

'Superhumans who are extraordinarily sharp and exhibit unimaginable prowess… The valley of Abghar in Arabia is renowned as the seating place of djinns. They were muses for creative souls… and it is a valley of poets now.'

'Ummu William, listen to this now!'

In Abu Dhabi, there was a fisherman called Ali. A good, decent man. He was good friends with his relative, Ahmad. They went fishing together and spent a lot of time with each other.

'Shamsa, stop! Is it a tale or…?'

Shamsa leaned over, and playfully pinched Rosa's cheeks.

'This is a real story, Ummu William…trust me!'

Rosa became enthused. Sitting up straight, she seemed ready to gobble down each of Shamsa's words.

Ah…so one day, both friends decided to meet at the seaside for fishing. Usually, the fish shoals could be sighted either early morning or at twilight. They had decided to meet at a rather forsaken spot near the shore before twilight set in. When Ali came in the evening, Ahmad was seen walking away towards the sea.

'Ahmad, stop a bit. Where are you off to?' Ali shouted.

Ahmad turned back, smiled and started racing away faster. 'Stop your game, wait for me!'

Ali panted. Ahmad ventured into the sea and soon disappeared into the waves. Ali followed him until he was neck-deep in the sea waters. He did not know how to swim, and could only cry out after his dear friend. Then he heard a voice hailing him from behind, 'Ali, what are you doing in the sea? Why are you here?' It was Ahmad! He had overslept after the dhuhr *prayers and could not make it in time.*

'So, who was it who had taken the guise of the first Ahmad?'
'Was it a djinn, Shamsa?' Rosa's eyes grew wide.
'It was Bu Darya, the devil of the sea! He wished to lead Ali astray!'
'Has anyone seen this djinn with their eyes?'
'Both fishermen and pearl divers have seen him, Ummu William! This Bu Darya or Baba Darya tries to frighten those who fall asleep in their skiffs at night. He drags them under the sea. That is why one or two men always keep watch while the others sleep. When there is a sudden turbulence, the watcher will shout, "Come fast with machete and sword!" The djinn Bu Darya disappears on hearing those words. He is monstrous in form, but due to his proclivity for appearing at night, nobody has seen his face clearly. Hiding in the dark, he snares *jalbut*s (pearling boat with capacity to carry tonnes of cargo) and boom ships in the middle and breaks them into halves, and pull them to the sea floor. Didn't that ship sailing from Ras Al-Khaimah to India sink on a windless, serene night? Sometimes he lures people on the shore to the sea using tricky lights and throws the corpses back onto the shore!'

Mariam interjected sleepily: 'Ummu William, don't believe Shamsa's tall tales. Bu Darya was a black slave. He is just taking vengeance against the atrocities perpetrated on him by his cruel owner. Can't a slave wreak retribution?' Shamsa snuffed out the lamps.

It took them another day's travel to reach the bait al-sha'ar encampment. Chhota Kishan had readied it for their stay. He had friends everywhere. It was a black fur tent with stripes of white. Among the multiple rooms inside, the majlis was for Rosa. An inner room was readied with woollen partitions for Mariam and her sisters. There was a room covered with date palm leaves where food was stored. Butter, flour, rice, et al., were stocked there. In the middle of the room was a huge sandy pit, meant to be a fireplace, surrounded by stones.

'I gave birth to William in India. There, in Calcutta, how many creatures appeared near the kitchen area: crows, cats, mice…but here not even an ant can be seen!'

'Memsahib! The partakers arrive when there is food to spare! Here in the desert, food is insufficient. So, all animals prey only on specific creatures according to the food chain. The chances of seeking anything from outside is meagre.'

Hearing Chhota Kishan's percipient words, Rosa felt that he wasn't as stupid as she'd presumed him to be. He posed for many pictures before Rosa's camera. Chhota Kishan forced her to climb a sand dune while inveigling her with the photograph of the sunset. When he returned to the tent, Shamsa was milking Anoud. Edging near her and desperately trying to start a conversation, he muttered, 'Shamsa *behan*, Anoud is soon going to stop lactating, right?'

'Don't worry, I haven't told Soraiyya yet!'

Chhota Kishan did not disclose that he ardently wished someone would tell Soraiyya about his heart's yearning! Just like Farhad was dwelling in Mariam's heart and Yakub in Shamsa's, there was nobody in Soraiyya's. Chhota Kishan was sure of that fact. But not a single woman had left Bait Al Banat for a man. The only one to leave was a man, the girls' Baba!

Rukhia Sultana

When I woke up in the morning, the book was by my side. Having enthusiastically read two chapters at one go, I mulled over taking a day off from work and continuing the reading spree.

'Today I am applying for sick leave,' I announced loudly enough for Sandra to hear.

Varun entered the room, while trying to fix his tie. When I struggled to sit up straight, he sat by my side.

'Don't worry too much, dear! First you finish the book. We will decide on further course of action later. Sandra is really anxious about you.'

'I have started reading, Varun. But the going is very slow… After reading a bit, I find myself lost in thoughts…'

'No worries, take your time. Let me leave now. Take care.' Patting me affectionately on my shoulder, Varun left the room.

Of course I know the three Emirati women—Mariam, Soraiyya and Shamsa. I have been to Bait Al Banat. No doubt, that was only after the house was turned into a museum, a women's museum! When I stepped into it for the first time in 2017, the laughter, tears and peeves of the three women had risen like water vapour from the walls and enveloped me. Though there was no picture of the trio, I imagined their faces based on the objects they owned. With great accuracy, I inscribed within myself all the love that they had given and received. The man who had taken me to the house had sworn that nobody would be able to understand the women as much as I would.

Sandra made some sandwiches before leaving for office, and placed them on the table.

'Make a cup of tea for yourself, Naz. I am sure you'll be on the bed grappling with this book even when I return in the evening.'

I curled up tighter, avoiding her gaze.

I was sinking into the warm familiarity of a lap. My face pressed against the yellow flowery polyester dress. Someone was caressing the tendrils of my hair. Her long fingers, adorned with many rings, were exploring my forehead. They gave off the scent of ittar and curry spices.

I could hear a slow hum…

Aap jaisa koi meri zindagi me aaye
Toh baat ban jaaye…

The famous song by the Pakistani singer Nazia Hassan.

I opened my eyes, and Rukhiyami stopped singing. It was my aunt Rukhiyami, or Rukhia Sultana, sister of my father, who named me Nazia Hassan. 'Rukhiya Mami' had coalesced into 'Rukhiyami' right at the beginning. Like the girls in Bait Al Banat, I too had lost my mother very early in life. Rukhiyami was everything to me, and she had found the name for me. She was an ardent fan of the Pakistani singer and had cassettes of all her Hindi songs. When Nazia died of cancer on 13 August 2000, Rukhiyami had lamented deeply. She had shed tears as if I had died when my namesake passed away.

My parents had wanted to name me 'Sumiya'. Complaining that it was a name ridden with termites, Rukhiyami started calling me Nazia, without seeking anyone's permission. Soon, everybody followed suit. My father had to enrol me in school under the same name. Vappa had acquiesced unaware that Nazia Hassan was a teenage girl popular for singing disco songs. Else he would never have granted his only daughter the name of a girl who sang pop music on stages across the world, with her head uncovered. Truth is, my name itself is a tad tricky!

On the days Vappa wasn't at home, Rukhiyami and I would sway to the tunes of Nazia Hassan's music. After dancing around to the song 'Disco Diwane', we would be brimming with wild energy. Rukhiyami's husband Taha and my Vappa were business partners. Whenever they travelled to Ceylon and Tamil Nadu for procuring raw material for their business, the women would be left alone at home. My Umma was a silent creature. Probably that's why I did not miss her presence later. Or was it because Rukhiyami was always there by my side with the lusciousness of an eternal spring? I have no idea.

Rukhiyami is now aged, and stays with her son in the family home. In between, she travels to Qatar to stay with her daughter. When I asked her why she chose to name me Nazia instead of bestowing it on her own daughter, she smiled, 'You are the one with light.'

I sat on my bed, nibbling the sandwich Sandra had made. The curtain stayed in its place; I would rather not have light today. I love chewing on my childhood memories in the dark. Inside the family home with a low-tiled roof and small windows, darkness was rampant. The only light Rukhiyami could see was perhaps me! Most of us tripped over objects inside the rooms. Mice, cats, lizards and cockroaches encountered us regularly. Nobody could ever discover their hideaways.

Rukhiyami and I slept together on a cot, and most nights would be cacophonic with mice orchestra. Rukhiyami would quip: 'A house-warming ceremony of a mouse is happening underneath this cot. Madam mouse is serving *payasam* pudding to her honoured guests! Now, one little mouse starts puking. Unfortunately, he has eaten the sweet with strains of rat poison! Now his mother and relatives are carrying him off to the hospital…' That was how Rukhiyami began her fabulous stories. It began from any random thread, travelled through miscellaneous ways, and I would often slip into sleep before it culminated somewhere. She would refuse to divulge it the next day! She took delight in weaving a new story every night.

How can I, used to that storytelling, read a book? After reading two pages of any story, I complete it in my own imagination. When I return from my ruminations to the book and read the real story,

I get flabbergasted at the different turn it has taken! I would have packed off the characters mostly to other places. Having merged someone's story into my own, I would stand baffled, unable to separate the twain.

The distance between Shamsa and Rukhiyami is very short. The writer who took me to the women's museum, the same writer once commented that I had woven Shamsa from Rukhiyami.

Maybe if my mother were alive, I would not have been so intimate with Rukhiyami. When I was twelve, one night, I asked my aunt whether my Ummi too narrated stories. 'Not all mothers are alike. There are mothers different from yours and mine,' she had replied. And followed it up with yet another story.

Although it was with the preface that the story was based on an Algerian folktale, I gravely suspect that it was of her own making! The very script flowed in such a way.

Once upon a time, there was a woman. Whenever twilight set in, she would stand on her terrace and ask the moon: 'Hey moon, is there anyone prettier than me?' The moon would retort: 'You are pretty, I am pretty. No one prettier than you though!'

Meanwhile, the woman became pregnant and gave birth to a daughter. She named her Lalla. The next day, she came to the terrace and repeated her question: 'Hey moon, is there anyone prettier than me?' The moon replied, 'I am pretty, you are pretty. No one prettier than Lalla though!'

The woman blazed with jealousy. 'Prettier than me? Shall I kill her then?' The moon responded calmy, 'Sure, but after she stops breastfeeding.' Thus, one year passed. The woman repeated her query: 'Shall I kill her then?' The moon said, 'Not yet. Let her learn to walk and run.' After a few years, the woman started pestering the moon again. The moon replied, 'Let her learn to cook first.' After a few more years, the reply was, 'Let her learn to sew clothes.'

Lalla grew into a beautiful young woman. This time, when the woman asked the moon the question, it replied, 'Lalla is of marriageable age now, and you can kill her if you wish.' The woman sent Lalla to the forest with a butcher after gifting him money and ornaments. She ordered that Lalla's blood be brought back to her in a bottle as proof of her murder. The butcher could not bring himself to kill the lovely girl. He left her inside the forest and returned to the woman with a bottle full of goat's blood. The woman drank it and expressed her satisfaction.

Lalla, meanwhile, became devastated at the loneliness, hunger and thirst which surrounded her and sought refuge in a tunnel. When she woke up, she heard seven demons howling over the prey they had killed. She hid herself in terror. After the feast, the youngest demon said, 'I can smell human blood.' His brothers reprimanded him, 'You are a fool. There's nobody here.' When everybody slept, Lalla sneaked in and retrieved a bit of food and water for herself. When the youngest demon woke up the next morning, he started hollering: 'Told you, didn't I? A man has stolen our food and drink!' They searched everywhere but Lalla stayed hidden and safe.

'Rukhiyami, isn't this the story of "Snow White and the Seven Dwarves"?'

'Can't there be any other Snow Whites in the rest of the world? This is the Snow White from Algeria. Shut up and listen. No questions in the middle of a story!'

The demons started howling… 'If anyone is hiding, come out immediately!' When Lalla stepped out in fear, her astounding beauty floored them. They swore that they would treat her like a younger sister. She cooked for them, made clothes, cleaned the house, looked after them…

Lalla's wicked mother stepped out to the terrace and asked the moon: 'So tell me, who is the prettiest of them all?' The moon laughed, 'I am pretty, you are pretty. But Lalla is the prettiest of them all. She lives in the forest with seven brothers.'

The woman could not bear the shock of that revelation and died then and there.

In course of time, all the seven brothers fell in love with Lalla. 'I will marry her; I am the eldest!' said one. 'No way, I will be her husband, I am the youngest,' retorted another. Lalla found a way out of the conundrum. 'The one whose hands redden most with the henna paste shall become my husband.' She slathered the henna paste on all their hands but none had red hands at dawn. Lalla had cleverly made a paste of other herbs and not of henna.

One day, all seven brothers went hunting but did not return at eventide. When Lalla got tired waiting for them, she started eating some boiled beans. Then a cat wandered into her room. 'You have eaten my beans,' it meowed accusingly at Lalla. Lalla was outraged and emptied a whole sack of beans in front of the creature. 'I want to eat my beans!' It purred angrily. 'I have eaten your beans!' Lalla lashed out spitefully. The enraged cat pissed into the smouldering embers. Now Lalla had no fire to cook food or keep the cold at bay. Lalla stepped into the forest searching for fire.

Seeing the glow of fire afar, she went closer. It was the hut of a demoness. She gave Lalla some embers in a pot. Cinders fell wherever Lalla trailed. The demoness followed that trail and reached Lalla's home. She pummelled seven long nails into Lalla's head. Lalla became motionless as if she had died.

When the brothers returned, they mistook Lalla to be dead and started wailing in despair. They did not wish to bury her and so tied her up on a mare and let the creature loose in the forest. The mare reached a palace and the crown prince ushered it inside. The king remarked, 'Why, this is a corpse!' They entrusted the body to a woman for readying it for customary death rites. When the woman removed the seven nails while readying her, Lalla regained her life. The prince insisted on marrying the pretty girl. Finally the king obliged.

Lalla gave birth to a son. Once, when he was playing with the children of ministers, a squabble broke out amidst them. 'Your mother is a wastrel with no clan or home!' The young boy came crying to Lalla. She was agonized and spoke up: 'Tell your father that your mother wishes to see her seven brothers.' After a few days' search, the soldiers found the seven demons. Their heads were bowed, cast down with the pain of loss. They were invited for a feast to the palace.

After the repast, the son asked Lalla to narrate a story. Lalla started speaking about her life.

The seven brothers embraced her happily at the end of the tale. They went to the house of the wicked demoness and killed her. The demoness had seven beautiful daughters. Lalla got them married to her seven brothers.

'Married them to demonesses?' I protested vociferously and Rukhiyami snapped, 'Not possible to marry off demons to human women, right?' I felt that one's own mother thirsting for her daughter's blood was a bit too much of an imaginative twist. Perhaps, stepmother stories hadn't picked up pace by then. That was something the Brothers Grimm brought into vogue later. Whenever she narrated stories, Rukhiyami's face became rosy, her eyes sparkled, and the drape over her head slipped away due to the excitement.

■

When I fell in love with Samad at fourteen, Rukhiyami was the first to know about it. Samad was three years senior to me at school, and we became close when I was in the ninth standard. When Rukhiyami wished to see him, I invited Samad home for Eid. My uncle and father yelled at him and asked him to leave. Rukhiyami, who had prepared biriyani for him, watched the young boy with sprouting moustache go away with tearful eyes.

I have no idea how I fell in love with Samad, who belonged to a lower economic stratum, and how our romance blossomed for so long. But Rukhiyami knew. Indeed, she knows me more than my own self.

On the night I eloped with Samad, Rukhiyami had let me out through the front door. She had helped me pack my bags and was the only one to wish me the best for a bright future. She gifted me a gold bracelet, in case I needed money. My father never accepted the daughter who ran away with a wastrel at eighteen.

Rukhiyami is the lone link I have with my home. Vappa always hated Rukhiyami for supporting my elopement. Though they lived in the same house, they were distant, like two distinct satellites moving around a planet.

There weren't any problems in Samad's house. However, on the day our marriage was registered, Samad insisted that I shouldn't call him by his name anymore. I was shocked but I told myself that it was too silly a matter. Soon, the question 'what will others think?' became dominant in our relationship, turning every natural affection between us into mere formality. I dislike thinking about those incidents.

After a few months, when he received a visiting visa, Samad left for Dubai. He got a job in a relative's shop. I too embarked for Dubai without much delay and got a job as a receptionist. Samad assured me that with my twelfth standard education, it was one of the best jobs around. After five months, Samad started his grocery shop near the Al Karama Bus Station and our economic status improved steadily. Soon, many people, including Rukhiyami, started asking why we were not thinking of children. 'Why should kids have a kid?' I would retort.

Last week too, when Rukhiyami called, she teased, 'You are a kid, after all!' Yes, that's true. I have not been able to grow up till now. That's why Samad's constant consternation, 'What will others say?', leaves me cold. Now that I am staying away from Samad, my childishness seems to have gathered strength. When he forced me out of the house that bitterly cold night, I had sought Sandra's house, feeling like a discarded object. But in a few days, that feeling of desolation left me, due to the untrammelled freedom bestowed on me by both Varun and Sandra.

I am clueless about Samad's whereabouts. Rukhiyami kept calling me back home. But I know that my father would not want me there. Rukhiyami is still bedevilled by accusations from both her husband and brother for intentionally misleading an erratic girl who leapt into a wrong relationship at an immature age. When I separated from Samad, Rukhiyami sighed: 'Our decision was wrong, wasn't it, dear?'

'I realized it and hence corrected my mistake,' I laughed it off and ended the chapter effortlessly.

I realized that it was only afternoon when Sandra called me.

'Are you still immersed in the book?'

'No dear! I was busy brooding over the past...was thinking about Rukhiyami and Samad...'

'Why are you imagining melancholic stuff after taking the day off? We will go out when I return.'

As soon as Sandra's call was over, Dr Peace Amin rang me up.

'What happened to you? A sudden leave of absence?'

'Not feeling too good, doctor.'

'Is it the body or the mind which isn't feeling too good?'

There was no point in being evasive. I promised that I would discuss the matter the next day.

I remembered the cat in Lalla's story. The one who insisted on her own beans, and wasn't willing to accept the sack of beans offered. '*I want my beans!*' Sandra is very much like that cat. She always asked for what she wanted and never accepted an alternative. How many Christian boys her father had lined up for her to choose from! The number of boys who pursued the smart Sandra in school! Her attitude was always the same. 'These are not my beans.' She had wished to be an architect and her father had forced her to get married. Sandra had worked part time and pursued her studies. Though she got many job offers, Sandra chose Dubai to live freely with Varun. 'What will others think?' was a concern which became irrelevant in this place. Sandra became the cat which purred, '*I want my beans!*'

I had to freshen up before Sandra and Varun arrived. We would go to the Deira creek this evening. I sat down on the sofa with a soft drink and two cookies. As I opened the book and bit into the cookies, the yellow crumbs scattered like sand on the open pages.

∞

Mariam woke up very early. Mixing *sikkam* charcoal with *zaatar* leaves and salt, she cleaned her teeth. She prepared breakfast even before

Rosa awakened. It was Zahran who informed that Farhad's parents had left for Bahrain from their home in Shindagha. Farhad's twin children were staying with them at Bahrain. Soraiyya had immediately piped in: 'I had always known that! He is in Germany with his wife and is planning to educate his children in Bahrain. That's why he has asked his parents to move there. What is the need to while away time here with blisters in their heels? Trampling around these darkened shacks by the seashore, buzzing with mosquitoes and flies?'

Mariam interjected in between that soliloquy: 'The first time Farhad had gone to Bahrain was to our Uncle Abdullah's house. He had been so thrilled that day. I wanted him to have opportunities in life and not waste his life here. But Soraiyya, I had no inkling that he would never return.'

'He returned from Bahrain after two months, didn't he? We should have fixed your *nikah* (marriage) at that time! But our Baba was least interested in such matters. His whole focus was on minting money from pearls...spending six months at sea and another six in Bombay and other places... You also waited for Farhad, oblivious of the months and years passing by.'

Mariam went to the majlis. Sweeping clean the Haseer mat with the date palm-leaved broom, she spread the breakfast items on it. Then she waited for Rosa to wake up. Sighting the round *mahalla* bread with honey and butter as toppings, many houseflies started buzzing around. Mariam drove those away and covered the food with a *mikab*. She lit the fragrant *bakhoor* incense, whose perfume wafted all over the majlis.

Leaning against the round cushion, she closed her eyes. In the first homecoming from Bahrain, Farhad's beard had been shaved clean. When he arrived with a handsomely trimmed moustache and rosy cheeks, he had resembled the Egyptian actor Rushdy Abaza.

'*Habibti*, Bahrain is a totally different world! Roads, highways, majestic buildings... The souks are overflowing with crowds...! There are so many alluring objects we haven't even seen... Most are imported, exquisite pieces of clothes, ornaments with intricate craftsmanship, toys for children, radio, household implements, mouthwatering delicacies... The port is magnificent and many ships are anchored there. There are many trucks which arrive to transport material. I went to my friend's baba's place. There is an air conditioner which causes cool air! Typewriters, desks, clerks... everything a modern office needs! You have to climb into a box at the bottom to reach the top! Like magic, it conveys people from one storey to another. Until the watchman scolded me, I kept getting inside it and stepping out...haha...'

Mariam had been delighted to see Farhad laugh. She hoped that like the magical box he had described, their life together would also ascend to wonderful heights very soon.

Mariam wished to tell him about the special Dana pearl her Baba had brought, and about the *tawmina*—a festival to celebrate children completing their Quran lessons—when Soraiyya finished hers. She wished to narrate about how she tripped over a sackful of dry camel manure when she had rushed to meet him and how the seller had cursed her as *Ya Sharmootha!* (You dirty rag!) But not allowing her to interject, Farhad kept on speaking.

'I went to attend a sheikh's feast with my uncle. What variety of food items! A room full of variegated sweetmeats and fruits for a handful of visitors! I stood flabbergasted, as if caught inside the tapestry of the Arabian tales from the 1001 Nights! Sparkling vessels, gigantic chandeliers, exotic majlis, men wearing golden filigreed overcoat over snow-white kanduras... I could hardly eat anything because I was so overwhelmed.'

On the day Farhad returned to Bahrain in a ship, Mariam sat near the Khor after the subhi prayer. Passengers were being transported in small abras to the ship anchored at deep sea. Farhad was wearing a black coat. He kissed her fingers. Then he started massaging his collar bone. 'After a few days of sleeping on the ground, my back has started aching badly.' How could Mariam, who lived in the barasti made of palm leaves, guess at the softness of the mattress in Bahrain?

'Bathing in Deira's saline water, I have developed an allergy,' Farhad said. He had told Mariam about the pure water sprinkling down from the shower in Bahrain.

'Bahrain is our closest neighbour, but we are unable to catch up even with her. This country will never improve!' Those were his final words.

When Rosa nudged her, Mariam opened her eyes. Rosa was wearing the abaya that Mariam had stitched. She would pull it up while walking through the sand. Shamsa would tease her then: 'Ummi William, one should walk gracefully on the sand, like the Saluki hounds. You should not be stumbling around…'

Rosa went out and wished Zahran *Sabah-al-khair*. Zahran raised the stick in his hand and pointed it to the distance.

'Can you see a camp there? There are Bedouins there. Yesterday I watched them hunt a doe along with their Saluki hounds.' He had hardly finished speaking when two dogs came running like the wind and started sniffing around them. Rosa started howling with delight: 'How sexy!' The Saluki hounds had high thigh bones and narrow waists. Their almond-shaped eyes were covered with thick eyelashes.

'Salukis are more beautiful than you three girls! But I thought you were not allowed to touch dogs,' Rosa said and raced to retrieve her camera.

Zahran elucidated: 'Bedouins consider these creatures their very lives. They will never go hunting without them; they always accompany them in their travels… These creatures stay near the women in encampments. They subsist on anything, very low-maintenance animals…'

After clicking pictures of the Bedouins who came searching for the Salukis, Rosa tittered, 'The caption for this photograph shall be: Aborigines of the desert.'

Zahran stood confused, not understanding the word 'Aborigines'.

Chhota Kishan approached Soraiyya, who was washing plates behind the tent. 'Didi, the worker in the British steamer coming from Bombay brought these…wear on your toes, it will look good!' He gifted her with toe rings known as *fakht* rings.

'When you walk in the camp, hearing the jingle, I will make out it is Soraiyya Didi.'

'Chhota Kishan, not just me, it will make a sound if worn by anybody.'

'But I wish to hear the tinkle coming from you, Didi.'

'Why?'

Chhota Kishan held Soraiyya to himself and pressed his lips against hers. Soraiyya, who was sitting on her haunches, lost balance and tumbled backwards. Her abaya turned into the colour of sand.

'*Harami* sinner, I allowed you near like a Saluki! Have you behaved so atrociously with my sisters too? Tell me the truth!'

Chhota Kishan hurled the fakht rings far away and made himself scarce. Soraiyya entered the tent, agitated and trembling.

Rosa made the beleaguered Soraiyya sit on a cushion, and lay a consoling hand on her shoulder.

After listening to the matter, she murmured, 'Chhota Kishan is a decent person. To love is not a despicable thing.'

Rosa went back to the majlis. Shamsa had never expected Chhota Kishan to open his heart to Soraiyya directly. When she climbed a tall sand dune next to the tent, Shamsa saw him move away with the donkey. On returning to the camp, she saw Rosa crush coffee seeds with Soraiyya, while chattering with her.

'I don't need a man to protect me, Ummu William. We survived even after Baba deserted us, didn't we?'

'This is not an issue of offering protection, Soraiyya. It is a matter of love.'

'Perhaps. I don't feel any love for him.'

'Then I have nothing more to speak on the topic.'

From the gigantic *Yasra* leather water bag, Shamsa poured out water into a small *Yahla* pot and started washing the rice for cooking. Chhota Kishan had carried the heavy Yasra bag on his donkey all the way to the camp. When Soraiyya went out to clean the fish, Shamsa again returned to the topic. 'Ummu William, Baba's desertion of our family and Mariam's unfulfilled love, both have embittered Soraiyya. That's why she behaves like this...'

'I can understand that, Shamsa. She hasn't found love in the way I have.'

'Ummu William, every person should discover love like coffee seeds! Do you know that story?'

One night, a Yemeni goatherd went to sleep after corralling all his flock inside the fence. But even after midnight, the goats were not sleeping and were frolicking all over the place, instead! The goatherd was astounded since he had no clue about the source of their never-ending energy. The incident repeated the next night also. The goats were jumping around like children. The dumbfounded man approached the village wiseman. The old man observed the goats carefully. They were hovering around some shrubs in the hillside and eating up red berries and seeds voraciously. The wiseman plucked a few red berries himself and chewed on them, and experienced bountiful energy in his body.

That was how humans discovered coffee and became addicted to its pleasure!

'We should discover love like the goats found coffee seeds, Ummu William! Without understanding the whole thing, one should melt in its joy...'

'Shamsa, your mind is deeper than the Mariana Trench in Pacific Ocean.'

'Haha... We wake up seeing the shallow Persian Gulf. One can even see the atolls and coral reefs. Our sea is a mélange of both pure and salt waters. Perhaps we are able to accept any visitor with welcoming arms because we are born of such a sea! Any culture can mingle with us, with the perfect balance of salt and sugar...'

'Shamsa dear, I am familiar with this fact. Brighton had discussed it years before. Now tell me something new! I am eager to hear about your Yakub.'

While Shamsa started chattering about Yakub, Zahran stepped in seeking permission. There was a sandstorm outside. He sat in an obscure corner silently. They could see Anoud's yellow colour in the furiously circling sandstorm. Her long eyelashes stopped the sand specks from harming her eyes. Rosa suddenly caught on that the people around also were graced with luscious eyelashes. She hailed nature's innate knowledge of granting gifts appropriately, especially suitable to the circumstances.

Anoud shut her nostrils to evade the sand. Rosa was watching a creature who could do that for the first time in her life! She staggered outside to capture a photograph of that phenomenon, struggling to lift her legs which were getting swallowed by the sand. But she was soon rolling down the dune due to the brute force of the sandstorm.

'The storm is going to get stronger at night. We should leave the camp,' Zahran started packing hurriedly.

'Stronger than this one?' Rosa was bemused. She carefully placed her camera back in its cover. They all clambered up the camels. But in a short while, everything became invisible. The world which existed before seemed to have been part of some fairytale. Zahran stood still with the camels and the four women. When the dust subsided, they could see the façade of a building ahead.

'The Sheikh's palace!'

'Palace? This one?'

Rosa's mind had quickly compared the vision ahead with the palaces of England. Except for the huge courtyard inside the compound wall and the rather big house inside, there was nothing exceptional in that sight. Zahran took them to an unfinished building outside the wall.

Rosa remembered the great black smog of London in 1953.

'London was enveloped by pitch-black smog for three days in December. Even the ambulance service was shut down. So many died because of the pollution caused by the deadly black smoke.'

'Ummu William, this sandstorm vanquishes every one of man's inventions. Sand will spread inside any fortress; the thickest metal windows cannot keep it out. Nobody can evade it.' The smatterings of sand caught in Shamsa's throat made her melodious voice gruffy.

Rosa felt the grit inside her mouth; the taste of sand which no spitting could remove! Caught in the swirling, great force, houses, walls, trees all seemed to vanish inexplicably. Though Rosa covered herself with a blanket, it was futile. The house shook, and the sand rained on them. In the afternoon, the storm started abating, gasping to its grand finale. Like snowflakes, sand could be seen shrouding walls, houses, date palms and dresses. Dust covered everything human-made and naturally crafted. Rosa felt disappointed that there would be no rain to wash it all away. It would take days to sweep all that dust away. For the green to reemerge from the earth, it would take weeks. How many more days they would have to wait, until all that had been caught in the grips of the storm returned to earth!

The Creek

I SCRUBBED MYSELF SQUEAKY CLEAN WITH a loofa. There was this feeling that I was swathed in dust and grime. With shampoo, I washed my hair. That day, wouldn't Rosa have dreamt of luxuriating in her soap bubble-filled bathtub, back in her London home? Perhaps not. After all, she was a persevering, resilient woman. She relished facing novel experiences with an adventurous spirit.

From the almirah, I chose a dupatta and a kurta which had not seen the light of day for months. My usual attire at work was the uniform. During any shopping trip, I preferred to don jeans and shirt. I wear a salwar-kurta only when I feel like dolling up. Sandra arrived before long. Without waiting for a cup of coffee, she woke up Varun who was busy snoozing on the sofa, and we moved out.

'Please leave the book inside.' I was carrying *Bait Al Banat* along. Implicitly following Sandra's command, I went back to the flat to deposit the book.

'You look gorgeous! How long since I've seen you like this!' Sandra pinched my cheeks affectionately. Varun sleepily crept inside the car. He was still in his T-shirt and shorts.

'At least you could have changed that T-shirt! Do you know what I am planning to do when I cannot endure you any longer?' Sandra asked as the car stalled at the traffic light.

'Float me up in a hot-air balloon, I presume?'

'Nope! I shall tie you inside one of these boats near the creek. Let the seagulls peck you mercilessly!'

'How cruel, Sandra!' Varun started pulling at the fraying threads of her sleeves. When Sandra tried to slap his hands away, the car swayed on the road.

'Naz, aren't you watching this? Wake up, girl... What about having some *pav-bhaji*—blend of spicy mashed potatoes served with butter-toasted buns—from the chaat corner at Ghusais?' Even as she was speaking, Sandra changed lanes.

'No, let us go to the Gold Souk.'

Sandra lowered her blue shades and pretended to glare at me.

'See, I don't feel like eating anything right now.'

There was a heavy rush at the Gold Souk. Sandra slowed the car when we neared the Women's Museum. When the vehicles behind us started blaring their horns relentlessly, she parked the car to a side.

'Come on, let's walk.'

We dived into the congested souk. In a small shop nearby, they were selling kohl. It was this *surma* (kohl), made of powdered Ithmid stones, which Shamsa, Soraiyya and Mariam might have used. After dipping the tip of a long pencil into the kohl powder, they would use it as an eyeliner. It must have been their Jadda who trained them on how to keep their eyes beautiful and fresh. I wished to purchase a bottle, but Sandra had gone quite far ahead by then. In a matter of minutes, she would start scolding me! I ran to be by her side.

'What were you gawking at?'

'Oh, nothing...'

As I made my way through the narrow street leading to the museum, I sensed an inexplicable presence. *Arms around my shoulders, the scent of cigarette, the roughness of a linen shirt, the slow gait, his body leaning to the side...*

Bait Al Banat—Women's Museum

The black letters were inscribed on sand-tinted walls.

Sandra asked, 'Do you wish to go in?'

'No, let us go and sit by the creek.'

In the area where the boats were moored, there was a milling crowd. We sat on a bench which was rather isolated. It was twilight time. Making ripples in the cobalt-blue waters, the abra water-taxis were competing with one another. There was a queue waiting to board the boats in order to reach the other shore. Across the waters, at Bur Dubai, where old buildings jostled with one another, lights were coming to life.

From the boats thronging with foreign tourists, boisterous music and sounds of revelry were rising. White-winged seagulls roosted on the handrails. Varun and Sandra were bickering over a packet of popcorn. He was stuffing her mouth with fistfuls of popcorn and she was pinching and clawing affectionately at him. In spaces where the question 'what will others think?' does not blare itself hoarse like a siren, men and women are like that. They remain themselves.

I had sat on this bench before. I had not been alone but with my second love. Was it love? I am not sure of the answer. Perhaps it is due to my own apprehensions that I am silenced by many of Sandra's questions. Was it love that I felt for Samad at the age of fourteen? Ouch, I feel dizzy thinking about it. Should I talk to Rukhiyami? No, she will become agitated on hearing about the book.

Unexpectedly my eyes welled up. When I mopped the tears using tissue paper, the eyeliner spread on it, doodling the shape of a seashell. Only one man had told me that my eyes were like seashells: Solomon Cyriac.

Solomon had entered my life neither like a storm nor the sea, nor as fire or rain. It was comparable to a derailed train. For six months, I had moved around with him, my feet above the ground. Familiar places had turned exotic and the voices I had been familiar with, had become distant. Hitherto unknown elements opened before my eyes like a treasure chest from the deep sea. My life can easily be divided into two parts: before Solomon and after Solomon.

It was on a busy evening, like the day when the novel came by courier, that Solomon entered the hospital. I have become habituated to replaying the first encounter in my mind. However, for the week before *Bait Al Banat* arrived, I hadn't thought of it. A natural biological process, which dumps people into memory's recycle bin, must have happened inside me too. But after the courier's arrival, my mind started replaying that first day.

I saw Solomon when he was being shifted to orthopaedics in a wheelchair, his fractured leg in need of plastering. When Sister Lizzy wheeled him out of the lift, she stopped near me and asked me to prepare his file. A bear-like man, with long, curly hair, beard and thick eyebrows! The never-vanishing smile playing on his lips didn't seem to suit him at all. Especially one who was supposed to be writhing in the throes of a fracture! When I finished the file and wished them, he read aloud my name pinned to the uniform.

'Nazia Hassan! Where are you from?'

'Kerala, Sir!'

'Ah, you don't look like a Malayali,' he grinned.

'What should I do to look like one?'

'Oh, don't bother!'

I was incensed. I have seen many folks in Dubai who think it is a compliment to say, 'You don't look like a Mallu.'

'This girl loves tapioca, fish, rice and sambar, Sir! True-blooded Malabari!' Sister Lizzy joined in the fun.

'I adore snake's flesh, Sister! Do I look like a Mallu?' Casting a surreptitious glance at me, the man teased Sister Lizzy.

I wondered whether he was really the 'emergency' patient!

After some time, the doctor called for the patient. He was bruised all over and the nurse was supposed to administer medication to him in the examination room. I stepped out of the reception area and went in search of Sister Lizzy in the orthopaedics department. As I moved through the corridor, someone hailed me.

'Nazia Hassan!'

It was the same man. He was in the examination room where they were preparing to apply a cast on his leg.

'Where is Sister Lizzy who accompanied you?' I asked.

'I don't think she likes those who eats snakes. Escaped with her life, I should say!'

As I turned back, pretending that I have not heard it, he hummed a tune, '*Aap jaise koi meri zindagi me aaye*... Do you know who sang this?'

I was stunned.

'Nazia Hassan, the Pakistani pop singer. Have you heard it, Madam? The song to which Zeenat Aman swayed so alluringly in the movie *Qurbani*?'

Though I managed a 'yes', the sound was subdued.

'Wow, what a lovely girl...amazing grace! Well, whoever it was that named you, chose it perfectly. It suits you.'

I suddenly felt an urge to clutch Rukhiyami's hand.

As I was about to move out of the room, another nurse arrived with Dr Peace Amin. The man laughed, 'I told you that Sister Lizzy would not come anywhere near me again, didn't I?'

'Her duty got over. Let me take a look at your bruises...' The nurse started examining him carefully.

'Doctor, your receptionist has the name of a famous music artist!'

It was for the first time that Dr Peace Amin was hearing about Nazia Hassan. Solomon started showing him YouTube videos.

The nurse started grumbling that nobody but Dr Peace Amin would indulge any patient to such an extent.

'How innocent she looks! More than her music, her personality appeals to me...' Observing that Dr Peace Amin was still discussing Nazia Hassan with the man, I walked back to the reception.

I read his name from the patient file once again: Solomon Cyriac. Visiting visa, age 44. The address was of a flat in Deira.

After an hour, the nurse and the patient emerged from the lift. There was somebody else with them. Perhaps a friend. When Solomon pointed at me and said something to him, the friend pushed the wheelchair towards me.

'What can I do for you, Sir?'

Then, Solomon formally introduced me to his friend.

'This is the girl I spoke to you about, Nazia Hassan.'

Mahesh, his friend, shook hands with me and struck up a conversation.

'We went to see the waterfall in the Wadi Al Shees near the Oman border. He slipped from the rocks. This guy came here on a visiting visa for a movie discussion. You know, back in Kerala we have the sea, and the lagoon. Why, even the gutter is full of water! But this man insisted on seeing that thread-like waterfall. Maybe he had never glimpsed Athirappally Falls back home? Since he is a writer, I thought his creative energy must have demanded such a tryst. I took him there and he fell flat on his face.'

I ignored Solomon looking on my face smilingly as Mahesh gabbled on. I felt something very familiar in that smile, as if I had known it for years. Whenever I am embarrassed or discomfited, I tend to pinch my nose and rub my neck. Suffice it to say that I unwittingly enacted such odd gestures until I finished their billing formalities.

As they departed, Solomon hummed the Nazia Hassan song yet again. Then he raised his hand, grinning at me. But my own hand rose in response only after he disappeared from sight. That night, until Samad returned from his shop, I listened to each of Nazia Hassan's songs. I also called Rukhiyami.

'I met someone in the hospital today who asked about the person who named me…'

'What is the name of the interrogator?'

'Solomon Cyriac…a writer apparently…writes for movies too.'

'I know that name! Hmm… I have seen his photo in the newspapers once.'

'Oh, really? Is he that famous?'

I started searching for his interviews on the internet.

'I am not familiar with modern-day writers. But I am acquainted with his name, though I haven't read anything he has written. What happened afterwards? What did he say?'

'That Nazia Hassan is very graceful.'

'That's not a compliment meant for the Pakistani girl, but for you.'

'For me?'

'Of course! Wait and watch...he will come again!'

Samad had arrived by then. After having dinner and washing up the plates, I sat in the kitchen watching Solomon's videos. Most were old. His hair was not very long then and his beard looked trimmed. As he elucidated on art and writing, he mentioned about a temporarily delayed project. It was something which he planned to take up with a friend based in Dubai.

Minimizing the sound, I simply watched his gestures and smiles. I did not wish Samad to hear anything. After some time, I felt slightly strange and put away my phone. Why was I hell-bent on searching for Solomon's news and other updates? What was the use of knowing how many awards he had won, and the list of his movies and books? This was Dubai...and many such passersby came and went every day. Regretting the time wasted, I went off to sleep. Samad slept as soon as he hit the bed. I could hardly sleep that night. Rukhiyami had teased that he would return soon. *For what?*

The first thing I checked in office the next day was Solomon Cyriac's file. The date for the follow-up visit, I examined especially and noted it down. *For what?*

That day, during the lunch break, I got a call in the hospital's landline. Solomon Cyriac was glibly enquiring about Nazia Hassan!

'Remember me? *Aap jaisa koyi...*' When he started to sing, I stopped him.

'I am busy working. Why did you call?'

'If any patient calls you, as a hospital professional, shouldn't you be enquiring about his health?'

It sounded right to me. I apologized to him, since I had been unduly harsh, as if trying to evade a roadside Romeo. He gave me the address of his flat and his number. Then he extended an invitation that I was welcome to visit his place anytime.

'I am not in a position to move about. That's why I invited you over to my place. Do come if you feel comfortable.'

I did not look at the address until evening. But when I walked to the metro station after work, I found myself in two minds. For a moment, I wondered about calling Rukhiyami. The next moment, I shrugged off that idea. But I got off one stop before my usual one. For a little while, I stood bewildered, unsure of my destination. Then I took off straight to the target. By the time I reached Solomon's flat, I demurred like a cow with a halter around its neck that pulled it back. I must have spent almost ten minutes there. Fearing that the security personnel might find my tarrying odd, I caught a taxi and went home.

On reaching the house, I took a shower and made chapati and potato curry. While waiting for Samad, I searched whether Solomon's number had WhatsApp service. The display picture was of his friend Mahesh, clearly indicating that it was a borrowed number. Now, I would have to wait till the follow-up day. Surely Solomon would come then.

As I served food, I realized that most of the chapatis were burnt. I offered Samad the not-so-bad ones.

'Did you have dinner?'

'Yes'

'This potato curry is too watery...not tasty at all.'

'Then don't bother to eat it.' I took away the vessel and stomped off to the kitchen in a huff.

'Huh! You have become so touchy-feely nowadays... It is all due to lack of children.'

'And what if we had? Would they come and empty the water from this curry?'

Once the dialogue reached that stage, both usually slumped back into silence. Most nights ended that way.

The next day, I called the number from the hospital's landline. It was Solomon who took the call.

'I could not come yesterday...got rather busy.'

'Well, I know you won't come even if you weren't busy.'

'Why?'

'That's how it is.'

'That means you were testing me.'

'The probability of your coming is less because it is a house. One doesn't need too much intelligence to conclude that. It is a question of understanding human beings.'

When I did not reply, he continued: 'I felt like seeing you again, Nazia! Why should I hide that wish? I think you also have a lot to tell me... Why can't we meet and have a good chat?'

I placed the phone back speechlessly. However, that evening I wasn't held back by anything.

My finger pressed the doorbell on the second flat on the eleventh floor.

It was Mahesh who opened the door. Inviting me inside with obvious pleasure, he ushered me to Solomon's room. Promising me coffee, he disappeared from the scene. The room was rather bare, the main furniture consisting of a cot, a table and a chair. A few books lay open on the bed. I could see two liquor bottles inside a glass-panelled almirah.

Solomon sat up, leaning against the head of the cot and pulled a chair close to himself.

'Please sit down.'

There was no semblance of irritation on his face. Apparently, his plastered leg did not bother him at all. An unperturbable attitude, as if that limb did not belong to him!

'Tell me something about yourself.'

'I have nothing to say. You are a big-time writer, I know. I couldn't recognize you at first.'

'What is bigger? The writer or the writing?' I could see his sharp incisors, akin to Dracula's fangs, between his moustache and his beard.

'Neither. The reader is bigger.'

'Okay... What sort of a reader are you?'

His way of speaking seemed suddenly casual. I did not object, since I found it oddly intimate.

'I don't read much...because of a tendency to drift away... While I am reading something, I wander off to some place and rewrite that story in my own mind. By the time I return from my peregrinations, the story would no longer hold any interest for me.'

'Then why don't you write?'

'I am no writer...can't do such stuff!'

'Hmm... So, Nazia's job is to draw the tails of others' tales. Interesting indeed! At least, one can break away from this world for a certain period.'

'Anyway, I don't reside in this world all the time. Is there anyone who doesn't transgress boundaries occasionally?'

'There are many like that. Those form the majority. They live implicitly following all limits.'

By that time, our coffee arrived. Mahesh leaned against the table and started conversing with us. Solomon had come on a three months' visiting visa, which they planned to extend depending on the completion of their project. I gleaned this information from their conversation. I also felt that many women and men visited that house regularly. Mahesh hardly seemed taken aback at a woman's solitary advent. Neither did I feel any twinge of apprehension inside a house where two men, comparative strangers to me, lived by themselves. That day, before I departed, Solomon gifted me some books.

'It doesn't matter whether you read ten pages or a hundred! But scribble down your thoughts thereafter. Just for the heck of it!' Though I nodded along, I thought it was a futile suggestion.

The next time we met was on Solomon's follow-up day. I accompanied him to the flat that day. His bruises had healed and he could sit up by himself to read and write. Soon, it became my habit to drop in at Solomon's flat after work. I would be back before Samad returned from his grocery shop at eleven at night. Taking a hasty shower, and preparing dinner, I would be seated in front of the TV by the time of his arrival. Let him see for himself that I hadn't changed!

One day, Solomon read aloud his screenplay to me. There were a couple of Arab characters in that script written against the backdrop of Dubai.

'I want to visit some places when I am able to walk. It is needed to finish my work. You should come too.'

'Sol, even though I have been in Dubai for a few years now, I haven't seen many localities. Since Samad runs his shop even on holidays, I'm used to spending it alone at home. I don't know where to take you.'

'Nazia, you need not show me. I shall do the needful. When you call me "Sol", I should endeavour to be your soul, right?'

I rested against his chest. Embracing me and kissing me on the forehead, Solomon said: 'Nazia, do you know the story of King Solomon of Jerusalem? During his sleep, Jehovah asked Solomon, "What should I give you?" Solomon answered, "I am young and do not know how to rule your people righteously. Jehovah, grant me the wisdom needed for my task." A pleased Jehovah proclaimed, "Since you did not demand a long life or prosperity and asked for wisdom, I shall make you the wisest among men who had ever lived!" Likewise, this Solomon is going to ask Jehovah, "Please give me the boon, make this girl called Nazia Hassan mine! Allow me to love her limitlessly and the opportunities to see her without any obstacles."'

My face was pressed against Solomon's heart. Why did two drops of tears moisten my eyes? It was the pristine water which had welled up from within. That night, I got on a videocall with Rukhiyami. Like a flow, everything which happened after meeting Solomon gushed from my heart.

'Your voice has changed, Nazia. Your eyes sparkle like it once used to…when I told you stories in childhood! Your body radiates like it did when we danced to the disco tunes. There is a rosiness in your lips which wasn't there before. Rukhiyami is very happy, darling.'

'I feel so brave now. Though am I not doing something which should make me scared? Yet...'

'I shall support anything which makes you bloom, which makes you joyous! Stay like this forever. Nazia, one doesn't get love, consideration and acknowledgement always in life. Enjoy it while you can. When they are no longer there, at least let your heart be overwhelmed with the memories,' Rukhiyami smiled.

The westering sun sank slowly in the creek. The orange colour melted and turned black. The abra taxis were still running. Varun wished to have dinner before leaving but I refused. I yearned to reach my bed and start reading.

∞

Rosa was feverish when she returned from Dubai. Her eyes became red and swollen, and the face looked sickly. Shamsa commented that it was because of mosquito bites. Kohl helped keep those bugs at bay. She applied kohl on Rosa's eyes from a tiny bottle.

'This is some infection, Shamsa. The kohl will do it no good.'

'No, Ummu William. This is caused by mosquito bites.'

Even when she was unwell, Rosa continued to click photographs seated on Anoud's back. Seeing kids play in the sand, she stopped the camel. They were dragging a makeshift cart made of date palm leaves. Running around and playing was not possible for them. They were sucked into the sand knee-deep. Some of them were swimming in the sand, as if it were water. Lying on top of sand dunes, they dived making...shrrrr...shrrrrr sounds.

'I shall never forget this sight! Swimming as if in water! So surreal...'

The first thing Rosa did on reaching Deira was visit the Al Makhtoum Hospital. Mariam went along with her. Col. Dr Makoli, retired from the Indian Army, was at work. When Rosa entered, the doctor was examining an Arab woman's teeth. The lady had not removed her burqa. The doctor slowly lifted it, and turning his face away, inserted his finger in her mouth, probing tentatively.

'What a sophisticated way of diagnosis, Doctor,' Rosa teased mercilessly.

'See, Mariam! Merely on getting her medical prescription, Ummu William has started regaining her health! How enthusiastic she is!'

Mariam smiled, 'Ummu William, we have never touched English medicines in our lives! We have been kept alive by Khadeeja's and Jadda's herbal concoctions till now. Just take a sip of water boiled with *za'atar* herb-spice mix, and you will soon get well.'

After helping Rosa into a taxi, the girls went to Bait Al Banat. Some children were playing with tops near the house. The door was wide open. Thinking that Jadda or Khadeeja might be inside, they stepped in and were shell-shocked. Their possessions were scattered around. Shamsa's abaya was trodden on, and lay abandoned, dusty and dirty, to one side. Mariam's needles and threads were strewn all over the floor.

'What nonsense is this? Has any djinn visited the place? Or have evil spirits started sleeping inside?' Soraiyya burst out in fury.

They ran to their grandmother's place. Both Jadda and Khadeeja were unaware of anything untoward. The previous afternoon when they were in the house, everything was in its place.

'This occurred last night. Just check if anything is missing.' The fifty-five rupaiyya which Soraiyya had tucked inside the pillow cover was there. The forty rupaiyya which Mariam had hidden inside the rice pot was not missing either. Someone had forced their way in the previous night.

There was no custom of locking doors in that region. Even the shops in the souk did not have locks. The children of Deira wore kanduras without pockets, stitched by Mariam. They never had anything to slip into their pockets. The few coins they would come by were during the feast-day celebrations, once a year. They had nothing to purchase with that pittance in the souk! What was the need of locks then, in such a land?

Soraiyya painstakingly collected the gnarled skeins of thread.

Looking at Shamsa sitting hopelessly by the side, she said, 'It is that harami, Kishan! He has done it as an act of vengeance because I spurned his advances!'

Jadda intervened then. 'Nobody dares to act against the master in these lands. He does not have the courage to do so.'

'But we cannot let this go so easily. I shall find that blasted Kishan.'

'Would he have escaped with the car?' Shamsa raised a tentative query.

'Where will he go, leaving Deira? I will teach him a lesson!' Soraiyya was incensed. Shamsa got a boy to check whether their taxi was somewhere in the souk. However, Jadda obstinately refused to believe that Kishan was behind the incident.

'In these parts, no man has ever done anything to a woman for rejecting his love,' Jadda vouchsafed.

'As if any woman will reject a man in these parts! Jadda, tell me a single name!' Shamsa raised her voice.

Seeing Shamsa, many children started trooping near Bait Al Banat.

They teased her, 'Shamsa, Shamsa, did a camel enter your home?'

'No dears, it was not a camel which entered my home.'

'Shamsa, Shamsa, did a donkey stray inside your home to graze?'

'No dears, no donkey strayed inside my home to graze.'

'Shamsa, Shamsa, please tell us which creature entered your home?'

'Neither a camel nor a donkey. The one who entered Bait Al Banat was a handsome man called Shanakh Bin Anakh!'

'Shamsa, Shamsa, who is this Shanakh Bin Anakh? Will he kill, will he kidnap, or will he eat you up?'

'Listen now, dears!' Shamsa grinned and began her story.

Shanakh Bin Anakh is a giant. The houses, the humans, the hens and goats appear like tiny dolls to him. Since he has a monstrous body, he will need to eat twice as much as we do; so he enters all houses and fills up his tummy. When such a gargantuan person enters our small homes, his limbs strike against the furniture and everything shatters to smithereens. But he never harms anybody. Once a year, either from faraway India or Sindh, he drops in for a visit, crossing seas and bays to reach our land. When he demands food, what will the poor people do? Finally, he will eat up all the sugar, rice and tea available in all houses. We will all go hungry!

'Shamsa, do not waste time spinning yarns! Let us go to Mutawa and inform him of our problems,' Soraiyya insisted. The children dispersed.

'What will that old man do? Except teaching the Quran, what is he capable of?'

'Then let us go to the judge, the Khadi.'

'As if you have seen women visiting him! We are not going anywhere.'

'Hmm...but one day, I will catch hold of that damned Chhota Kishan!'

■

Rosa sat in her airline's hotel, sipping whiskey and holding a diary in her hand. When she offered a glass to the waiter, he demurred.

'No Madam, if a Muslim dares to sip liquor, the punishment is eighty-five whip lashings!'

'Well, I'm not forcing anybody. I got it under the liquor permit,' she replied affably.

He reiterated apologetically, 'See, in front of the Sheikh's palace, there is this huge cannon. One is tied to it with the hands stretched taut. Almost eight hours, one will be subjected to intense sunlight and then the scourging begins... It can go up to one hundred and five lashings too!'

Rosa slapped her head mockingly, 'Oh no! I cannot bear to visualize that scene. Please don't drink! I am withdrawing my words.'

The lad started grinning at her play-act and retreated from the room.

Rosa started jotting down in her diary a few observations:

Dubai, previously known as Debai, was first recorded in 1822 as being a mud-hut town on the Gulf Coast, with about 1,200 inhabitants.

She re-read her words before criss-crossing them with her pen. What was the need to travel with the girls if she had to write such piffle? Then Rosa started again.

What an extraordinary people! We dismiss them historically as Bedouin herders, traders or fishermen, but they were engineers, sailors, builders, navigators, farmers and soldiers.

The next day, Rosa, who was waiting for Chhota Kishan, got no information about his whereabouts. Though the hotel arranged for another taxi, she waited for Chhota Kishan. But he did not arrive. Soraiyya too had reached the souk in search of the man. She watched the hordes whisper among themselves. The British tourists were relentlessly seeking tinned food.

Soraiyya was near a fishmonger now. The woman was fast gathering her dried fishes. Apparently, police would be arriving soon in the area. Soraiyya loitered around the shop selling kerosene, oil and glass bottles. People were crowding near the fragrance shop and speaking about some driver. Noticing that many eyes were on her, she hurried inside the Fakri Al Hind shop. That was the place from which she purchased hair clips and henna. The salesboy, who hailed from Bombay, told her that a skirmish had broken out near the souk's entrance the previous night. Since the police had arrived, the din was brought under control. The cops had been marching through the gullies of the souk since morning.

The police forces had come into existence hardly two years ago. Before that, it was the Bedouins, the henchmen of the Sheikh, who were in charge of law and order. Jadda used to narrate tales of Bedouins perched atop watchtowers near Shindagha and Murakhabad, and raucously shouting 'hoy, hoy' to all passersby. If anyone did not reply 'hoy', he would be shot dead immediately.

Two policemen could be sighted now. They wore white kanduras and red belts strapped majestically across their chests. One shopkeeper was bragging that each gun held five bullets. After the souk shut at ten at night, the cops would not allow anyone entry till four in the morning. The next guard duty began at six o' clock. In that two-hour gap, something malevolent had taken place. Soraiyya did not dither further; she hugged her abaya close to her and raced back home. Nafisa Jadda and Khadeeja were waiting in the foyer. Everyone was aware of the police party in the souk.

That night, as the women were getting ready to sleep after the *ishah*, nightly namaaz, Khadeeja knocked on the door of Bait Al Banat.

'Did you know, that was Chhota Kishan!'

'What?'

'There was a knife fight earlier today at the souk. His corpse is lying in Naif Police Station.'

Soraiyya stared at Shamsa. She was wide-eyed with horror, her mouth covered with the shayla. Mariam muttered *Ya Ilahi, Ya Ilahi* (O God) and went inside.

It was Chhota Kishan's newbie tradesman friend who was behind the murder. The onlookers swore that the stabbing was premeditated and ruthlessly executed. There were witnesses to his threatening Chhota Kishan about the money due to him. Such crimes were not so uncommon among Indians in Deira. There were frequent scuffles over not paying back money lent to someone. There would also be fights over backstabbing during the course of a business.

Soraiyya made arrangements to inform Rosa about the incident, before settling down to sleep. As she tossed and turned sleeplessly, the wooden cot carved from mangrove logs cried strangely.

Solomon Cyriac

AFTER SOLOMON'S LEG CAST WAS removed, we regularly visited the creek at Deira. Though I had crossed that area in car with Samad, never had I ever sat down in that place. Even on holidays, we never went out anywhere. Samad used to bring home groceries from his shop. I used to get out of the house only to go to work. Even if I wished to get a beauty treatment, I would visit the salon in the ground floor of our flats. Once, I asked Samad whether he was scared someone would steal the house if we ever stepped outside. Whenever I thought about my relationship with Samad and the time spent together in the past, it threw me into acute discomfiture.

Solomon and I sat down near the creek, as if we were in some other world. He would ask me many things and I would respond as I deemed fit. One is astounded that all the words he captured in the book were actually mine!

On seeing the relentlessly moving abra water taxis, Solomon quipped, 'This waterway is the Venice of the Gulf. Look at those old buildings on the other shore. Nazia, don't you think there might be women waiting for their pearl diver husbands even now?'

'Expecting that the man of the house would be back after the diving season that lasts four or five months, with his wallet full of money and pearls, the women would look towards Mecca, and spend time stitching clothes, selling fish and doing small businesses,' I replied.

'Living in houses made of seashell-mud mixture, they might have counted days based on the protruding cowrie shells,' Solomon remarked.

'In a land with no pebbles to count, women lived by counting shells! Caressing the grooves on the sea shells, they might have dreamed away many nights.'

'Nazia, can't you write something about these women?'

'As the proverb goes, the stone scattered with the jasmine pollen too shall turn fragrant! Sol, you are the writer. I am a mere stone enveloped with your scent. Maybe I exude fragrance too. But it needn't be that of stories!'

'Then what? My cigarette?' Solomon guffawed. The seagulls roosting on the handrails near the creek took flight in unison.

'Care to take a puff?' Solomon stuck a cigarette in my mouth once. 'You should experience everything. Enjoy the ecstasy of smoking a cigarette now.' I coughed until I reached home that day. The next day, he got the milder version—Virginia Slims—for me.

You've come a long way, baby
To get where you've got to today
You've got your own cigarette now, baby
You've come a long, long way.

The advertisement of that brand ran like that!

When I held a cigarette for the first time, my fingers became enervated as if they couldn't bear the burden. Solomon straightened my fingers and gently pushed the cigarette into my mouth.

'Girl, try to breathe from your lungs, not your cheeks,' he laughed.

I coughed the first time I took a puff. Afterwards, there was no coughing or any trembling fingers!

'Don't make it a habit. Just for occasional fun!'

'Sol, are you afraid that I'll turn into a chain smoker?'

'Hey, I am free of any such worries. You don't need any inebriant since you are already intoxicated!'

One day, when we were loitering around the Gold Souk, Solomon noticed the board, 'Women's Museum'. It pointed to a rather narrow gully. With his hand around my shoulder, Solomon turned in that direction.

'What's a women's museum?' I asked curiously.

'Let's take a look at how Arab women lived in the past, eh? You have no objections I hope.'

'Arab women are no ancient relics! I am yet to see females who take more meticulous care of their bodies and minds. They pay immaculate attention to their food, beauty and clothes.'

'These women have money, Nazia. There are solid reasons behind why our women drape their sarees shoddily and stand despondently at bus stations, holding old handbags.'

'I am not negating that fact at all. But I firmly feel that our women should start paying attention to their own needs more. Even if they are educated and employed, they do not look beyond their kids and kitchens!'

'Ah, that's because you are yet to see women of substance! Come with me…shall show you a few of those stalwarts!'

'If you are intimate with such awesome women, why are you bothering me?' I slapped away Solomon's arm, which was lying on my shoulder. The next moment, it curved itself tightly around my waist.

'Who do you think you are? You are an artist, a storyteller, a revolutionary…'

'Stop, I am none of those…just a simple girl.'

'That title has been heaped on your head by others…that you are just another simple girl. Nazia, you are totally unique.'

We reached the museum. 'Bait Al Banat' was written in both English and Arabic.

'Does "Banat" mean museum in Arabic?'

'I have no idea, Sol. "Bait" means house. Clueless about what "Banat" implies.'

There was a ticket counter when we crossed the wooden door. No visitors inside the place. I read the leaflet standing near the reception counter. It was written 'The girls' house'.

'Ah, "Banat" means girl,' I called out to Solomon.

'House of girls? Fine name for a women's museum.'

In the building with three storeys, they had displayed pictures of women power right from the time the UAE had evolved from the Trucial States. Remnants of kitchen implements, their clothes, specimens of their occupations… Items showcasing the trades Emirati women had engaged in from the nineteenth century, their property documents…all of those were exhibited.

'You mean women had property rights in those times?'

'Dear Sol, it is to convince the sceptics that they have displayed all material in glass enclosures, with proper lighting!'

'Hmm…whatever!'

Burqas meant for women of varying ages were on display.

'This looks like metal work…'

'These are clothes, and I read somewhere that colours from the burqas used to stain the wearer's face when she sweated.'

The perfumes they used were stored in small containers.

'Most look as if they were imported from Iran or India.'

'Of course! Will cloves, cinnamon and cardamom sprout in this area?'

They had collected the artefacts from ancient Emirati homes. Typically, museums were meant for exhibiting collections dispassionately. But over here, the scheme indicated that emotions were being ensnared subtly.

'Look at the implements for stitching. A round cushion…what on earth is that?'

'Did you read the inscription below? It belonged to a woman who lived in this house. The house belonged to three sisters.' There was an amazing collection of the coins and dresses in their possession. They had a Butterfly sewing machine.

'Butterfly sewing machine! Good fun…' Solomon laughed.

'So, this museum is in remembrance of those three women. It is written that they were spinsters.'

'I am astonished…three women who lived and died in these lands, staying unmarried, back in those days?'

'Read what's written about the businesses they conducted.'

Biting at the edge of my dupatta, I mumbled, 'Mariam, Shamsa, Soraiyya…'

'Eh? From where did you read that? Sly girl, you know how to read Arabic, don't you?'

'No, I did not read Arabic. Just telling their names. The eldest is Mariam, the youngest Shamsa. Soraiyya is the middle child.'

'Ah, the names you have endowed them with!'

'Yes, don't they suit them?'

'As you wish...' Solomon caught hold of my fingers and dropped a kiss on them.

'Look at the pictures of the women on the walls. Aisha Yusuf, she apparently was into active trading with India; remember which era we are talking about....!'

I was pressing my face against the wall when Solomon waxed eloquent.

'Well, this is not feeling like a public space. Rather, I feel I am at home.'

'The title has worked out well. You ended up saying these words!'

'Bait Al Banat becomes a house not merely due to its nomenclature. Other museums teem with cold formality. Somehow, I feel as if I am...'

'Home?' Solomon gently touched my head with his forehead. I nodded. For the first time after being banished from my home, I was feeling at home in another place.

There were many artworks in the upper storey. Many sculptures and photographs starting from the seventies. Depictions of dancing forms using the clothes of Emirati women from the past. The name of that installation was 'Dancing in the Light'.

'Maybe they meant to say that their past was not dark. It was the start of all the present joys.' Whenever I made a remark, Solomon gazed affectionately at me, with the usual playful smile on his face.

Ousha bint Khalifa Al Suwaidi's poems were inscribed on either side of the twisted tunnel-like structure. The mellifluous voice of the poetess could be heard reciting her verses as one stepped into the passage. I gently caressed the lines on the walls. When the honeyed voice fell on my ears, I remembered Rukhiyami. I stood still, my fingers clutching Solomon's hand.

On emerging from that poem-tunnel, I felt faint. The pictures displayed could not attract my attention. Suspecting that I might stumble on the steps, I clutched Solomon's shoulder.

'I feel afraid, Sol!' A breathlessness muffled my voice.

'No worries, let's go.'

'Just a moment...let me take another look at the threads and sewing machine.'

Solomon waited at the reception. I stepped inside and caressed Mariam's yarns. I sniffed my fingers that were smattered with some powder. The perfume called Dehn El Yasmin, scented like jasmines, prepared by the female perfumers of Al Ain Oasis! This red abaya must have belonged to Shamsa! Mariam stitched colourful clothes only for her. There was a box with a ring of keys inside. On it was pasted an inscription: '*Sanduk,* box purchased from Oman'. Surely it must belong to the enterprising Soraiyya who ran her own business!

I got out of the museum and ignoring Solomon who was puffing away at a cigarette, moved ahead.

'Hey Madam, excuse me...do you have any idea of who I am?' Solomon clapped his hands to catch my attention. I turned back, shocked out of my wits.

'What happened?' Solomon noticed my bewilderment and gently hugged me close.

'Sorry, I felt at a loss momentarily. Shall I call Rukhiyami?'

'Nazia, these are pretty normal. Why do you phone Rukhiyami every time something happens? If you sit quietly for some time, it will pass. Relax...'

Solomon walked with his hand draped around my shoulders through the Gold Souk. The three sisters who lived in Bait Al Banat assumed gigantic proportions, appeared before my eyes and hid the view. These three women meant nothing to me; they did not speak my language and they were clueless about my land, Kerala.

Not in their wildest dreams had they supposed that their home would one day turn into a museum.

'Sol, how did their names come to me so suddenly?'

'Nazia, those are not their real names.'

'I know that. Can I call them Mariam, Soraiyya and Shamsa?'

'You can call them anything you like. Because they are characters in your story. It is true that they lived once upon a time but now they are yours. Now you can weave their lives into a story…'

'But how…?'

'How you can do that? Just like you did now. The way you found their names.'

'Shamsa is a storyteller. Her mind is like pure water. Soraiyya's nature…well, it is like that sweet and sour taste which fills your mouth on cracking a melon seed in your mouth.'

'Haha…Nazia, love you. You're outrageous! I have no idea who you truly are.' Solomon's eyes turned moist that moment.

I sat brooding over many memories…

'Why are your eyes brimming over?' I hadn't noticed Sandra stepping inside the room.

'Nazia, weep if you must. Let it all flow out.'

Varun was close behind, twirling the vehicle keys around his finger.

'First, you finish reading the book. Then we'll decide what to do next.'

'Varun, do not force her. Let her read at her own pace. Come on, let's go to sleep.'

I opened the next chapter. But I could see nothing. The tear-dampened letters did not stay in control, and seemed to flow away somewhere.

⌘

'Who on earth killed him?' Soraiyya wondered sleepily. Mariam, who was doing her subhi prayers, thought to herself: 'Compared to those who disappear without even a farewell, Chhota Kishan's ending was far better.'

Shamsa said, 'The souk is full of gossip that it is one of those banias from his group.'

'Whoever it is, the cops will catch him. But why did he go to the souk at that time?'

'Maybe they called him there! Now, are you convinced that I'm right? If he was murdered at the dawn, how could he have sneaked into this house?' As Jadda hissed, the three girls dropped their heads.

Soraiyya started searching for a new driver soon after. All the men she found in the souk were either Indians or Baluchis. Whoever knew about Chhota Kishan seemed to demur from taking up the job. Things brightened up a bit when a young Pakistani was found. Though he knew Arabic, he was laconic and averse to even the slightest overtures of friendliness.

One day, Soraiyya was returning in the car from Al Raz with Mariam's new sewing machine and perfumes for her shop. It must have been around seven in the night; the time for the ishah prayers wasn't imminent. As the vehicle neared the creek's end, she saw a crowd on the road. There were more than five men, dressed like fisherfolk. They were clothed in vests and lungi, and looked formidably huge. It was not difficult for them to halt the crawling vehicle in the road where salty sand spread all around, inhibiting any speed. After pulling the driver out, they slammed the door shut. They conversed with him in the dark. When Soraiyya felt stirrings of misgivings, she got out of the car. The driver was yelling hoarsely. Soraiyya's feet froze in terror. After a while, the Pakistani driver could be seen running for his life, rushing past Soraiyya in the opposite direction. The five intruders vanished into the night, hardly having noticed the frozen Soraiyya standing by the roadside. Regaining her composure, she gathered the packages from the car and started making a painful journey forward. In apprehension of the strangers coming back, Soraiyya was walking at a quick pace. Mariam's sewing machine wobbled on her head. She breathed normally only after stepping on Sikkat Al Khail Road.

The next two days, Soraiyya hardly stirred out of the house. After hearing about what had transpired, Jadda insisted that the taxi business be stopped once and for all. Soraiyya decided to wait until a suitable replacement was found. She packed the perfumes in separate packets. When Shamsa set out to meet Yakub, she asked her to hand over the perfumes to Ali who worked in her shop at the souk.

Shamsa searched for Yakub near the customs office. It was the place where most of the ships were anchored. He was nowhere to be found. Next, she scoured the shops dotting the neighbourhood of the Al Fahidi Fort. She meandered through the paths surrounded by abras and barastis. Shamsa went to the houses made of seashells where the pearl merchants lived. Could Yakub have gone to Al Ain or Ras Al-Khaimah? The desert travellers often took him along as a helper. But he always informed Khadeeja before he left. Finally, Shamsa returned to the creek and sat waiting for him.

Some old boatmen were smoking at a distance. Logs of teak, brought all the way from India, could be seen piled up nearby. She clambered up the logs and looked around. Huge Bedford trucks were chugging in logs from Oman. Those were meant for crafting the insides of boats. A couple of lads were swimming in the sea. Apparently in the house of a sheikh at Bur Dubai, there were crimson Lavoos fruits. The boys were probably racing towards the luscious fruits.

The mechanical hammer was deafening as it pounded away. The sound of the machines installed for the development of the creeks was all-pervading. As the metallic parts forcefully clanked against one another, Shamsa felt as if someone was tearing her hair out from inside. Rosa had observed once that these machines were emblazoned with the words 'Overseas Australian Company Limited'. Due to the accumulated slush, big ships could not anchor near the port.

When Rosa told Chhota Kishan that day about the King of Kuwait sponsoring the money which financed Halcrow Company's ambitious project, he had cheekily asked how it would be repaid. Rosa had spoken about the tonnes of money which would flow into the land when the creek transformed into a huge port. About the gigantic ships from across the world that would sail to their shore. The question probably took life inside Kishan because of the several debts he owed others.

When the work was over, huge ships would purportedly anchor at Dubai! Shamsa found it a rather fanciful idea.

There were rumours that oil had been found in Bahrain. Now attempts were being made to discover oil in their area too. Shamsa, however, was averse to the whole idea. Didn't Farhad flee to Bahrain like a moth attracted to the flame because of the oil? Poor Mariam had been abandoned ruthlessly. Shamsa loathed the slimy black liquid. For her, the way the natives lived now—by catching fish, diving for pearls and unloading material brought in by the ships—was good enough. Nobody should go anywhere else, and the land should not change the way of its life! People left their homes when money proliferated: like Farhad, like Baba.

Disappointed at not meeting Yakub, Shamsa dejectedly made her way back home. The ship workers were applying whale oil on the wooden planks of old boats. The tummies of the boats gleamed red in the oily shimmer. Sensing that someone was nudging her from behind, Shamsa turned. But there was nobody around. When she reached the place where Chhota Kishan had invited them to taste samosa, Shamsa paused for a moment. The snack roasted in piping hot oil was evocative of Chhota Kishan.

On reaching home, she saw Mariam caught up in her sewing machine experiments. Shamsa did not share her disappointment on not meeting Yakub. But when Jadda and Khadeeja came by at night to chat, they observed Shamsa's face scrupulously. It was dispassionate, with no inkling of any turmoil.

Mariam ended her stitching work, after lowering the hurricane lamp's wick. On hearing the news that electricity had arrived in Dubai, many people had stopped cleaning their hurricane lamps and crafting wicks. The hope that either today or tomorrow the electric bulb would shine in their huts glittered in the eyes of the inhabitants of the Sikkat Al Khail Road.

Shamsa searched relentlessly for Yakub the following three days. The places he used to frequent, the place he stayed along with workers like himself… One day, she boarded an abra and went to Bur Dubai and wandered about in the souk. There was a shop by the jetty: Tulsidas Lalchand Trading Company, which Yakub used to visit for work. The shop was run by a merchant called Bhatia, and the workers consisted exclusively of Indians. Shamsa felt that most of them resembled Chhota Kishan. She enquired about Yakub. Since black slaves were not known by real names, nobody knew Yakub.

It was a week since he had gone missing. Yakub used to visit Khadeeja every Friday without fail.

On Friday evening, the children from the neighbourhood came to Shamsa's place. They knocked boisterously on her door shouting, 'Shamsa, tell us a story!'

Shamsa suddenly remembered Rowan, the expert diver.

Rowan worked in a ship which was used for pearl diving. He was hard working, smart and loyal. Besides, he was popular and got along well with everybody. But Rowan had two sides to his personality. He was a kind soul with friends, neighbours and family. But he also had a dual identity unknown to them—a dark one! He appeared forlorn and silent on certain nights, often disappearing from sight inexplicably.

The story went that he was a slave who had come from South Africa around 1900 to that shore, at the young age of twenty. He spoke Arabic in a stilted manner, heavily accented with his native Swahili. Ever since his arrival, the black dwellers of the sea shore felt a strange discomfort. A djinn had come in the form of a black man and was killing the fishermen. When the rumour became rife, people stopped going to the sea. Children went hungry, people started moving only in hordes and kept weapons with them for self-protection.

While fear and doubt permeated the air, one night, an Arab, healthy and well built, set out in the night for some urgent work. Suddenly, he became aware of hurried footsteps and heavy breathing behind him. Someone brawny leapt on him. Now, as mentioned before, the Arab was a physically strong man. He fought back with ferocity. They wrestled with each other until dawn, when the subhi prayers were announced. Suddenly the attacker disappeared. The exhausted Arab slipped into sleep. The devotees going for their morning prayers saw the wounded man and helped him to his house.

After a few days, the Arab was invited to attend the diwan of the Sheikh where he narrated his experience. He revealed that it was Rowan who had attacked him. Rowan was called to the Sheikh's palace. On arrival, he politely wished everyone. After enquiring about the Arab's health, he stood humbly. Everybody was flabbergasted at his behaviour. When the Sheikh asked him about the attack on the Arab, Rowan heartily wished that God would punish the perpetrator! The members of the diwan were dumbstruck. The Sheikh allowed Rowan to leave. Everyone realized that Rowan was not aware of what he did on certain nights. He transformed into someone else. It was the djinn's doing!

When the people understood that Rowan was innocent and was helpless when possessed by the djinn, they sympathized with the unfortunate man and became more friendly with him. They kept watch over him to guard him from more suffering. In course of time, when Rowan became old, his health deteriorated and the episodes of the djinn ceased totally.

The children left after listening to Shamsa's story. But a darkness spread within Shamsa's mind. Why did she choose to tell that particular tale today? Did she compare Yakub's disappearance with Rowan's? If she were around, Soraiyya would have scolded her soundly for slipping into melancholy and troubling herself.

That night, the three girls woke up on hearing a ruckus at their door. When Shamsa opened the door, nobody was to be seen around. But something was writhing on the ground. A blood-soaked foal! The baby donkey's head was severed halfway. The helpless creature was shuddering in the throes of death, unable to even make a whimpering sound. Shamsa shouted in horror and raced inside the house. By the time Mariam and Soraiyya came out running with the lamp, the flailing foal was inside the house, thrashing around in agony. Soraiyya ran to Jadda's barasti. By that time, the shudders of the creature had stopped. There was a sickening pool of blood on the floor.

'*Ya Ilahi!* After your Ummi's death, I'm seeing so much blood inside this house for the first time,' Khadeeja sat on her haunches and wailed, clutching her head desperately.

'This is a warning for us...a deadly caution,' Soraiyya affirmed.

'There has been a series of unfortunate incidents after Kishan's death. The attack on Soraiyya's driver, the disappearance of Yakub, and now this...!' Mariam walked to and fro, her mind fraught with anxiety.

Khadeeja interjected, 'Who said Yakub has disappeared just because he didn't visit one Friday? He must have gone to work somewhere... He'll be back soon.'

Khadeeja and Shamsa dragged the carcass and became busy in burying it inside a sandpit. Soraiyya and Mariam were washing the floor clean of congealed blood.

As she dug the hole, Khadeeja cursed bitterly, 'May Allah grant *jahannam*, hell, to the devils who placed a dead creature at the door.'

The foal was lying on its back, its four legs stretched upward; the huge teeth projecting skyward. Many flowers embroidered on Soraiyya's abaya were coloured blood red. The foal's tail was covered with manure and urine. Flies were buzzing all around. The marks of rope could be seen on the severed neck. All burdens ceasing, the donkey lay inside the pit peacefully. Yet the flies were not leaving it alone. Shamsa wondered if those would chase the creature to the heavens!

'Mariam, I shall be going somewhere tomorrow. I might be late in returning,' Soraiyya said while applying drops of Oudh perfume on her hands, after washing away the blood. Mariam stared at her with trepidation. Soraiyya's clear eyes, filled with determination, seemed to contain all answers.

■

As she had said, Soraiyya returned from her perfume shop rather late the next day. She had a cloth sack in her hand.

'*Alhamdulillah* (Praise be to Allah), she has arrived! Where were you till now?' A vexed Jadda started scolding her. Hushing Jadda, Soraiyya took out an object from the sack. It was a battle axe.

'Huh! The weapon of that monstrous clan? How dare you hold the axe of the Shihus? Go and throw it away,' Jadda cried in distress.

'We badly need one. Do you know how much I paid to secure this from a Bedouin?'

'That's because you are not aware of the cruelty of that murderous gang! Even on their wedding eve, they need an axe! The bride stands behind the door with a close relative. When the bridegroom enters asking for his bride, the relative hacks at him with the axe! Only the one who manages to dodge the deadly weapon gets the girl. What utter barbarity! Soraiyya, why did you have to desecrate this home with such a damned object? Astaghfirullah!'

'Well, one whack with this axe, and someone's head can be cleaved into two! Do you know that? Let it remain here. When we are discussing Shihus, let us not forget that we have houses, businesses, water and food in abundance. Those Bedouins live in the most miserable conditions without water or food amidst mountains, the wind and sun. They have to battle every moment for their existence. Let us not forget the rampant poverty. The truth is, every moment their very lives are at risk. It is a matter of survival; let us not unduly blame them, Jadda.'

Digging a hole in the sand, Soraiyya hid the weapon that she had purchased. The foe that the lethal axe would be used against, remained unknown.

Solomon and I

I HAVE NEVER SEEN DONKEYS IN Dubai. But I know the place where Shamsa buried the donkey's carcass. It was beyond the Spice Souk, behind the Gold Souk. In the olden days, luxurious stretches of sand filled that vicinity. Now it abounds with monstrous buildings. On the night Shamsa and Khadeeja had dragged the donkey's carcass, there had been a red tide. Red algae had bloomed under the sea. It was the night when the sea had turned blood red.

After keeping the book aside, I listlessly watched an old video of Solomon on YouTube. I remembered those days when we met each other daily. We relished every day as if we were meeting each other for the first time. I had told Rukhiyami everything. However, I did not disclose all details to Sandra, though I had hinted that such a story was playing out in my life.

'Don't fall too deep! You should be able to pull yourself out without anybody's help. Never get lost in the depths. Be sure to perch at a place from which you can glimpse the light overhead. Never let go of the rope to escape!' Sandra's sagacious advice went thus.

She has a practical heart, which I do not possess.

Meanwhile, Dr Peace Amin caught me red-handed one evening. When I bid him goodbye, he said, 'You are not headed home!'

'Why do you say that, Peace doc? Where else shall one go after work?'

'To Eden maybe?'

He caught my fingers and squeezed them tight. 'Look, even the tips of your fingers are vibrating to the rhythm of the leaves in Eden.'

I used to keep away from Lizzy Chechi and Matilda then. The old habit of gossiping with them, and bitching about the manager, had been long lost. I did not have the time for anything. I was so overwhelmed with myself those days, intoxicated by the fragrance wafting from within!

After the hospital shift, I would go straight to Solomon, either to the flat or meet him at the creek. We went for tours with Varun and Sandra too. The visits to Al Ain and Ras Al-Khaimah had been with them. I used to fib about working overtime on such days. Samad was happy that I was making more money.

In Al Ain, we had visited a museum and Solomon had become fascinated by a hand axe displayed as an artefact. Despite exploring many antique shops, we couldn't find a replica. The hand axe was crafted by the tribals who lived in the isolated mountains in Ras Al-Khaimah. The wooden grip was about three feet whereas the head of the axe, extending to either side, was two-and-half-inches long.

'Sol, whose head do you want to split with this axe?'

'Many back home…stinging wasps! I would like to gently knock their heads with this beauty,' Solomon grinned at me.

'But this is not meant to knock sense into someone's head, writer! The brains will spill if you use it,' Varun cautioned jocularly.

'Well, the expected victims don't happen to possess brains! Anyway, I want one of these!'

Finally, we got a hand axe from an antique shop in Bur Dubai. An aged Sudani was the salesman.

'This is the weapon of the Shihus who live in the Hajar Mountains, Sir. It's a real axe, an original!'

He was an expert in selling stuff to tourists.

'Would there be any Shihus around still, brother?'

'What's the matter with you? They've been an ostracized lot even in the past. Whenever somebody encroaches upon their territory, they make a peculiar sound which echoes across the mountains. Then the signal gets passed on. If you wish to enter their premises, a gunshot is fired as a warning. If one gets a reply shot, it implies that it is fine to step into the area. Else the answering bullet will be on your chest!' The Sudani gabbled on.

Varun interjected, 'I say, why do you need such a horrible thing? Leave it and come along!'

Though Varun was trying to persuade Solomon to leave, the Sudani salesman was inveigling him with more anecdotes. 'A very interesting episode happened once upon a time. A small group of British explorers entered the Shihu habitat. Of course, they had no clue about the ways of the people. The tribals kept them imprisoned and fed them with bread and water. After three days, after teaching them some discipline and good habits, they were left at the borders, stark naked. How is that?'

'Cool! It was written in the museum that the Shihus take their battle axe with them even while visiting the Sheikh. The axe will be at hand's length as they sit talking with any stranger. Perhaps it is an alertness which their perilous life has taught them.'

When Solomon stepped out with the axe, he looked like a conqueror.

While reading *Bait Al Banat*, especially the part about Soraiyya's axe, I had remembered that incident.

Parallel to Solomon's screenplay, the story of the women in Bait Al Banat kept progressing in my imagination. When I spoke about Mariam's lost love, Solomon objected. He insisted that no story progressed when one character was relegated to an abyss. But in my mind, she was an emotional girl. When she realized that Farhad had been lost to her forever, she started greying, her youthfulness becoming irrelevant.

'I want Shamsa to tell a lot of stories, Sol.'

'How many does she know?'

'She can weave more yarns than Rukhiyami. You scratch at her and a story will ooze from her skin! That defines her very existence!'

'What about their parents?'

'I told you, didn't I? That their Ummi died while giving birth to Shamsa. Their Baba married another woman and left them.'

Solomon pushed a notepad and pen towards me. I scribbled something on the sheets. Not bothering to read what I had jotted down, and discarding the sheets on the bed, I returned home.

Another day, as I started narrating the story of the girls, Solomon asked, 'Naz, who is like you in the story?'

'Sol, you told me that there wasn't anyone like me! I am unique...'

'Good one! Who taught you to give such sharp repartees?'

Solomon was a bachelor and never intended to give up that status. He had fallen in love while studying but the love affair had failed. He even argued that he wouldn't have fallen for the erstwhile sweetheart had he met her now.

'Why? How come she was acceptable then and not now?'

'No, no, Naz. People change, don't they? The person I was then, has travelled much distance to become the person I am now. What I preferred then, are no longer on my preference list now. Today's Solomon follows an entirely different philosophy of living and thinking. Humans should always renew themselves. It is immaterial whether it is for good or bad. But change should definitely occur!'

'What will happen if there is no change? Will mould set in?'

'Mould, verdigris...anything can infect, can't they? We evolved from monkeys to two-legged creatures. Well, one should progress further...at least mentally.'

'But in my case, I remain the same girl I was years ago.'

'That's your assumption. Did you ever plan to love an extremist like me? Did you know that I would fly in, break my leg and we would meet?'

'Nobody can predict the future, can they?'

'Dearest, we haven't reached that stage yet! Who knows whether you shall become a famous writer in future?'

'That's a great leap of imagination! But I never expected to fall in love again. It has been hardly two months since we met...but it feels like I've known you for years.'

'Don't turn mushy...try this wine.'

With every sip, I plummeted deeper into *Bait Al Banat* and Rukhiyami's tales. During my fall, Solomon supported me like a feather bed.

Songs of Solomon: 'Let him kiss me with the kisses of his mouth, for thy love is better than wine.'

I turned my lips into grapevines. Wherever they clambered, thrilling coolness spread. Those were moments when I realized that the heart's way was the most accurate.

'How beautiful you are, my darling! Oh, how very beautiful! Your eyes are like doves. How handsome you are, my beloved, oh, how delightful! The soft grass is our bed. The beams of our house are cedars; our rafters are fragrant firs...'

'Just because someone sees a few old pictures, nobody can imagine such a history, Naz. Bait Al Banat has taken full possession of you! Is it Dubai that's filling your mind?'

'Yes, Sol! My girls played, grew up, fell in love and lived by themselves on this shore...here, in the Venice of the Gulf.'

Solomon was recording all my words in his mobile unobtrusively. When I asked him the reason, he said he wished to sleep listening to my voice.

I am feeling exhausted now. Hardly can I read anymore tonight. Besides, I have to go to work tomorrow. If I stay sleepless, a headache was sure to trouble me the next day. Tomorrow, I shall return from the hospital early and finish two more chapters.

⌘

Yakub's father Hilal too had vanished inexplicably one day. He had left to dive for pearls in some island of Bahrain. When the ship named *Jalbut* returned after four months, Hilal was not on board. Rumours were rampant. Some said that he was helping around in a shop at Abu Dhabi's Yas Island, and also helping sell drinking water. Some hissed that the *nukhadh*, the captain of the ship, had murdered Hilal. Apparently, Hilal had stolen a costly pearl and the captain had found him out. He was killed instantly and his body thrown into the sea!

When Khadeeja went to draw water from the sattwa well, the women around gossiped relentlessly. Many had seen Shamsa and

Yakub together at several places. When they mocked venomously, telling colourful tales of the Arab girl flirting with the slave boy, Khadeeja feigned indifference.

When three weeks elapsed with no news of Yakub, Mariam confronted Shamsa. 'Are you setting out to make life an endless wait, just like me?'

Rosa was back on her yearly visits. The very next day, Shamsa met her at the hotel and updated her on the spate of events. When it sank in that Yakub was a slave, Rosa's thoughts meandered in many directions. She had heard about the pact signed by the sheikhs with the British in 1856, putting an end to slavery. It had been made a punishable offence. Yet, slaves were common in most households. They could be seen toiling in public places too.

'But Ummu William, Khadeeja and Yakub are like our own family members. Jadda always ensured their welfare.'

'Could be so, Shamsa. But it need not be the same in all circumstances. The slaves who wish to seek liberty under the pact have to cling beseechingly to the flagpole at the British Consulate, and then they are freed, with a certificate! Thereafter, they are beyond anybody's dictates.'

'Ummu William, many of those who sought freedom returned to their masters! When the pearl business became less lucrative and started picking up losses, many slaves were freed voluntarily by their owners. However, they loitered around the owners' premises. What could they do without any job or income? At least, they were assured of food with their masters,' Shamsa argued.

'Shamsa, freedom is a human right. You don't understand what it means and that's why you are speaking in this way.'

'I understand perfectly, Ummu William. The British who arrived at our shores promising help to the poor Arabs, what did they do for us in reality? I have no idea what they did in India.'

Rosa sighed deeply. 'True, under the name of a protectorate regime, colonization was the real goal. For the last 150 years, the entire marine commerce through the Strait of Hormuz has been under Britain's control.'

'And they gave an epithet to our shore: mocking it as the shore of pirates!'

'Yes, Pirate's Coast! I have never seen any pirates in these shores...neither have I seen any potential marauders! I am yet to meet someone who thinks of anything beyond the daily food. That was a British ploy to control the Strait of Hormuz exclusively.' Rosa lit a cigarette. When the curl of smoke arose, Shamsa stepped back.

'You are from Britain. Why do you sound so indifferent then?'

'Are you trying to relegate me to a single country, dear? I can only stand with truth and justice in my life. Nobody can stuff me inside any "box" whatsoever!' Rosa laughed wryly.

Snuffing out her cigarette, she moved closer to Shamsa.

'Shamsa, do you have any photograph of Yakub? I shall try searching for him.'

Shamsa stood bewildered. Nobody she knew had ever taken a photograph.

'Okay, let me meet the British political agent. If I get any information, I shall let you know.'

Many apprehensions floated in Rosa's mind. They rose like curls of smoke and subsided within her own self.

Shamsa set off from the hotel with a mind full of hope. After boarding an abra, she proceeded to Bur Dubai. She walked through the gullies near Al Bastakiya neighbourhood where most of the Iranians lived. A wedding was being celebrated there. People were carrying food from the groom's home. It was meant for the wedding repast to be held at the bride's place. Singers with Mirwah drums and girls who were to perform the Khaleeji dance were walking near her.

In the wedding celebrations lasting seven days, every day the bride would adorn herself with golden filigreed dresses in different colours.

Shamsa peeked into the room full of women. The bride was adorned with a golden headgear with sparkling coins dangling like festoons, thick bracelets, huge earrings and a nose ring. There was a huge necklace covering her chest. Shamsa felt suffocated. Noticing that many eyes were darting towards her, she slipped away to the place where the banquet was being prepared. Hoping that some slaves who worked with Yakub would be there, she dallied around for a while.

At twilight, Shamsa watched a troupe of women, referred to as *sanghardoon*, carrying cardamom covered in colourful, lustrous threads, displayed in attractive small vessels. They entered every house in the neighbourhood, spreading the fragrance of cardamom. It was the invitation for the marriage ceremony. From the sanghardoon women, one fifty-year-old approached Shamsa surreptitiously. Her left eyelid was drooping and she gazed at Shamsa through her right eye, turning her head like a crow.

Raising her burqa, the woman stared at Shamsa intensely, and then dragged her outside the majlis, into a deserted area.

'You are Nafisa's granddaughter, aren't you? Khadeeja lives in your house, doesn't she?'

Shamsa nodded.

'Ask Khadeeja to be very careful,' the woman whispered, trying to open her drooping eyelid and raising her eyebrows in the process.

'They are searching for them—Khadeeja and her son. I heard some people talking when they were returning after the Juma Friday prayer. They stood talking in front of my barasti and I could hear their words.'

'What were they saying?'

'They were speaking about your house. Three girls, a slave, then some accident...'

'Was it about a taxi?'

'Something like that...about killing someone, burning down a house... I knew that Bait Al Banat was your home and the slave woman was Khadeeja. Binti, I never expected to find you here. Be careful.'

'Listen, could you catch a glimpse of anyone in that group?'

'One was wearing a fine white keffiyeh and kandura like sheikhs.

The rest were fisherfolk… He was busy issuing instructions to them.'

The woman then hurried away to join the others. Shamsa thanked her profusely.

'*Shukran, shukran, Ma'a salama…*' (Thank you so much, goodbye…)

Shamsa ran towards Bait Al Banat like the legendary headless camel, Bayer Bela Ras… There was a story of a camel about to be slaughtered in Sharjah market. The meat shop was near the seaside. The butcher got his appurtenances ready and the hatchet severed the camel's head. But when they lowered the carcass, the headless camel sprang up and raced forward with blood dripping from its torso. The mad rush ended in the sea. It sank in the waters. The camel's spectre still appeared on afternoons, frightening children. Blood would be oozing from its headless carcass.

Shamsa ran into the house. Not seeing Mariam and Soraiyya around, she rushed to Jadda's barasti. Nobody was there either! Where on earth did Jadda, who hardly moved out of her home, go?

One of the children, who came to listen to Shamsa's stories, went up to her and said, 'Jadda felt unwell and lost her consciousness. They took her to some hospital in a taxi.'

There was confusion about which hospital Jadda had been taken to. Was it the Makhtoum Hospital or Dr Shareef Al Mulla's clinic? Shamsa went to the clinic first. It had a room where deliveries took place and a pharmacy for selling medicines. It cost five rupaiyya to call the doctor on a home visit. Apparently, Jadda hadn't been brought to that place.

Mariam and Soraiyya were at the foyer of Makhtoum Hospital. Jadda seemed fine. She opened her eyes and started chatting. Khadeeja was sitting on her haunches, her hands clutching her head. Before Shamsa could speak, Jadda burst into tears.

'Binti, I am feeling afraid. Call Sayyid and get an amulet tied around everybody's wrist. *Ya Rabbi,* O my god…there are ominous signs around.'

Shamsa stood blank and confused.

'Shamsa, Baba and a few friends dropped in to meet Jadda,' Mariam informed her, while wiping the perspiration from her face.

'Baba? How come he felt the longing to see his old mother after all these years?'

'Longing? No way! He wanted to throw his weight around and so he came to see her. But we do not need any head of the house to manage us!' Soraiyya's face flushed red with fury.

'Tell me clearly why Baba came,' Shamsa became agitated.

'To issue a warning! Apparently, Jadda did not bring up his daughters properly!'

Khadeeja raised her hands to the skies, and gazing up, said plaintively, '*Ya Allah*! Didn't you see how we brought up these three motherless girls, watching over them closely every moment? Who are we supposed to convince now?'

'And what provoked that sudden caution?' Shamsa asked.

'He accused us of being promiscuous women! A litany of complaints! That I call anybody and make him the driver of my taxi… I trade with non-Muslim males…and lots of scurrilous stuff like that,' Soraiyya ground her teeth.

'What Muslim and what Arab? How many diverse people have landed on these shores! Does Baba trade only with Arabs? Think of all the nations the commodities are purchased from! Think of those carrying them to the shores from the ships…the people who come to buy those!' Shamsa raged.

'No point discussing this, Shamsa. Apparently, we have been flirting with men in the creek and the seaside,' Mariam sighed bitterly.

Shamsa was assailed by doubts. Someone had gossiped about her and Yakub. Everybody knew about the expected wedding between Farhad and Mariam. And it had ceased to be news when he left the shore. Besides, Farhad was a proper young man, desirable as a groom. Shamsa concluded that Baba had been speaking about herself and Yakub. There was some connection between Yakub's sudden disappearance, Baba's unexpected visit, and the information given by the middle-aged woman in Bur Dubai. The rich man whom the woman had seen was Baba himself!

History

Sandra asked me for the book even today. I made an excuse that I was yet to finish reading it.

'How many days do you need to finish such a slim little book? Instead of munching at it, try gobbling it down in big bites!' Sandra mocked me.

She was in a hurry to read the novel. However, I preferred to munch delectably, bit by bit. After reading one chapter, I found myself travelling to Solomon. It took much time for me to return to my moorings.

Varun was forthright, 'I am not going to bother reading the book. I know exactly what's inside!'

Sandra punched his tummy playfully.

'What? Come on, tell me what's inside the book.'

'Dearest, whatever Solomon feels for Nazia will be inside that book. I am very sure about that.'

Before meeting Sandra, Varun had been in a relationship with a Russian girl who worked with him. They have a child together. After giving birth, the woman entrusted the care of the infant to Varun and left the country. Varun took the next flight home and handed over the baby to his mother. The blue-eyed boy who should have listened to Russian folk tales was listening to Panchatantra stories now. I have seen his photographs. Whenever I meet him, I am going to tell him a few old Emirati legends.

Once I asked Varun, 'What drew you to the Russian girl?'

'Oh, she was a marvellous cook!'

'But you are not a foodie! Then how come you fell for her?'

'You should have seen how prettily she sliced red bell peppers and violet brinjals! Lady's fingers and potatoes transformed into something else after they passed through her fingers. Everything she made was a piece of art! Her pizza...a moon-like surface, and the garnishes, chunks of chicken and olives, artfully spread over cheese slivers! Wow...it was like a painting! Once, she made our Kerala beef curry based on a YouTube video. It was so appealing!'

'Felt like dipping a paint brush in it, right?'

'Exactly! Maybe, because I am a designer, she reminded me of a crafting machine.'

'She also crafted a son for you...'

'Yes, she did...let's say, an unforgettable experience! My house turned into an art gallery. The clothes were folded in strange patterns. Well, she even designed a new tie-holder for me. There was art in washing and drying the dresses too. The woman had some kind of magic about her,' Varun sighed.

I opened the book again. But my thoughts were caught in yet another 'Solomon Day'. There was a female Arab character in his screenplay. Though it was planned that a Malayali actress would enact her role, more details had to be collected. When we started out, Solomon shared an idea.

'Naz, do you remember reading about the founder of the museum, Bait Al Banat? An Emirati woman...now, what was her name?'

'Dr Najah Mahar. We saw her photograph there. The brochure mentioned that she had grown up in the same neighbourhood, and knew the women of Bait Al Banat from her childhood.'

'Try for an appointment then. Let's meet her.'

That was how we became acquainted with Dr Najah Mahar. She welcomed us warmly in her beautiful office room, and had a hundred tongues when it came to describing her days with the women of Bait Al Banat. The museum, which she owned, was just one of her projects for empowering Emirati women. The woman looked at us with her large eyes. On hearing that Solomon was a writer, those eyes grew wider. Dr Mahar told us that for the first time someone from India had got in touch with her to ask for her views about the museum. There was a special thrill in the experience. She had an ever-smiling face. What a vibrant woman!

'My house was situated in the Gold Souk. I grew up seeing how the world arrived and left via the sea! The haul of fishes, pearl diving, merchandise being brought in by ships, people coming to our shores from different nations...these were daily sights. Right from my young days, I realized that *"sea was life...life originated in water"*. I was fortunate to live in the most significant part of Dubai. As one saunters down the street, one is assailed by the smell of food, the scent of perfumes, the Arabic spoken in different accents by people from different nationalities... I could experience everything. Dubai's soul is here... Everything began from here. You see, I started the museum to introduce the new generation to their ancestors. Without knowing the origin of a nation's people, can anybody hope to understand its soul?'

'Madam, did you ever see the women of Bait Al Banat?'

'Of course! When we were dawdling away our time, Ummi would scold, "Go to Bait Al Banat and listen to a story...go get this or that from Bait Al Banat..." Those days, people were very close to one another. I grew up in that neighbourhood. Not a day went by without meeting those three women. They managed their lives by themselves. You see, they showed the females of the Gold Souk, as well as the future generations, that women could live well even without marrying.'

'Did their home exude the scent of perfumes? Did flocks of kids gather around their home to listen to stories? The thawb, the free-flowing garment elaborately decorated and vibrantly coloured, used for weddings, for the brides in the neighbourhood, were stitched in that house, right?'

Hearing my enthusiastic query, the dignified lady stared at me in wonder. Dr Mahar informed us that many wives of British officers who had settled in Dubai used to frequent Bait Al Banat and maintained close ties with the women living there. They also took them along on their tours. 'Rosa' germinated in my mind at that moment.

I told Solomon about Rosa's entry in the story when we were at his flat. Solomon was reading something and I was reclining nearby.

I said, 'Rosa is very loving by nature, unlike other English memsahibs. Emirati women looked after the children and did household chores for the British living in the concrete buildings at Deira. One could find twelve-year-old Emirati girls babysitting the children of white women.'

Solomon shut the book and moved closer to me. Hugging me tightly, he asked: 'Rosa! What a lovely name…where did you get it from?'

'It just came to me. A sympathetic voice and a pleasant face. A character who is open-minded about everything, welcoming one and all.' On Solomon's notepad, I scribbled much that day. As was the practice, I never bothered to check on those again.

Before meeting Dr Mahar, we had researched a bit about Emirati women. I had read that once, there was an army of women at Ras Al-Khaimah and that they had fought against the British navy, alongside male compatriots.

On being asked about it, Dr Mahar responded, 'That was in 1819. The British attacked the forts and port at Ras Al-Khaimah. The Qawasim clan who ruled the area did not surrender. For four days, the battle raged relentlessly; the soldiers including the female army, fought from the shores. A naval captain, part of the war, had recorded all the events in his diary. He has described how the women fought from the front, fetched arms and ammunition, took care of the wounded… Finally, using cannon balls, the British destroyed the Al Dayah Fort, 15 kilometres south of Ras Al-Khaimah. The Qawasim had to concede defeat then.

'In 1820, there was a treaty between the sheikhs and the British. Though marked as a peace treaty by the British, it was not so for the Arabs. It was an agreement that British ships would never be attacked again. The British were not interested in conquering our land; there was nothing worth attracting them over here. They were on the lookout for a free passage through the gulfs of the sea, and with that treaty, the British got exactly what they had wished for.

'But even today, this region is referred to as Pirate's Coast. Though history has provided enough evidence to the contrary, the results have not been visible. Those days, there was nobody to challenge British hegemony. The Qawasim ruled as kings of the sea in that era. They had earned the name not just as one of the finest sea powers but also as one of the most benevolent.

'Yes, Nazia Hassan, the unique insights about the sea that the Qawasim possessed, stirred much envy in the British. They insisted that other than the East India Company or any of their cronies, nobody should control the Persian Gulf. Do you know how many ships of the Qawasim sailed to India? But India was under British rule then, and they stopped all our maritime relations with the country.'

'Madam, if you read Sindbad the Sailor's stories, those mention *dhow* boats, which I feel are the same ones those Arabian traders used. There are so many similarities! The wood for their construction came from Nilambur in Kerala. The British put an end to that practice. The boat constructions were badly affected. Afterwards, they probably procured the logs from countries not under the subjugation of Britain,' I said.

'I am not sure about the Sindbad connection. But if you are keen about such facts, you should know about the great navigator Ahmad ibin Majid al-Sa'id. He was a great sailor, who lived in AD 1400. The magisterial book he wrote on the art of navigation, *Kitab al-fawa'id fi 'usul 'ilm al-bahr wa-l-qawa'id,* is still used as a reference book by seafarers. It is full of poems and allegories. There are detailed guidelines on how to navigate the Red Sea, the Indian Ocean and the Persian Gulf. He has described 70 ways of controlling the ship's direction after checking the position of the stars in the sky. The fixing of location vis-à-vis the Pole Star was perhaps the ancient GPS system! They determined the position of the Pole Star using a set of wooden chunks tied up with a piece of rope, which the sailor bit hard using his teeth! There were many other tricks to get them to their desired destinations...one has to refer to the book!'

Solomon, who had been a silent listener till then, exclaimed:
'The British usually followed a strategy for conquering a region. If you study the pattern of their invasions, they would have fabricated many lies about the Qawasim to discredit them before destroying them. Because it was true that their naval strength was no match for the Qawasim then!'

Dr Mahar stood up, and then moving to the window, looked down at the vehicles racing on the six-laned roads below.

'There is definitely truth in your apprehension. Since they had no reason to attack the Qawasim, the British fabricated issues. Whenever a Qawasim boat neared a British ship, they would announce the sighting of a 'pirate' before attacking it! Thus they created the imaginary Pirate's Coast. The beginning of 1800s was a bad time for the Qawasim. The British destroyed Ras Al-Khaimah. They set fire to many houses on the coastline of the Persian Gulf and in Sharjah. The British recorded proudly that they destroyed 184 ships of the Qawasim!'

'But every sheikh signed the treaty of 1820!'

'Yes, as per Article 5, all "friendly" Arab ships would fly a British flag. The words did not imply "friendly Arabs" but "defeated Arabs"! Though the treaty speaks about ensuring peace for every province ruled by the respective sheikh, it was all on paper! Reality flowed in another direction.'

'Madam, I read that pearl diving was the main source of Dubai's income till 1930s. The men would be working in the sea for almost five to six months. The women and children would be alone on the shore. I realize it was a laborious task. But tell me, weren't women included in the work?'

'Of course, women were involved in the pearl-diving business. The famous pearl merchant of Abu Dhabi's Dalma Island was a woman named Assa Al Khubaisi. When she went to the sea in her own ship, other ships would raise flags in honour of her! There was another woman, Ummu Abdullah. Her real name was Shamsa Bint Sultan Al Mura. She flourished as a pearl merchant in Abu Dhabi for a decade. The woman travelled with her father and brother, right from childhood, in pearl-diving boats. She worked alongside her family members, diving into the deep sea for pearls. The famous Dana Pearl is credited to her exploratory skills! It seems one sailor asked her baba, 'Why does your son wear a red kandura like a woman?' She never pretended to be a man or dress differently to dive for pearls. She wore clothes that women wore at home. In 1950, when she was twenty, she got married. Afterwards, she became renowned for travelling to the sea to catch fish. Ummu Abdullah caught fish using gargour traps, nets and spears. After selling fish first in the souk, she would sell the rest to the British households around.' Gargour traps are dome-shaped trap used to capture fish unharmed. It is weighed to the seabed with rocks. Fresh or rotting fish are placed inside to bait larger fish into a one-way tunnel.

After spending time with Dr Mahar, I felt as if I had known her since a long time. And that I was deeply affiliated with Bait Al Banat. The joy of meeting someone who had known my three girls right from her childhood!

'Good, you did a decent interview! Let your talents emerge one by one from their hideouts!' Solomon quipped.

'Interview? I was simply clarifying my doubts,' I replied.

I had actually forgotten the very purpose of approaching Dr Mahar! Solomon's screenplay and its requirements had been relegated to the wayside! In fact, I had been guiding the conversation towards getting my questions answered, and Solomon had willingly allowed me to do so.

⁂

Shamsa was busy trying to find the house of the sanghardoon woman with the drooping eye. She wandered across the Khor region, chock-a-block with hovels. Except for the dreariness of withered date palm leaves and the yellow of the desert sand, no bright colours were discernible around. A young woman stepped out to gather dry camel manure into a sack. A child's wail rang out from within the home. Shamsa went to the front of the hut and coughed discreetly.

'*Aslamu alaikkum!* (Peace be upon you.) I came in search of a woman.'

'*Va alaikkum asalam!* (And upon you too.) Which woman?'

'She had some problem in her left eye…must be around fifty years of age. The one who goes to help during weddings…'

'What's wrong with her eyes?'

There were many in Deira with eye issues due to the blazing sunlight, because of fly bites, the sting of the saline waters…

'See, her left eye droops…and she looks at you at this…' Shamsa mimicked the woman, turning her head and screwing up her left eye.

The young woman started giggling, and covering her mouth, she pointed at a distance.

'Go this way until you reach a hut where a goat is tied in front.'

Shamsa moved on, searching for a shack with a goat tethered near the door. A passerby was wrapping a plantain in paper. Obviously, he was taking it to a patient somewhere. Plantains from India were very precious. They were much in demand as nutritious food for boosting the health of invalids. Suddenly, Shamsa caught the glimpse of a young man carrying a bunch of dried Ghaf wood on his head. He had a pallid face and was dressed in grey clothes. Shamsa followed him. He was now feeding Ghaf leaves to the goat.

'Oh, you are Ibrahim, aren't you?' Shamsa raised her voice inadvertently. 'Is this your house?'

The lad turned to stare at her as if she were someone unfamiliar. A woman, undoubtedly his Ummi, stepped out of the hut. Turning her head, she tried to look at Shamsa with her one good eye. Shamsa had found the person she was searching for! On seeing her, the woman sneaked back into her shack.

Ibrahim pretended not to have noticed Shamsa, and started stroking the goat's head.

'Ibrahim, Aslamu alaikkum, why do you act as if you don't know me?' Shamsa confronted him.

He wished her politely and continued to feed his animal.

'Tell me the rest of your Ummi's story,' she demanded.

'What story? Do not waste my time,' Ibrahim growled.

'You know where Yakub is! You were the one to see us together for the very last time.'

The woman came hastily towards her and pulled Shamsa into the hut. Seating her on a mat, she said in a hushed voice, 'See, do not get us into trouble. If you loiter around this place, we will end up in big problems. We have done nothing to your Yakub!'

'Who is behind all this? Didn't you speak about some people chatting in front of this hut about my house and a slave? You know everything!'

When the woman got up to prepare tea, Shamsa forcibly stopped her.

'I will not accept your hospitality. Tell me the truth.'

Casting a glance around to see that Ibrahim was no longer around, the woman whispered, 'I know my son is involved in wrong activities. The whole village knows what he is dealing with!'

'Good that his Ummi is aware of his misdeeds,' Shamsa mocked.

'Twelve years ago, his baba died in the war at the border of Dubai and Abu Dhabi. My son has been looking after me well. I work too and earn whatever I can. We are living comfortably,' the woman explained.

'Comfortably? After disturbing the lives of others? Didn't your son drag that beheaded donkey in front of Bait Al Banat?'

'Donkey? We don't have any!' The woman objected weakly.

'From whom did he take money for that? Tell me the truth.'

'I have been trying to help you. Ibrahim was the one who spoke about sighting you and Yakub together. I don't deny it. But if not he, someone else would have spoken about it! How long could you hide such a love?'

Shamsa did not reply.

'Listen, the man is a slave and his mother is a servant in your house. You will get many good proposals. Your baba is a big shot, isn't he? You forget about Yakub. Good riddance!' The woman said harshly.

'We have no baba! It has been years since he abandoned us.'

'But your father is your father! Aren't you girls responsible for upholding his good name and reputation?'

'Oh, and when he married again and moved away, was that good for his reputation?'

'That is our custom! How long was he expected to moon around after your dead Ummi?'

'I need to find where my Yakub is! I don't care about the obstacles. Yakub is everything to me and his mother brought me up.'

'Perhaps...but you can never marry a slave. Have you seen such a couple anywhere in these shores?'

Shamsa became quiet.

She felt that it was better to be a tree in the desert. A tree capable of drawing water from the depths of sand using its long roots. A tree with the forbearance to continue thriving for decades without rain. Or perhaps a sand fish which slipped in and out of the desert soil. It survived by slipping out of anybody's sight. What if she were a desert cat? With claws that wouldn't plunge too deep into the sand? Having slept throughout the day in some hidden cave, it could emerge fearlessly at night to catch prey. Or else, one should become the small fishes seen in the small ponds near the Wadi. Once the rains were over, the temporary 'water jails' dried up and they died off along with it. Yet they had the satisfaction of having lived happily through an autumn! If she were to turn into Agama lizards of the desert, which dived into sand and camouflaged themselves on sighting foes, it would be delightful! She felt miserable thinking how fortunate even the tiniest creature of the desert was, compared to herself. There were deadly vipers with two hoods, and they could slither quickly through the blistering desert sands scarcely touching their body on the ground.

How pitiable that she was not born as one of those!

God did not grant her the ability to race towards her beloved on her two legs! Her two eyes were unable to gauge the distance he had travelled away. Her nose failed to sense the remnant of his scent and find him! Unlike the desert chameleons, which could thrust out their tongues to double their body's length and ensnare their prey, Shamsa could not extend her hands and reach Yakub either. She started sobbing bitterly.

Hearing her sobs, Ibrahim entered the house.

'I heard whatever you said.'

'I know you are pretty good at eavesdropping, Ibrahim,' Shamsa retorted.

'Yes, I have eavesdropped on your lovers' banter many times. But whatever happened to Yakub is not my fault at all. I just did my job. I cannot be blamed for your baba's abnormality!'

'What did Baba do?'

'Well, I spoke about you both to my friends. They gossiped about it and the news reached your baba's ears. One day, some people took me to Ahmad Manzuri's house. I was offered money and I took it from him. Of course, I do not feel guilty about that even now. I was asked whether the news of Shamsa and Yakub happened to be true. I admitted it was true. I was asked to point out where Yakub stayed and I agreed. *Khallas*! (That was that.)'

Shamsa stood dumbstruck at his words.

Ibrahim's Ummi spoke, 'Your baba thirsts for the blood of his daughters, am I not right, binti?'

Shamsa hurried out of the hut without bidding anyone farewell. Near the goat, she saw a coil of rope. She saw a helpless neck, with the rope tightening around it, on a night when the sea turned blood red. Next to the piece of rope was a travelling seat affixed to donkeys, now lying dusty and orphaned.

Love

I THOUGHT ABOUT IBRAHIM'S DONKEY FOR some time. Its severed head seemed to be dangling from the rafters of my room.

Today Sister Lizzy had a baby. Dr Peace Amin and I went together to see him. Sister had not taken a single day's leave even when her confinement was near. She felt the pain begin, and in between her work, went and delivered the infant!

'Naz, my wife's last childbirth was like this. I still remember the scene of her running through the streets of Cairo, with my fifth daughter in her tummy! We were returning after attending a wedding. There must have been a dozen relatives along with us. As we sauntered back, laughing and joking, suddenly my wife clutched her tummy and started running. Passersby looked at us astounded! A heavily pregnant woman racing ahead, followed by a group of marathon runners behind her! Tell you what, she stopped only on reaching the hospital gates.'

It was ten years since Dr Peace Amin's wife had died. She had been suffering from cancer. He took care of her till the last moment, singing to her, massaging her feet, caressing her... He had retrieved a few strands of her hair from her cot as a keepsake.

'Look at this...the final thread of love she gifted me. I will treasure it!'

'What do you feel when you look at it now?' I asked. Keeping mementoes was a habit I did not possess.

'When I see this...well, a deep love wells up from the heart and spreads all over my body... I can feel it even in my breathing.' Placing his hand on his heart, Dr Amin took a deep breath.

'Is there any shortage of love in your case, Doctor? Every day, all the time, love is in the air... Tell me, I haven't seen your

Egyptian singer girlfriend for a while now.'

Many women came to meet Dr Amin. He had introduced most of them to me.

'Oh she? Hahaha...her name is Maha.' He hummed a song unfamiliar to me. 'She is a nice girl like you.'

'Am I that nice, indeed?'

'Of course! If I had met you in my youth, then...'

'Then what?'

'I would have been your Solomon!'

I laughed, and so did he.

■

On a day when Solomon was feverish, I got some medicines from the hospital and went to meet him. I snuggled up against the burning body which had a temperature of 102 degrees. That day, he showed me the picture of a house.

'Which house is this?'

'A house which I call my own.'

'Who resides there?'

'A few birds, one dog and four cats. They were entrusted to my mother's care when I came over to Dubai.'

'What about your mother?'

'Amma stays with my chechi.'

'Can't you ask her to stay with you? Why live alone with all those animals?'

'It is much better this way. I cannot adjust with my mother. She will force me to have the food she makes, take an oil bath, sleep on time, reach home every night... I will become that old schoolboy again. Rather, Amma will try to make me one!'

'Problems of having a mother! My problems are because I do not have one.'

'You have an aunt much better than any mother. It was your Rukhiyami who made you what you are today. She assisted you in recognizing your true self, didn't she? Naz, that is a great fortune.

To have mentors who help mould your personality at a young age... That is a great stroke of luck.'

I kissed Solomon's forehead and started perspiring due to his feverish body heat. Solomon murmured that vodka was the best prescription during fever. I poured him a drink. He never partook of any drink without sharing it with me. Solomon's motto was: 'When you are together, share everything.' Whether it was liquor, story or passion....we shared all of them.

In the daze caused by the combination of paracetamol and vodka, Solomon's hazy tongue asked, 'What news of your Mariam, Soraiyya and Shamsa? Are they keeping well?'

I felt as if he were asking about three people who lived with me.

'Is your Shamsa's love flaring like a wildfire?' He tweaked my lips with his fingers.

'No, she is inconsolable nowadays. After all, she is in love with a slave. And he has gone missing!'

'Huh! When did that happen? You never told me about it.'

'Well, it happened that way,' I shrugged.

'Naz, tell me the truth! When are you going to write it down?'

'There he goes again! I do not know how to write a story. But I do think of stories.'

'Writers struggle terribly to weave stories from their imagination. And having written a decent book, they preen as if they have upended the whole world! And you, you shower stories as you move! A girl who creates a veritable feast of tales while gazing at the sky! Who are you in reality?'

Till today, I have not been able to find answers to some of Solomon's questions.

As I sit holding this book entitled *Bait Al Banat*, and see my name inscribed on it, I find myself looking at a hitherto unknown me.

When his fever abated a bit, I got ready to leave.

'Don't go today, please Naz!'

'I am not a free bird. I will have to find convincing answers if

I don't reach home in time. See, I haven't ever gone to a store just by myself to purchase even sanitary napkins! If I don't go home one night, the event will be telecast as an apocalypse.'

'You may go. I just expressed my wish, that was all. Maybe not physically, but you are definitely free mentally. You don't need anyone's permission to let your mind fly high. Let it be unfettered and allow it to wander wildly. Let your mind travel to all the places where you cannot reach physically.'

I sat there for some more time.

'Sol, why did you enquire about Shamsa?'

'You were so flustered about her yesterday.'

'I'm terrified about her future...how far she has to travel to get her love.'

'And then? Will she reach him finally?'

'No idea... Their baba will not allow that to happen. He has entered the scene, has he not?'

'Why did he have to step in just now? Couldn't you have kept him away?'

'That's not possible. The lives of the three girls and their personalities were crafted by the sea. Didn't Dr Mahar speak about water being the very soul of the common people? The rhythm of their lives is created by the movement of the sea and the siren of the ships. Their lives have been born from the pearls and rubies which their baba, Ahmad Manzuri, retrieved from the depths of the sea. They are entwined in their intricate origins. See, Mariam opens her baba's old pearl bag every night. Without such nuances, the girls will lose the pulse of life.'

I slowly sank into Solomon's chest. Indeed, I was aware of him stretching his arm and pressing the button of the recorder.

I was babbling: 'Ahmad Manzuri was an ordinary man who dived into the depths of the sea in search of rubies and pearls. He left his family on the shore for four months every year and gazed exclusively at the sea waters! Early dawn, after consuming a small cup of coffee and two date fruits, he would start diving for pearls.

Every time, he took a deep breath before jumping into the water, and he would hope that the mother oyster shell on the seabed would be keeping a precious pearl exclusively for him. Attired in gloves, cap, a clip on the nose crafted from goat's horn, a heavy stone tied on the ankle, he would dive into the sea. He would keep filling the *diyyin,* the bag on his waist, with oyster shells. Once it was filled to the brim, Manzuri would tug once or twice at the rope around his waist, the other end of which was held by the boat labourer called Zayib. He would immediately haul Ahmad Manzuri up. That was the daily routine. But something else happened in the shipping vessel going to Iran for trade. Ahmad Manzuri's life was turned upside down that night. The nukhadh had come to check on Manzuri, who emerged gasping from the sea, his eyes popping out in terror, mouth wide open and tongue flickering as if possessed by a ghost. "Let him rest for some time," the man shrugged. Ahmad Manzuri lay on his back staring at the dark sky. "*Ya Allah,* what sort of sight had I seen at the depths of the sea!" He pressed his hand against his heart.'

'Naz, what sight did Ahmad Manzuri see?' Solomon asked, fondling my forehead.

I woke up as if from sleep, and became aware of the surroundings.

I entered the name of the novel in Google and pressed 'Search'. It was just a passing fancy. Except for details on the Women's Museum, nothing else popped up. Thereafter, I tried to search for the publisher's website. I could not see *Bait Al Banat* in the 'New Releases' section either. The search engine also informed me that the writer hadn't authored any other book.

⁓∞⁓

Shamsa returned to Deira from Ibrahim's hovel. She looked like a skiff caught in high tide. She hesitated to go to Bait Al Banat. Trying to placate her mind, turbulent with whatever she had seen and heard, Shamsa sat down on an earthen mound near the creek.

On the loamy sabkha soil was a ghoulish crab. With its bleached outer shell and bulging eyes, looking as if they were propped up on two sticks, the creature scrambled past Shamsa. It had a morbid aura. The crab was busy digging holes in the sand, searching for prey. It dived into a pit, among the piles of sand resembling Egyptian pyramids, even as she gazed. Ahmad Manzuri was also hiding in some secret pit and trying to manipulate the lives of the girls living in Bait Al Banat.

Shamsa started walking towards home. The Iranians, seated in abras awaiting passengers, were busy smoking *narilla*. Inside the dried coconuts brought from India, tobacco would be filled. At the bottom was a hole attached to a small pipe. The contraption was used for smoking. Shamsa felt dizzy due to the pungent smell.

As soon as Shamsa entered her home, she fell down exhausted. Jadda and Soraiyya quickly got her into bed. When she updated them about meeting Ibrahim and his mother, Soraiyya declared: 'See, I was so sure it was none other than Baba who was behind everything! But nobody listened to me.'

Jadda sat down, stretching her legs. Khadeeja edged closer, always an appendage. 'Ahmad's sense of honour is deep,' Jadda spoke. Khadeeja murmured, 'Where is my Yakub? *Ya Allah*, could something bad have befallen him?' She burst into tears. Jadda consolingly stroked her hair, 'Khadeeja, he will return from wherever he is...'

The previous night, a neighbour had warned Khadeeja. She should not make solitary trips to the souk or to the well. Slaves were disappearing unexpectedly. Whoever stepped out into the night was trapped and bundled away in a sack! A gang from Dubai was all set to resell slaves. Khadeeja too had been pondering on such possibilities when her son vanished. But now, going by what Shamsa had narrated, it was evident that Ahmad Manzuri was involved.

Shamsa remembered that whenever it rained anywhere in the desert, the oryx would sniff it out! They would set forth in search of a downpour which happened one hundred kilometres away, yearning for the moistness of the fresh sprouts which would have emerged afterwards. She too wished to travel in search of Yakub in that way. Jadda spoke up suddenly and it jolted awake Shamsa, who sat with shut eyes, meditating on the sky's reflection in the wide eyes of the oryx, which walked in groups, gently shaking their long horns.

Alaik bardarb lau talat vo bind al amla barat: Continue undeterred on the path even if it is very long, and marry the child of your father or mother's brother even if he or she is sick or older than you. Jadda sighed.

Marrying one's relative was a tradition of the land. It was an old saying which Jadda was muttering, trying to remind Shamsa that she was not intended for Yakub.

Soraiyya immediately countered with another proverb: *Agrab luk, agrab luk:* Might be your relative, but beware, he is a deadly scorpion!

Jadda understood what she was hinting at. One's relatives knew every weakness of the person. They shall attack us fully armed with that knowledge. Just like Ahmad Manzuri had latched on to the weak points of Shamsa and Mariam!

Jadda proffered yet another axiom, *Farat al habuyifi shitha:* The circular waist rope used for climbing date palms gets dumped during winter. Date palm trees flowered and gave fruits in summer and consequently there was no need for any implements during winter. There were those who abandoned their ageing fathers after becoming self-dependent.

She snapped back with a new aphorism: *Kil udwa feeh dukhan:* Every twig has smoke within! Even the feeblest had a kindling spark within him.

Mariam intervened when the contest became heated.

'Enough, enough... I don't think we need any more needling with proverbs! We wish to know Yakub's whereabouts. Shall we achieve that by verbally wrestling with one another?'

'What should we do?' Shamsa whimpered.

After the pearl business collapsed, many slaves were freed, as the owners could no longer afford to feed them. Many of them were like Yakub, surviving by working for British households, or labourers in the port, or in boat-making units. But apparently there were human traffickers who were out to trap these South African slaves who were wandering around without the protection of their owners. They transported the men to far-off Zanzibar and Saudi Arabia. Once they reached Saudi, their lives depended on the type of Arab master they got. If he was kind, the slave was fortunate. Else, it was disastrous. Even so, among those who were beaten and starved and shipped away, some ended up with compassionate masters.

The chances of Yakub being kidnapped were negligible. At least there would have been one witness to such an incident. He would have managed to sneak out a message to Shamsa even if he was holed up somewhere. Shamsa felt sure that her father had killed Yakub.

Soraiyya stepped out. Khadeeja followed her.

'Where are you running off in the night?' Khadeeja howled after Soraiyya in the darkness. She was furiously rushing past the covered commodities in the souk, like the Shamal wind. Soraiyya's abaya became entangled in unknown material in the wide path of the empty souk. Khadeeja chased after her. She was moving without a burqa for the very first time in her life. Soraiyya paused at the junction where the path merged with the deserted road to the creek. She noticed Khadeeja and growled, 'No, don't follow me!'

Khadeeja became motionless like a recalcitrant camel. Soraiyya raged, 'I know what to do! Please go back.' The old woman did not respond. Soraiyya's shayla moved in the gentle breeze. The curls fell on her forehead and entwined with her thick eyelashes.

On the rock cleft next to Khadeeja was a pair of sea snakes. These had wide tails and lay tangled, awaiting the next tide to carry them back to sea. They would not survive unless they reached the waters. In the morning, some predator birds would swoop down and make a meal of them. Soraiyya gazed at the direction in which Khadeeja's eyes were drawn. Pity welled up within her on catching the sight. Let the tide flow in and carry them back to their home... Poor creatures, how miserable they looked, unable to either swim or crawl!

'These are poisonous...else I would have dropped them in the sea,' Soraiyya muttered.

'Yes, poison...stay away from poisonous creatures,' Khadeeja spoke pointedly. Soraiyya ignored her and walked ahead.

'Binti, don't you know the blood-drinking father of the girls in the tale which Shamsa narrates often?' Khadeeja persisted.

'I know him very well... I am going to meet a father very much like him.'

'No, I have seen Ahmad Manzuri as my master ever since I turned four. I know him very well. Please come back!'

Soraiyya walked ahead indifferently, pulling up her abaya. At a short distance, near the freshly crafted flagpole of a ship, a solitary man was keeping guard. On the burning embers next to him was a vessel of boiling coffee. There was a superstition that if an infertile woman leapt over a new keel, she would soon conceive. But the heavy price to pay would be the life of the ship's captain. To protect the Captain's life, the man was sleeplessly keeping watch over the keel. He was guardedly observing Soraiyya from his seating place. When she tried to cover her face with the shayla, it slipped off and fell down. As she stooped to pick it up, something fell from her waist knot from inside the abaya. It was the axe of the Shihu clan!

'Binti, hurl it away into the sea,' Khadeeja screeched as she raced forward. Soraiyya tucked it underneath her abaya once more.

'Let the folks know that there are girls who hack off their father's head and it's not just fathers who drink their daughters' blood,' Soraiyya snarled.

Like a lightning flash, three intruders leapt between her and Khadeeja. They were yelling as they turned on Soraiyya. In the faint light of the creek's lamps, she saw that one of them was

Ibrahim. Before she could utter a word, they lifted her up and raced toward the road. Before Khadeeja's stunned eyes, the vehicle rocked and swayed through the sand dunes and soon vanished from sight. Meanwhile, the tide had dragged back the entwined snakes into the depths. Khadeeja started running desperately, as if all her senses were diverting the entire energy to her legs. As if blinded and deaf, indifferent to everything else, she rushed to the doorsteps of Bait Al Banat.

Jadda was seated on her haunches in front of the house. Shamsa was vexedly walking to and fro. After listening to Khadeeja, Jadda wilted and leaned against the walls. Shamsa shook Khadeeja furiously.

'Tell me, who were they? It must be Ibrahim and his goons! It was a revenge for my visiting his house. They wish to destroy the three of us!'

'But for what? They have already abducted Yakub, haven't they? Why should they be after us now?' Jadda asked with utter weariness.

Khadeeja spoke, her heartbroken state evident from her voice: '*Ya Rab!* (O God!) Where shall we find Soraiyya now? Should we reach out to Ummu William? Or should we go to Ibrahim's house?'

'I think she is with her baba now…at his home.' Jadda spoke coldly.

■

Soraiyya lay in a heap before the ornamental teak door of a house situated amidst many similar ones in Jumeirah, near the seaside. Inside the house, some men were involved in a serious discussion. Ibrahim was sipping kahwa, seated in the front yard. A few people were surrounding him. All those henchmen had been with Ahmad Manzuri ever since he had stopped his pearl business. Nobody knew about his new business except that he was rolling in money.

Ahmad Manzuri came near Soraiyya and helped her stand up. Ushering her inside his house, he made her sit on a chair. Then he asked in an affectionate tone, 'Binti, why do you resent me so much? You are the smartest among all my children!'

When he lifted her chin, ignoring the fluster of seeing her father for the first time in many years, Soraiyya pushed away his hands. The dark blisters in his hands, a remnant of the days when he rowed his boat, had long vanished. Soraiyya remembered the old voice of her baba, as he narrated the tales of the sea in her childhood. It was as if some sophistry had appended itself into that serene and firm voice of yore! Baba had never worn a kandura nor a keffiyeh made of such exquisite material before. Above all, never before had there been such a troupe of hound dog-like henchmen, ready to commit any atrocity, awaiting his orders!

'Look, Soraiyya, do you think Shamsa did right by cavorting with that slave boy? Is he suitable for her?'

'You had found a suitable boy for Mariam once. Farhad! And where is he now?' Soraiyya raised her voice.

'Softly…women should not raise their voice! Well, Farhad left. But Mariam remained unmarried because she refused to consider anyone else.'

'Of course, you would justify Farhad! You also abandoned us, for another woman, didn't you?'

'Soraiyya, I remarried only after the death of your Ummi. I made a house for you girls too. I have carried out all my responsibilities perfectly well. Now stop arguing.'

'Why did you bring me here? Let me go or else I will scream for help,' Soraiyya warned.

'All three of you should live in this home with me. We shall bring Jadda too. You have a nice Ummi here. Let me call her.'

The strong sea breeze made Soraiyya's throat go dry. Fortifying her faltering voice, she rallied back: 'No, we don't have a life away from Bait Al Banat. Why should we live here with your wife?'

'This is a palace compared to your house! Let go of that house; come and settle here.'

'I know, you wish to do some business in that house. I am against that. We are no longer willing to live under your subjugation.'

Ahmad Mazuri hurled the hot tea he was sipping at Soraiyya's face.

He snarled, 'When I demand that you vacate my house, you should obey! Your arrogance is because you earn your living! There is no need for it anymore. Come here and curl up in some corner!'

Ibrahim edged closer to her.

'That sister of yours, the famous storyteller, she dropped in at my house today. She is aggravated because she misses her slave lover. If you care for your life, vacate that house. We have planned for some expensive projects based on that place. Without wasting anymore time, get out from there.'

'Ah, you were the one who cut off the poor donkey's head! So that you could scare us out of Bait Al Banat,' Soraiyya railed.

'Yes, I was the one who created that mess in your home! The one who murdered your Indian driver, do you wish to see him? Look, there he sits!'

Soraiyya cast a glance at the direction in which Ibrahim pointed. A bania trader, with a prominent paunch and thick moustache! She was familiar with his face, and knew that Chhota Kishan had some business dealings with the man.

'Better go home and pack your paltry stuff! Get here before it is too late!' Ibrahim pushed Soraiyya out of the house. She fell heavily on the sand outside.

Spitting out the sand particles which entered her mouth, Soraiyya walked about like a mad woman in the darkness.

Her feet were sinking in the sand. As she made her way panting and heaving, she saw three dark forms approaching her from a distance. Her sight dimmed, but the faces exposed in the dark coverings were gleaming as if the phase of the new moon was over.

'Allah, did they hurt you?' Khadeeja wiped away the blood dripping from Soraiyya's nose with the end of her abaya.

Soraiyya had seen her father after decades. His greying beard stuck in her mind like a coral reef. Every memory connected with her Baba was inexplicably linked to the sea. Baba was a ghost who emerged from the sea, once every four months, with a bagful of money! The pearl trader was immensely rich now! Who would dare fight him in a land where people struggled to make ends meet?

Khadeeja, Shamsa and Mariam helped her to walk home. Jadda was waiting impatiently for them.

'They killed Kishan and chased away the Pakistani driver in the hope that we would leave the place after losing our financial independence. They marauded our home and took away Yakub. Yet, we did not go in search of Baba. Hence, he staged the abduction of Soraiyya,' Mariam wept.

Jadda made Soraiyya lie on her lap. She gently wiped away the perspiration on her face.

'I don't care who opposes us, but we are not going to leave Bait Al Banat. My girls will rule this place. Ahmad is my son. Unless he comes here and kills me, he shall not be able to evacuate you forcibly.'

Jadda was speaking against her son for the first time in her life. 'Khadeeja, just like my son is beloved to me, so is your son to you. There is no need to consider Ahmad as your master since he has harmed Yakub. Ahmad Manzuri is the enemy of this house!' Jadda choked.

Nobody slept that night. When someone knocked on the door early morning, though scared out of her wits for a moment, Soraiyya opened it, confident in the power of the Shihu axe!

It was Rosa, and she had arrived to bid her goodbye. It was only after she assured them of her next trip that Soraiyya smiled.

Shamsa asked, 'Ummu William, what are you going to write about us?'

'The three lovely ladies of Bait Al Banat... Oh, there is a lot to write about them! Your life is much more beautiful than the stagnating lives inside the palaces and mansions of England. However, the people who live beyond the seas consider your lives inside the burqa as something mysterious. Nobody knows what is happening inside it!'

'Well, our lives have the secretiveness of the precious pearl inside the oyster shell. Ummu William, anything connected with the sea is enigmatic. A pearl may not sparkle like a Cat's Eye but it has an ineffable beauty. It will not make you blink with its charm, neither will it make you flounder within its loveliness. But pearls shall engender a mysterious curiosity inside us,' Shamsa elucidated.

'It is that enigma which attracts the queens of Europe! There are umpteen pictures of Queen Eugene of France and Victoria of England adorned with pearl jewellery. In the case of Victoria, after her husband Prince Albert's death, she wore only pearls, avoiding ostentatious display. Avoiding flashy jewels, she chose pearls as a symbol of purity. They are colourless and melded well with her mourning clothes.'

'Ummu William, have you ever visited the houses of Tawash? They trade in pearls. A very interesting sight indeed!'

'I have taken many pictures of pearl traders, Shamsa. My camera is full of their photographs. Donned in pure white kandura, these men sit on the ground along with the Indian brokers. There will be shimmering red clothes spread in front of them. A similar red wrap would be around their heads. They will throw a fistful of pearls on the red cloth and start categorizing them. Then they start negotiating the prices. What surprised me was the lack of mayhem in fixing the rates unlike other trades. They were haggling over prices using sign language, in utter silence! How they guard the great secrets of the prices! The only sounds were the 'shurrr' of the falling pearls and the sibilant undertones as they rolled around. I was taken aback!'

Rosa rolled her eyes in wonder.

Mariam spoke up, 'Once the men finish with the business, someone else takes over. Ummu William, did you know that? After the men left, Ummi would scour the place with me and Soraiyya. We would gather the cheap pearls which they had discarded. Ummi would embroider those into the hems of our dresses, on the necks and arms.'

'Next time you visit, stay with us at Bait Al Banat,' Jadda invited Rosa.

'Let us hope this house will stay untouched till then,' Shamsa sighed poignantly.

'Why will it not be? We shall definitely stay here forever,' Soraiyya leapt into the melee.

Shamsa explained to a befuddled Rosa about the recent occurrences. Though she was shocked for an instant, she regained her equanimity soon.

'Well, it seems whether it is in England or Arabia, the plight of women remains the same. Here you wear abaya, there we wear skirts. But there is not much difference in fundamental matters. You own your property and conduct your business. The man who marries a girl has to pay her enough and in case she doesn't like him, the woman can return home! See, aren't you three women living confidently by yourselves, here? That's a great thing.'

Rosa informed them about the residences of the British political agent and the Head of Oman Scouts. She assured them that help would be provided at any time, and in case of any threats or fears, they were to approach them using her name as a reference.

Shamsa plonked herself on the floor after Rosa took leave. Mariam became engrossed in embellishing a bride's wedding dress. Jadda sat staring at the moon which was still visible in the sky. She used to address the moon sighted at day as the 'day thief'.

Sea

SOLOMON POSSESSED ME AS I became engrossed in reading *Bait Al Banat*. Varun remarked that I had changed much and was becoming terse in conversations. I was apparently not taking interest in cooking or even reading newspapers. He advised me to finish the novel and regain my normalcy.

Sandra, as usual, came to chat with me after dinner. While speaking about Lizzy Sister's newborn, she commented, 'It is great to have a child of one's own. Varun is fortunate.'

'It can happen to you too, Sandra. Might come about unexpectedly. See, like getting a book under my own name!'

'Yours? How can a book written and published by another be called your own?'

'Not entirely,' I admitted.

'Look, Naz, we read about so many scandals in social media. The lover writes a short story for his sweetheart. The girl gifts a poem to her lover. Somebody catches the fraud and there is a huge uproar… Certainly, there is something wrong in all this…'

'I have no clue! It wasn't at my insistence that Solomon scripted this novel. I have never wished for a book at all. The story inside me and Solomon's wish to see it published came together in this form.'

'Yet you have not given the book to me to glance through till now!' Sandra expressed her pet peeve again.

'I cannot finish it so fast, Sandra! I am caught in various thoughts as I read. See, I get lost and am unable to recognize the time and place even! Whenever I get ten minutes free, I reach out and touch the book to reassure myself that it is there. I feel all the precious things I have lost are within its pages.'

'What have you lost, my dear? You can see your Rukhiyami

any second you wish. Bait Al Banat stays firm as a museum even now. Well, Solomon…now, if you hardly take the pain to search, what can be said about him?"

'Didn't he make it clear on the last day that nobody should try to contact him? He wished to be left alone… Wanted to stay away from me,' I said.

'Yes, I remember what he said when we bid him goodbye. How does one search for a person who is not present in any social media?' Sandra mused.

'When he said he does not use a phone, I felt it was some sort of a joke! But he is not a Luddite who opposes technology either. After all, he writes using all the latest gadgets, doesn't he?' I replied.

'Naz, in this era, it is easy to find someone, provided you are determined enough.' Sandra became mulish.

'I realize that. It was my decision not to search for him. If the passion towards me has not yet died within him, Solomon will come back to me. I can wait till then.'

'It hasn't dwindled, my dear. This book, *Bait Al Banat*, is testimony to that fact.' Sandra started juggling the book playfully.

'Apart from the screenplay he was busy working on when I met him, *Bait Al Banat* is his latest creative work.'

'That means, all this while Solomon was hard at work on this book,' Sandra quipped.

'After granting me a few beautiful days, he vanished into the blue. Having given me many new insights, and transforming me completely, he disappeared from my sight,' I replied.

'Naz, every person we encounter has a predesignated role to play in our lives. This novel is evidence that Solomon exists.'

Sandra's father had called her today and insisted that she return home to Kerala. He was munificent when it came to promising her a bright future. Apparently, he would offer her anything in the world if she discarded Varun! How could a father offer to bribe his own daughter? Usually, Sandra tends to be depressed whenever her father called. But today, she looked indifferent. Perhaps she realized the pointlessness of being sentimental. Among her father's usual sob stories were how he bought her sweets in childhood, took her to the feast of the saints, of being deprived of sleep when she caught chickenpox… Her mother hardly had a role when it came to decision making in their home. If Sandra's mother had extended her strong support, her father would not have been so obdurate. But in Sandra's own words, her mother was a simpleton who knew only how to cook beef and tapioca!

Flicking through the pages of *Bait Al Banat,* Sandra queried, 'Do you remember the night when Samad threw you out of the house?'

'Yes, the night when Solomon left Dubai.'

'That night you should have gone with him,' Sandra sighed.

'Sandra, you are wrong. Solomon does not like any restraints which bind him down. He is a free spirit. Well, even his mother's love seems a bondage to him. He can never accept me as a lifelong companion. He must be flying about blissfully somewhere…'

'When we were at the Buddha Bar at Jumeirah, he gave an indication of this book. Well, at least I think so! Something about how you should continue to write…or how he would turn you into an author! Maybe I was a bit tipsy, I cannot recollect much,' Sandra shrugged.

'He would say that repeatedly, Sandra! That Nazia is a writer…'

'He has initiated you into the world of letters. It reminds me of how we hold the fingers of little kids and make them write! You will have to write your second book by yourself and send to him!' Sandra giggled.

'Oh no! I cannot do any writing.'

'Lord! I am totally unaware of the complexity intrinsic to writers! Anyway, Solomon knows that you are working in the same hospital. That is why he couriered the book to that address.'

'That's not tough to find. My grinning photograph is available on the hospital's website, isn't it?' I said self-mockingly.

'But Naz, he does not wish to meet you again. Else, he would have left a phone number or address in the book, right?' Sandra wondered aloud.

'Sandra, now that's Solomon! If I were a typical soap opera character who created a hullabaloo about seeing him and talking to him, would he have loved me so deeply? Tell me…'

'I have no idea, Naz. As I said, the intricacies of a writer's mind leave me befuddled. I take my leave, dear.'

Sandra draped her arm around Varun's shoulder and went off to the kitchen. They were attempting to make a chicken pizza from scratch. I had told her that I wasn't in the mood for any chicken pizza! But she was no weakling who would humbly accept such an admonishment, was she? She knew how to create a chicken pizza and forcibly feed me too!

Solomon had once observed humorously that Sandra was the network upgrade which had occurred to Varun's system! He had suddenly turned into 5G from 4G! She was so vibrant and vivacious!

Varun was busy preparing chicken while Sandra was readying the dough. I should have been helping them out, allaying Varun's grievance. But I just felt like sitting in the armchair, hugging the book. My father used to say that I was the laziest among all family members. But Rukhiyami would immediately interject that except my limbs which were sluggish, when it came to working, my mind was super active!

■

One day, when I was describing Ahmad Manzuri to Solomon, Rukhiyami made a video call. Seeing an unfamiliar flat and bedroom, she sharply queried about my whereabouts. I showed her Solomon, lying sprawled on the bed. They stared at each other in astonishment for a few moments.

Solomon asked Rukhiyami, who was watching us with a smile on her face, 'Were you the one to give such a lovely name to this young woman? Who had told you that anyone with this name would turn out to be special?'

'Nobody told me. But it turned out like that!'

'Well, it turned out to be supremely excellent!' Solomon kissed me on my lips. Startled, I tried to hold the camera away. Rukhiyami pretended that she had seen nothing. As we talked, the rain and thunder worsened back home and the call was abruptly cut short.

'You didn't tell me what happened to Ahmad Manzuri when he emerged from the depths of the sea! Go on…' Solomon prodded.

I moved away from the warmth of his body to the edge of the bed. Curling up like a centipede, I recalled Ahmad Manzuri.

'He must have been in his thirties then…a handsome and well-built young man. He had eyebrows joined above the bridge of his nose. He was the father of two daughters then. Right from his childhood, Ahmad was used to frequenting the sea with his father Shihab Manzuri. Back then, his duty was to help the *naham*, the one who melodiously sang songs and poetry, to relieve the labourers from their stress while toiling in the ship and the sea. The presence of a young child was a soothing balm in the eyes of those hardy workers who were forced to be away from their families for months on end. Ahmad would run around energetically, singing songs while distributing tea and dates to everybody. When the naham recited Nabati poems and sang songs of the sea, Ahmad would start playing on the small drum. The exhausted divers would slip into slumber. They were men who soaked in the saline depths throughout the day. With dry skin and red-brimmed eyes, they would curl up and sleep on the rough, scorching floor of the ship.

Sometimes, the nukhadh would assign young Ahmad Manzuri the duty of catching thieves too! He would ask him to keep a sharp lookout while the oyster shells were opened. If anyone slipped away a pearl, what a catastrophe it would be!

Once, young Ahmad had caught a Baluchi. He hadn't stolen a pearl but a sliver of dry fish meant for the nukhadh. The man had hidden it in his clothes. Ahmad had followed the trail of the fish's stink and found the culprit. The punishment meted out to the Baluchi was horrifying. He was asked to dive into the water for six hours without respite, denied food for hours on end, and whipped to boot. When he was on the verge of death, somebody kindly offered him some tea and dates. Had he died, they would have dumped him in the sea. The ships never returned to the shore because of someone falling sick or dying. They would simply wrap up the corpse and push it overboard. There were many sharks lying in wait to take over ownership of those!'

'Let Ahmad Manzuri's childhood alone for a while. Tell me what happened to him after he dived into the sea that particular day,' Solomon interjected.

'Well, I was about to explain. Ahmad Manzuri was a wreck that day. He was unconscious and on the verge of delirium. The onlookers had their own doubts about what had transpired.'

'What doubts? Some sea creatures might have attacked him, right?'

'No...'

'What else? That he was petrified at the sight of something? Are you hinting that he saw djinns?' Solomon asked.

'Not a djinn...but something more terrible than that!'

'What?'

'Salama and her three daughters. Ahmad Manzuri had caught a glimpse of them.'

'Is Salama beautiful?'

'Yes, Salama is gigantic but beautiful. Her three daughters are also lovely. They have fish tails, long trailing tresses and gorgeous lips.'

'Mermaids, am I correct?'

'Well, one can imagine in that manner too. Salama lives with her children in the Strait of Hormuz. Laden with goods, Ahmad Manzuri's ship was returning from Iran via the Hormuz. Everybody was fast asleep. Suddenly, the sea turned tempestuous. Huge whirlpools started forming, and monstrous waves arose. The ship swayed dangerously from side to side; the sail was about to collapse. The nukhadh shouted, "It is none other than her! Quick, throw all the goats and roosters into the sea." They offered the animals to appease her. Else, she would have eaten everyone in the ship.

'As the precious animals were being hurled overboard, somehow Ahmad Manzuri lost his footing and toppled over into the sea waters. The rest of the survivors were sure that the Strait of Hormuz had swallowed him up! But to the great astonishment of all, Ahmad emerged very adventurously from the surface after a while. Clutching a piece of log which the nukhadh had tossed to him, Ahmad neared the ship.

'This was what Ahmad Manzuri narrated to the others about his experience: "I saw with my own eyes…four dancing females! They wore colourful dresses, and were adorned with many bangles, gem-studded earrings, huge pearl necklaces! The biggest was Salama and she was twirling crazily always. The three small girls followed suit. Like a top, they were going round and round on the fulcrum of their fish tails! I became dizzy at that sight. The mother and daughters were howling with laughter as they stood arm in arm in a circle. They circled unceasingly and thus increased the circumference of the whirlpool. Depending on their dance moves, the whirlpool kept shifting in the sea. I have no idea how I emerged from that depth."'

'Salama is an interesting concept! It is evocative of an African dancer's body and dance moves. But Manzuri was in the pearl-diving business. This incident happened in a ship returning from Iran, right Naz?'

'Yes, it was after the return from Iran that the fear of the sea took hold of Ahmad Manzuri. Thereafter, whenever he dived into the sea, he saw Salama and her girls! Before they started dancing, he would desperately tug at the rope tied around his waist. Someone would haul him up. In the last dive, as Ahmad Manzuri lay exhausted on the wooden platform of the ship, he was frothing at the mouth. He did not divulge being petrified at the sight of Salama. Never again did he dive into the sea.'

'Have you wondered what Salama might actually be? Strait

of Hormuz is a gulf surrounded by huge mountains? One big mountain and three small ones…'

'No, I don't want to know that. Details spoil the tale.'

'There is a likelihood of strong tidal waves in a narrow strait… The probability of those turning into whirlpools…'

'I told you, I am not interested. Salama and her daughters fill my mind. They eat up captains and sink ships!'

'Ok, fine. Relish your belief. Sit atop Salama's shoulders and sway along with her, Naz!'

Solomon had been recording that conversation too.

'Why do you try to possess these sounds and safekeep them? Once they leave the mouth, words should not be stored anywhere else. They should dissipate in the air.'

'Your words, your voice…well, I am not keen on those dissipating. Let them stay with me. Might come in handy someday.' Solomon laughed.

'What use, Sol? I just chatter on and on… What's the significance of all these words?' I queried.

'I shall inform you on what they can shape into,' Solomon replied.

Solomon did inform me on what those shaped into. My sentences, stories, characters, scenes…my *Bait Al Banat*. But Salama and her daughters were yet to appear in the novel. Maybe they shall appear soon. Let me hope that what's yet to arrive, turns out to be more beautiful.

How many times might Solomon have replayed my voice? He collated all the notes I scribbled on, and meticulously kept track. The man who picked up every word from my mouth like a pearl and linked them together into a book-garland, would have thought about me incessantly.

Sol, a man who thought about me without bothering about whether I thought of him. He had given me back in words whatever I had ever offered to him. What more do I need in life?

∞

Mariam finished stitching the bride's thawb. She wrapped it up beautifully and set off to the house. With silver threads and corals embroidered skillfully, the dress was too heavy. A huge tent was being hoisted in front of the house. She walked into the marquee meant for female guests at the back of the house.

Zaleekha, the bride, was seated in the middle of the room on a wooden platform. As Mariam moved towards her, she heard the giggles of the girls from the makeshift room at the southern end of the tent. They were teenagers aged between fourteen and sixteen. Middle-aged women scouted for future brides for their sons from among them. Though each one wished that she would be selected, they pretended to be shy whenever someone stepped inside. Soraiyya would feel infuriated at all these manoeuvres, but Mariam was inclined to enjoying them. As she walked, she affectionately touched the head of one young girl who was squatting on the side. She lowered her face shyly.

Zaleekha, who was about to be married, had also been hoarding wedding dreams for a long while now. She would often gripe to Mariam that her mother would not allow her to apply make-up, or dress in fineries or gold, before marriage. If only her wedding happened quickly! She would be free to indulge all her whims and fancies! The contentment that her dreams were going to be realized was visible on Zaleekha's face.

The thawb's neckline and chest were embellished with gold and silver flowers. Seeing the exquisite *badla*, gold and silver thread embroidery, Zaleekha's eyes welled up with tears. Her Ummi opened the Omani dowry chest—the Mandoos box. It was a beautiful red box with filigreed handiwork and brass latches. In the three drawers, the bride's dresses, perfumes and gifts were packed. Zaleekha's mother was displaying the contents of the Mandoos box to everyone who dropped in to see the bride.

Mariam lifted Zaleekha's hand to see the henna design. The girl was drenched in perfume. The wedding preparations had started almost a month ago. Her hair had been oiled and washed with henna preparation, thus softening it. Different unguents were applied on her body to make it resplendent. Her feet were reddened with henna. Before donning the thawb, Zaleekha was supposed to wear a golden cap which had threads dangling with golden coins, reaching up to her waist. Then the ritual of wearing the golden rings on toes and fingers would begin.

Two years ago, in a great cyclone which wreaked havoc, Zaleekha's father died. All the dhows on the beach were devastated and a huge boom ship breached the shore. Many who were fast asleep in their hovels were crushed to death. Dogs, cats, goats were all caught in the terrible storm, and seagulls and pigeons were dashed against the stone walls of houses. Date palms were uprooted. The popular belief was that the head of the date palm was in hell and the 'feet' or roots were in heaven. The trees were rooted in sand under which were water reservoirs, even as they stood with their heads up in the blazing sun. Many humans who had sought shelter in the 'feet from heaven' were found dead, with bodies floating in the sea. One of them was Zaleekha's baba. Yet, her arranged marriage with her Ummi's brother's son was going to be solemnized. Zaleekha was a lucky girl indeed!

The women who saw the loveliness of the thawb stitched by Mariam embraced her, uttering *Masha Allah!* (Allah has willed it.) They wished that Allah would grace her gifted fingers with more magical powers. Amidst them was a woman with a prominent depression in her left eyelid. It was Ibrahim's Ummi, an unavoidable presence when houses celebrated weddings.

'See, I warned your sister because she was a woman like me. I had told her to be on her guard and keep low. Now there is no option but to suffer!'

'Keep low? Who are we supposed to be afraid of?' Mariam snapped back.

'Your baba is incensed and is in a mood to commit any atrocity.'

'Let him! First, you please try to correct the ways of your son before embarking on rectifying other people.'

'See, Ahmad Manzuri's second wife is a good woman. There are two beautiful children in that marriage too. Your siblings. Why can't you stay with them in that house? What is the need to struggle alone in that hovel of yours?'

'We are not getting out of Bait Al Banat. Even if another cyclone arrives, like the one which killed Zaleekha's father, and ploughs through Deira, we shall not move out. The three girls will die in their home. After removing our stinking, rotting corpses from our house, Baba can conduct any business there! Please do tell him that!' Mariam retorted.

'I have never seen such arrogance anywhere in this Deira! Why, no woman who believes in Islam will display such a hoity-toity attitude! Damn you all!' The woman shouted wrathfully.

Mariam walked away to the tent where food was being cooked.

Soraiyya, meanwhile, was busy chatting with old Ali who worked in her perfume store located at the souk. When she was lowering the hurricane lamp and getting ready to return home, the old man had stopped her.

'Binti, let me come along with you,' he said.

Shamsa used to quip that the hunch on Ali's back resembled the Hajar Mountains! His bald head rose above it like the bright sun. Ali, scared of Shamsa's teasing, would always wrap his head with a cloth before appearing before her.

'Soraiyya, why can't you marry my younger son, Saif?'

'How old do you think I am? He is much younger than me,' Soraiyya burst out laughing.

'So what? Many men marry women older than them.'

'The girls of Bait Al Banat do not need men. Neither are we of marriageable age,' Soraiyya declared.

'Yet, you need another generation, don't you?'

'We shall remain even after we depart. Everyone should remember Mariam, Soraiyya and Shamsa. Do you think otherwise?'

'Not at all. But Saif really likes you. It is well known all over Deira that your baba is insistent on occupying Bait Al Banat. He will definitely take over its possession. In one way, it is his house, am I not right, Soraiyya?'

'Baba is a very prosperous man. But his endless avarice... grabbing money through any wicked means, is that a good thing, Ali? We earn our own living by working hard. Maybe Baba feels that merely being rich does not enhance his reputation? To establish that, he needs to crush his three daughters and subjugate them. There is no other explanation, is there?'

Suddenly, they observed a great crowd rushing out of Sikkat Al-Khail Road shouting, 'Fire, fire!' People were running helter-skelter and some were trying to douse the flames. Ali and Soraiyya ran ahead.

'Fire in the wedding tent,' someone shouted. Soraiyya felt her heart go up in flames. Mariam had gone to Zaleekha's house with the thawb! There was no other wedding in the vicinity except Zaleekha's. Soraiyya lost her composure. Leaving Ali behind, she raced ahead. Except the fiery tongues of fire, nothing could be seen. People were struggling to save the hutments nearby. If fire swallowed the dried date thatch of the innumerable barastis around, thousands would burn alive! The wedding house was almost burnt to cinders.

A crowd rushed past Soraiyya, carrying a completely burnt Zaleekha, battling for her life. When Soraiyya tried to enter the premises, the crowd pushed her back and she found herself running towards Bait Al Banat. Jadda, Mariam and Shamsa were waiting for her impatiently near the neem tree.

'All is lost. I do not know what happened to poor Zaleekha!' Mariam cried.

'Thank God you are safe, Mariam! I saw them take away Zaleekha...she was unrecognizable! Her clothes and body were burnt to cinders,' Soraiyya replied.

'*Ya Allah*, I can't imagine... May those criminals be punished!" Mariam said.

'Which criminals?'

'Ibrahim and his gang! When his Ummi started passing snarky

comments, I moved away to the cooking area. That's when they entered the area meant for women, dressed in abayas, like women. Ibrahim's mother had showed them the way in and pointed out the sanduk, where the gold and money were kept. She had guided them inside, that damned woman!'

'But how did the fire start?

When they stood around the sanduk, a woman caught sight of Ibrahim's beard. She screamed and the women inside the tent panicked! In the ensuing mayhem, a hurricane lamp tilted and the flames leapt on the dresses. In moments, the fire had swallowed the whole place.'

'Alhamdullillah, you escaped, my dear!' Jadda sighed thankfully.

'Poor Zaleekha, how much she had dreamt of her wedding day. How come such catastrophes happen to the girls who dream so much about their weddings?' Mariam asked.

'Mariam, nothing tragic happened to you just because the marriage with Farhad did not occur,' Soraiyya did not mince her words.

Jadda stopped a group loitering nearby and queried after Zaleekha.

'What happened to the bride? Her Ummi?'

'The girl died before reaching Makhtoum Hospital. Her Ummi is very critical too. Four other women have died in the conflagration.'

A little later, they discovered from another cluster of women that Ibrahim's Ummi had died. The women in the neighbourhood sat on a woven mattress spread in front of Bait Al Banat and started chatting about the fire and the unexpected robbery attempt.

It was then that Shamsa asked Jadda, 'Don't you remember a mother and son like Ibrahim and his Ummi in our old stories?'

'Yes, in a Somalian tale...called "Mother's Tongue!"' Jadda replied.

The women spoke enthusiastically. 'How long since we heard Shamsa tell us a story! The men have gone to help the victims. Tonight we shall spend with you... Go on, Shamsa...'

Long, long ago, there was a woman called Habu in Somalia. Her husband died when she was pregnant. After four months, she gave birth to a son whom she named Hayan. Habu used to visit graveyards at night and steal the shrouds of the dead. In those would be the most precious objects, beloved to the dead person when alive. She would sell these and bring up her son. Soon, she started taking Hayan along with her during these surreptitious stealing sprees. If she left him asleep in the cradle and he happened to awaken at night, wouldn't the neighbours come enquiring and find that the mother was not around?

When Hayan was five years old, he came home one day with an egg stolen from an old woman living next door. Habu encouraged him warmly, 'Good job, little son! Say, you should have picked up two!' The next day, the little lad came to his mother with two stolen eggs. Habu said, 'You should have brought the hen with you. We shall then eat eggs every day.' Hayan followed his mother's instructions promptly and stole the hen.

Once, when Hayan was ten years old, he overheard a conversation in the Sheikh's home.

'The prophet says that we should always help our neighbours and the poor around us. We should be aware of the sorrows and needs of people who are in our vicinity.' Hearing those sagacious words, Hayan felt guilty. The next day, he marched off to the old woman and handed her a hen and two eggs. He stopped stealing from the neighbours after that incident.

When Hayan turned twenty, he told his mother, 'Ummi, now you should stop stealing.' Hayan stole only from the rich and helped the poor. One night, he planned to break into the home of the King's Representative. He crossed over to the palatial house after climbing the branch of a tree and stole a huge amount of money. When the guardsman slept, Hayan escaped through the front door. He kept repeating this adventure night after night. In a matter of a month, the King's Representative's coffers became empty. He fortified his home's protection and hired more security staff.

Hayan dug a tunnel from the wall to the house's interior, and covered the entrance with straw. One night, as he was moving around the bedroom, the King's Representative woke up and discovered him. Hayan lost his composure and stabbed him. Luckily the injuries were not grave. Hayan was caught by the soldiers before he could escape through the tunnel. Hayan was sentenced to death.

On the day of his hanging, one soldier asked Hayan, 'Do you have any final wish?'

'Yes, I wish to see my mother.'

Habu came to see her son. Then Hayan said, 'Ummi, can you please open your mouth? I wish to see your tongue.' When Habu opened her mouth, Hayan bit off her tongue! With bloodied lips he told the soldier, 'Now I am ready to die!'

When the soldier informed the King's Representative about the developments, Hayan was ushered to his presence.

'Why did you bite off your mother's tongue?' The King's Representative asked with great curiosity.

'Ummi was my teacher. It was her lessons which landed me in prison,' Hayan replied stoically.

After listening to the story of Hayan's unfortunate upbringing, the benevolent administrator let him free. He also asked the ironsmith of the area to train Hayan in his trade.

'Hayan, you should learn a new craft from this ironsmith and earn your living honestly.'

Hayan followed his wise advice and started a new life. He also started telling everybody about the greatness of earning one's living through honest, hard work.

Habu, meanwhile had bled to death when her tongue was bitten off.

'How was the story?' Shamsa asked.

'This is the story of Ibrahim's Ummi...' The women could not help laughing despite the tragedy they had witnessed.

Mariam alone was silent. Seeing the slivers of dress material, from which she had stitched Zaleekha's thawb, strewn on the floor, she felt enervated. How many of those giggling young girls, who were expecting to be chosen by their prospective mothers-in-law, had survived the fiery tragedy? Tears gathered in her eyes.

'Mariam, I am still befuddled why the woman warned me when I met her in the wedding function at Basthakia,' Shamsa spoke.

'To terrify us with the story that some unknown people were after our lives! Either take refuge with Baba or flee to Ras Al-Khaimah or Khor Fakkan and live incognito on mountaintops! That was her ploy all the while.'

Soraiyya did not participate in that lively conversation. She was thinking about Ali's younger son, Saif. She had never known that he had any feelings for her, since a word or signal to that effect had never emerged from the young man till now. Except for a formal greeting occasionally, they had never talked. Neither had Chhota Kishan ever made any lovestruck gesture towards her. In the desert, when Kishan had attempted to kiss her, she had not been able to sense any love either. She had reacted as if someone had attacked her. Soraiyya started wondering whether she possessed the capability to feel love. She was a dispassionate young woman, among two ardent sisters who oozed love at the slightest touch!

Message

I YEARN TO VISIT BAIT AL Banat again. When they see me all alone, I know how the three girls shall receive me. Besides, I wish to also show the museum director Dr Najah Mahar the novel. Unfortunately, she would not understand the Malayalam narrative describing Mariam, Shamsa and Soraiyya. If only the world had a single tongue—for humans, animals and birds!

When I was in love with Samad, I used to treasure all his love letters. A few months after my marriage, I flicked through those again and could not recognize my own self revealed in those missives. I had thrown them away that day. Of course, I did not burn those papers, because it seemed ridiculous and overdramatic. I dumped them in a dustbin with the same ease of cleaning a fish—scraping off its gills and fins. There is hardly one percent of that simple schoolgirl in me now.

This must be the transformation which Solomon was mentioning about. Man should change constantly; the greatest sign of life is change.

But the notes I had scribbled about Bait Al Banat, seated in front of Solomon, were unlike the letters I had written for Samad. Those moments made me realize that fiction was the best way to express oneself. The three girls continue to live within me. Even if Solomon had not caught them in words, they would never have let go of me.

Every time I saw the creek at Deira, I experienced their depths relentlessly.

That day, while booking Solomon's return tickets, I had queried, 'Need you go?'

'I have finished the cinema work. It is time to go back.'

'What if I get you a visa?'
'How long will you obtain a visiting visa for me?'
'Until you say enough!'
'Why should you force me to say enough? I shall never have enough of you, Naz! It will always stay the same.'

∎

'Pizza's ready!' Sandra yelled from the kitchen.

By the time I moved out of the armchair, Varun entered the room with a plateful of pizza. Sandra trooped in after him, carrying Pepsi bottles and sauce, and settled comfortably on the carpet.

I too sat down on the carpet. Though it did not have the Russian flair of Varun's erstwhile lover, the pizza was decent. Varun was taking a selfie even as he chomped on the cheese threads. I gobbled up all the capsicum bits and then sucked my finger after dipping it in sauce. As I browsed through my mobile, I noticed that many mails had overloaded my inbox—most of them promotions. I typically check the Amazon deals and delete the rest without a second glance. There was a new mail from the publishers of *Bait Al Banat*. I had subscribed to their website one day, while searching for publishers. Last week, a mail had arrived, an offer package for children's books.

I opened the mail. It was an invitation letter as part of an advertisement. The book launch of *Bait Al Banat* would be held at the bookstore of Rangeela Hall at 10.30 a.m., on the 16th of this month. The launch would be by writer Solomon Cyriac. Among the august invitees was my name! I zoomed in to check whether it was actually my own name. Ten thousand train whistles blared through my heart all at once. Dropping the phone abruptly, I raced to the balcony.

Sandra ran after me. I stood gazing at the moving colours of the vehicles whizzing through the road below. I felt dizzy. Melting in the tears of my eyes, the colours disappeared soon enough. Varun walked towards us and showed Sandra the invite for the book launch displayed on my phone.

'This is too much! I can forgive him for publishing your book without seeking your permission. But promising others that you shall attend an event without cross-checking with you?' Sandra was enraged.

'It is not a promise, rather, it is a piece of information. It is meant for Nazia too,' Varun intervened gently.

'Oh, is that so?'

'He was sure that Naz would notice it, Sandra.'

The pigeons which had laid eggs in the flowerpots on the balcony cooed at me. Their eyes were expressionless.

'Naz, come inside. We will chat comfortably.'

Was Sandra scared that I would jump off the balcony and kill myself? I sensed her tension. I wondered whether my legs were moving forward or not.

'Let us calm ourselves down. Have some water, dear.'

'I am fine, Sandra. Don't worry about me.'

'Solomon is waiting to spring a big surprise on you!'

'You mean I should go?'

'What's your opinion?'

'I don't know…'

I had no clue about how I would respond on seeing Solomon, who had remained hidden from my view for so long, suddenly on the stage of a book launch. What could I say?

'Look Sandra, Naz…let us be patient for a few more days. We have ten days before the book launch. Maybe Solomon might get in touch with Naz before the function,' Varun spoke.

Varun sat in front of the television. Sandra sat in a chair, with her eyes closed. The pizza was lying forlornly on the plate, like a total zero, seemingly asking us, 'What is my fault in all this hullabaloo?'

I called Rukhiyami. She replied without hesitation, 'You should attend, Nazia.'

'What then? What should I say?'

'Just stand there, my child.'

'I am the author, Rukhiyami. How can I just stand there?'

'Your presence is what matters.'

'Should I then claim that I am the writer? I cannot bring myself to say that.'

'Who else created it, eh? The book is in your name.'

Rukhiyami chuckled.

'Are you laughing at me? This is the most significant personal dilemma that I have been faced with in my life. I am not even sure of what I am anymore.'

Rukhiyami murmured many things. I heard absolutely nothing.

Varun insisted that I eat some pizza and carried a piece to the tea-poi on the balcony. In the light of the lamp, the eyes of the pigeons seemed to be focusing on me. Their eggs would hatch in eight to ten days. Would the hatchlings emerge before my book launch?

My book launch?

∽∾

When she regained consciousness, Soraiyya was lying on a wooden plank. The log was floating in an unknown sea. The sparkle of sunrise could be seen on the sea waters which reflected only the sky. Soraiyya could not open her eyes due to the intensity of the light. The serene sea, devoid of waves, rocked Soraiyya like a baby in a cradle even as she desperately gripped the wooden plank. She was not afraid. True, she was somewhere in the deep sea and was all alone, but her mind was calm.

As she lay on her back on the plank, she extended her arms to the sun. There was a bite mark on her wrist. As she brought her hand close, she noticed that they were human teeth marks. Wetting her hand, she placed it across her chest. Ouch, it hurt badly! There were scratch marks and clotted blood on her body. Her elbow had hit against some blunt object, and a blue-black welt spread from her shoulder to her neck. There were countless bruises on her lower body. Soraiyya shut her eyes and lay still.

The wooden plank stopped brusquely. The gentle breeze ceased suddenly. Only the painful stinging continued. She gazed around. It felt as if she had crawled to the bottom of the sea…she could perceive sea creatures. Her long tresses, caught in the tendrils of plants, hurt her scalp. Grotesque creatures seemed to be swimming towards her. She tried to swim away but her limbs did not accede. As if mutilated, she lay motionless like a piece of flesh.

Soraiyya's back was pressed against hard sea-grass. The horrible monsters had edged very nearby. Their fangs were exposed over their thick, fleshy lips. Gigantic fiends, swarming near her! 'Help me!' She wished to cry but no sound came out of her mouth. The monsters started grazing placidly.

Arus Al Bahar (sea-elephant),' she wished to scream. How many blood-curdling stories of the legendary sea-elephants had Jadda narrated in Soraiyya's childhood! 'Oh, how helpless I am!' Blood seemed to drip from her eyes.

When Soraiyya rubbed her eyes, the sea had long disappeared. Where was that wooden plank? She was lying on a cold, hard ground. Where was the horde of sea-elephants? They were still visible! An ugly, dusky face with small eyes. The sea-elephant's face was morphing into that of a human being. 'Ya Rabbi, who is this man?' Then she heard his voice, 'Abandon her in some empty boat on the Khor.'

Someone tried to pull at her legs. Soraiyya kicked out viciously and he suddenly let go. She struggled to get up from the ground, her hands frantic for a steady hold.

'Where the hell are you taking me?' Soraiyya screamed.

'What use are you anymore? Manichand bhai asked us to dump you somewhere.'

Manichand, that moustachioed bania tradesman from India! Ahmad Manzuri was planning to sell Bait Al Banat to him! The man usually spent his time in the godown where his goods were stored.

Soraiyya had gone to meet him to enquire about the taxi. After scaring away the Pakistani driver, the henchmen had discarded Soraiyya's taxi at a distance. For some time, it lay dust-ridden at the other end of the Ras Al Khor Port. Then suddenly, it disappeared.

Everybody in Deira had mistaken Manichand as the murderer of Chhota Kishan. But the man was moving around nonchalantly. It was then that the fisherfolk found out more about him.

'This is not Mahajan. It is his twin brother Manichand. Chhota Kishan's killer is in jail awaiting the gallows.' It was from her neighbour Layla that Soraiyya heard the news. Layla went to the shore daily with her date palm leaf woven basket, and returned with fishes which she sold in the souk. If the fresh fishes remained unsold until afternoon, the lot started rotting. Those who purchased the fish, had to cook it immediately or else the fish would turn bad. Often Layla resorted to selling dried fish, since that entailed lesser risk.

Layla said, 'Mahajan's twin brother Manichand is also a flabby man with a paunch and a thick moustache. He sells scraps in his godown. I am sure he must have smashed your taxi to smithereens and sold it as scrap!'

It was Layla's innuendo which had made Soraiyya go to the dismal place.

A burly man standing guard at the godown's entrance asked her about the purpose of her visit.

'I need to meet Manichandji...to enquire about my taxi.'

'Your taxi? Haha...since when have women started driving taxis in this land, eh? Or is it that you are not a woman?' The man cast a lascivious glance at her from top to toe.

It was an area packed with banias and Sindhis. They all had households in India and dwelled in Dubai for business purposes. Once or twice, they would board the British steamers and go home.

The watchman let Soraiyya in. As she stepped inside, she observed a lit lamp facing the door. The sculpture of a long-nosed creature attracted her. There was an alluring picture of a woman who held a large flower in her hands and wore a crown on her head. She was seated inside another flower, similar to the one she held. Soraiyya was wonderstruck. Who would be this beautiful woman who seemed to be emerging from a flower?

Manichand was seated on the floor, eating food. There was roti, dal and a glass of goat's milk near him. Soraiyya moved towards him. Manichand was breaking off large pieces of roti and tossing them into his cavernous mouth. She was familiar with the man's face! Soraiyya recollected seeing him in Ahmad Manzuri's house at Jumeirah. The bear-like person whom Ibrahim had pointed out to her as Chhota Kishan's killer! Soraiyya felt confused whether it was Mahajan or Manichand.

There was a commotion outside; three or four tradesmen wanted to meet Manichand. After asking her to go to the inner room, Manichand went out to meet them.

'No, unless you return my principal amount with interest, I shall not return any of your merchandise.' Manichand's roar could be heard.

They were small-time traders who sold tea, coffee and other household items in the souk. When they failed to return the borrowed money, Manichand confiscated all their stocks and brought those to the godown, using his henchmen. The poor fellows were pleading with him to return their commodities. After abusing them in the most pernicious way, Manichand shut the door. As the rusty door creaked shut, a chill went down Soraiyya's spine. The man climbed a coir cot and sat with his feet crossed. Red and black threads were tied around his hairy hands. There was a white metallic bangle on his right hand, which he twirled often. He also twisted his moustache intermittently. His head was dense with hair, shining with oil.

Manichand commanded Soraiyya to be seated next to him. She did not move at all. Before she could ask about the taxi, he taunted, 'It was my brother who killed your driver. Did you know that?'

Soraiyya nodded.

'Now who shall drive your taxi? Or are you planning to drive it yourself?' He started roaring with laughter. The guard outside also started laughing uproariously.

'Are you the ruling Sheikh of some place? Can't you live without a car?'

'It is my source of livelihood. Please return it to me,' Soraiyya requested.

'Ah, is that so? What shall you pay me in return?'

'You need payment for returning something which you stole?' Soraiyya retorted.

'A wild one! Come here!'

Manichand got up and pulled at her hand.

As he caught hold of Soraiyya's shayla, she lashed out. When she ran to the door and tried to open it, the guard stopped her. Except for the long-nosed figure and the woman who held a flower, there were no sympathetic faces around. A stench emanated from the room, where commodities were stacked helter-skelter. The terrible stink of camel urine and dried fish filled her nostrils.

'Let me go. You shall not touch me,' Soraiyya said firmly.

'How come? It is not for the first time that I am touching a woman. I know exactly where and how to touch…hahaha.'

The guard chortled too.

'I have heard you are a very brave girl. Let me see how brave you are!'

The man forcibly dragged her towards the cot. The awful smell of half-boiled dal reeked from Manichand's mouth. As Soraiyya slipped free from his grasp, he threw a gargour net to trap her. Soraiyya lay ensnared in that iron net which was hemispherical in shape. Manichand sat on top and it sank due to his enormous weight. She cried loudly, 'You dirty man, what harm have I done to you? Let me go!'

'You are the exquisite Hamour fish for my dinner tonight. My dear Hamour, with brown freckles on her fair body, today you are my delicacy!' Manichand grinned lustfully.

He threw away the net and lifted Soraiyya from where she

lay exhausted and shocked. Since she had lain under the gargour net, her limbs were yet to straighten out. Soraiyya struggled like a Hamour caught in a shark's jaws. Every hair end seemed to be spitting out blood.

'My dear Hamour, let me soak each piece of you with lemon juice and masala,' Manichand muttered as he stroked her body. Soraiyya stopped breathing. She imagined she was in some other place, and was another person.

'Now I am sautéing onion and spices. What fragrance…let me now apply the mixture affectionately to your beautiful body.'

Her eyes were closed tight; only her lips whimpered endlessly.

'Huh! Did some chilli paste enter my Hamour's eyes? Now, I am dropping you into a vessel with boiling rice and water. Let it cook well. Now I am shutting the lid of the vessel.'

When Manichand penetrated her body, Soraiyya thrashed about for a moment and then lost consciousness. When the perspiring Manichand lifted himself from her body, he bent to lick at her lips. He savagely muttered, 'The name of the dish I prepared is Machboos. My beloved Machboos, I have eaten you to my fill.'

There was no chance that Manichand had ever eaten the Arabic delicacy known as Machboos, made with Hamour fish. He jested with the guard that for consuming an Arab girl, he had temporarily converted into a non-vegetarian.

■

At that time, Mariam was participating in the funeral rites of Zaleekha. The unfortunate girl's Ummi had died too. Most of the women, whom she had seen the day before the wedding, were absent. The rites were being conducted by the groom-to-be and his baba.

Shamsa, along with Khadeeja, had gone to the house of the Political Agent mentioned by Rosa. The houses where the British lived with their families were very large. Bougainvillea flowers were abundant in many of these homes. The prams of their children, stuck in sand, could be sighted in the backyards. The address which Rosa had given belonged to an officer called Edward Simon. His wife was playing with the children in the courtyard. She was uttering some Arabic words. But in the very first conversation, Shamsa realized that her knowledge of Arabic was negligible.

Mrs Edward took them to the kitchen and served cold water. The visitors were amazed at the size of the eggs stored in the refrigerator—double that of the eggs which the hens laid in Deira! Shamsa also noticed the pomegranates. Iranian pomegranates were rare to be seen nowadays. Usually, they got spoilt during the long journey to Dubai.

'Isn't this uncomfortable?' Mrs Edward tugged at Khadeeja's burqa.

'I am used to it. In fact, it is far more uncomfortable to step out without it,' Khadeeja smiled.

Seeing Khadeeja look wonderingly inside the refrigerator, Mrs Edward offered her a banana When Khadeeja looked questioningly at Shamsa, the white woman offered her one too. Mrs Edward had no clue that bananas were considered a delicacy in Deira. On seeing bananas, people on the shore enquired whether someone had fallen sick in the house! Shamsa relished the banana while Khadeeja tucked it away, like a precious object, inside her abaya.

Mr Edward Simon was very conversant with Arabic. He called them to his office room. Rosa often quipped that the relationship between the British and the Trucial Coast was a strange one. It was like the symbiosis between the Gobi fish and the shrimp, abundantly sighted in the Persian Gulf (the Mediterranean Sea in West Asia). The shrimp builds and maintains the burrow at the bottom of the sea, in which both creatures live together. The Gobi cleans out the burrow daily, throwing out the slush and sand. The nearly blind shrimp depends on the Gobi for protection and its long sensors are always touching the Gobi. Whenever a predator passes that way, the Gobi warns the shrimp with the flick of its tail and pushes it inside the burrow. The alert watchman never leaves the burrow. It was difficult to understand who stood to benefit and lose from such a relationship. In short, the Gobi fish got a burrow to live in, and the shrimp got a protector!

Khadeeja told in detail about her son's sudden disappearance. Edward said that many such cases had been reported in the Trucial Coast recently. When he asked for more details, Shamsa pitched in.

'We have apprehensions that my Baba, Ahmad Manzuri, is involved in this disappearance. If you would kindly order an investigation along those lines…'

Khadeeja grabbed her hand and gestured her to be silent. Shamsa felt infuriated that while she was revealing information about her own father, Khadeeja was still being loyal to her erstwhile employer. When they left, Edward's children observed them with curious, narrowed eyes.

■

Soraiyya pushed open the creaky, rusty door of the godown. She crossed her arms across her chest to hide the torn abaya. In the moist sabkha sand, yellow crabs were scrambling after her footsteps. Drops of blood were oozing from her feet. Had Soraiyya fallen, the crabs would have harmed her with their pincers.

She took the shorter path home instead of crossing the souk. She felt as if thousands of locusts were following in her wake. When she turned, Soraiyya caught a glimpse of the 'brown carpet' of locusts humming and hovering near her. She walked as fast as she could, not possessing the strength to run. The ravenous flock would devastate anything in its way in moments.

Soraiyya wondered, 'Why am I seeing voracious creatures all the time?' On waking, she had seen grazing sea-elephants, then the sneakily blood-licking crabs, and now a swarm of locusts which was covering her from head to toe! What was happening?

The horde of locusts from Africa, which had alighted in Dubai the previous year, had turned the date palm trees bald. The lads in the hovels of Deira had set out to snare them, wishing to roast them for food. Jadda had quipped about its nutritional value!

After chomping on fried locusts thrice a day, the tummies of many children and their mothers had been satiated. As she reached Bait Al Banat, Soraiyya cast another backward glance. The locusts had vanished, and so had the crabs.

Wondering how she would show her face, Soraiyya stood flabbergasted for a while. Then she regained her poise, adjusted her shayla and walked in quickly. As she moved to the bathroom, Mariam called out to her.

'I was expecting you at Zaleekha's *Fatiha* (recitation of the first chapter of Quran during the wedding ceremony)! I waited for some time and then returned. I could not bear sitting there since I was getting overwhelmed by the memories.'

After pouring water all over herself, soaking from head to toe, Soraiyya stepped out and stood before her family. From the wet abaya, drops of water dripped, jostling against one another, wishing to be the first to fall. Mariam stuck the needle in her hand into the Kajuja and gazed at her, aghast. Soraiyya flinched as if the needle had penetrated her stomach.

Farewell

I BRUSQUELY SHUT THE BOOK. INDEED, I was remembering how Solomon said that he shuddered to imagine the agony endured by Soraiyya.

'Soraiyya has the resilience to handle any trauma, Sol,' I had replied calmly.

'How can you be so sure? In those times, a woman like her… how could she face it with equanimity?'

'She can! Soraiyya experienced it as the grazing of wild sea-elephants and an attack by locusts,' I explained. 'Hungry sea-elephants graze rapaciously through the grass at the sea floor and locusts decapitate the heads of date trees! After the creatures are sated, they withdraw. Something similar happened to her. Manichand sautéed the Hamour with spices, cooked it with rice and made Machboos. The first taste of non-vegetarian food which Manichand, the hard-core vegetarian, had. How he must have relished it!'

'Soraiyya saw the incident merely as a hungry person feeding gluttonously. Okay, I think I understand,' Solomon said.

'This event is enough to catch a glimpse of Soraiyya's character! She had never desired any man. Unlike her sisters Mariam and Shamsa, Soraiyya never nurtured any romantic fantasies either. But she was adamant about leading life well. Did she not take over the great responsibility of looking after her sisters and her grandmother?'

'Naz, how many Soraiyyas do you know?'

'I have not met many Soraiyyas in my life. She is neither me, nor Rukhiyami, nor Sandra. But any woman would aspire to be like her! She could effortlessly find a way to an island which many others would have never reached. Nothing, no one, can scare her now.'

■

I saved the invitation letter on my desktop.

'I got a personal mail too, Sandra. The same image of the invitation letter.'

'Who sent it?' Sandra queried.

'The mail was from the publisher's official mail id, copying many people. In fact, it cannot be seen as a personal invitation.'

'That means they are investing in a good advertising campaign for the book! How can they publish someone's photograph without their permission? I wonder at the daring!' Sandra said.

'Sandra, it was Solomon who gave them my photograph. How can I grumble about it?'

The day Solomon left Dubai, all of us met in the evening at the mellow ambience of the Buddha Bar. Like its name, there were beautiful sculptures of the Buddha inside. I had nothing particular to speak about. When they asked me about the wine of my choice, I gave a non-committal reply.

Solomon grinned, 'Try vodka today...not wine!'

We were on the top floor, at a table adjoining the balcony. Below us, on the ground floor, a huge Buddha statue could be seen. Many were climbing the steps of happiness surrounding it. A group of European women were sitting at a round glass table and clapping to Justin Bieber's latest song. The Indonesian at the next table was dancing with the barmaid.

Sandra poured the drink in my glass. Solomon's face blazed in the yellow light reflected from the Buddha statue. Nobody tasted the chicken dish we had ordered. I struggled not to display my unhappiness when Solomon smiled at me. As I started drinking, I became more cheerful. I did not protest when the glass was refilled many times. I was keen to divert my mind from Solomon's impending journey. After some time, I almost forgot about the departure.

The bartenders started clapping along with the European women. Everyone was swaying to the rhythm of the song. The barmaids wore figure-hugging gowns resembling mermaids. They seemed to have emerged from the sea, attuned to the rhythms of intoxication!

'What gift do you need, Solomon?' Varun asked suddenly.

'Dubai has given me a great gift. What else do I need?' Solomon looked at me tenderly.

'Anything typical of Dubai? Don't ask for the creek or museum, please!' Sandra laughed.

'There is nothing typical of any land, Sandra. Haven't you heard about the biriyani story? Have you read N.S. Madhavan's book, *Litanies of Dutch Battery*? There is a conversation between the Valiyasari, the head mason, and Edwin. When Edwin, who is a whiz in cooking, is asked whether the Arabs had brought biriyani to Calicut, he retorts that it was the Jonaka Mappilas of Malabar who had given biriyani to the Arabs! In their gigantic ships, they brought dates and carried back timber, tiles, yarn, and the ingredients to prepare biriyani. Edwin quips that when the Arab reaches his tent, after swaying on the camel's back for hours on end, it is heavenly to have a plate of biriyani waiting for him,' Solomon laughed.

Varun pitched in, 'In short, what had to be taken away, and what had to be given, all had happened early on! There is nothing left to give and take anymore, is there?'

'There is something beyond giving and taking, Varun. The magic of discovery! Wherever I have travelled, I have discovered more than I could ever measure. For someone like me, those are my most valued earnings,' Solomon said somberly.

I remembered Samad on hearing the word 'earning'. That was Samad's favourite refrain: 'earnings', 'we have to earn enough and build a huge house in the village', 'buy a car', 'make the days of childhood penury a distant memory…'

Samad's 'earnings' were actually the dreams of a typical Gulf emigrant. Nowadays, whenever I hear that word, I am reminded of houses and cars. When Solomon gave 'earnings' a whole new interpretation, I felt the awakening of something ineffable within.

'Once I leave, will you turn into a lovelorn persona, Naz? Like

Mariam who pines for Farhad, listening to Umm Kulthum's songs?' Solomon teased me.

I had absolutely no idea about my situation after Solomon's return. I stared at a smaller Buddha made of stone, meditating away on a corner, and remained silent.

'Who on earth are Farhad and Mariam? New avatars, eh?' Varun was astounded.

'Ah, they are characters who are currently hidden behind the curtains... Slowly, they shall make their appearance on the stage,' Solomon drawled.

'Varun, don't even bother! Part of creative complexities,' Sandra spoke, the effect of alcohol echoing in her voice.

The curtain Solomon referred to that evening, now stands drawn! All the characters are clearly visible.

We spent some time in Jumeirah Beach. Sandra and Varun got drenched by the waves as they sat very close to the sea. Solomon and I, we took a walk on the shore.

'Sol, what should I do when I feel like seeing you?'

'You should see me.'

'How?'

'How do you see Mariam stitching the thawb, Naz? How do you hear Shamsa telling stories? You watch Soraiyya pick up a fight with Jadda, don't you? In the same way, you shall see me and hear me too.'

'In today's age, do humans interact in such a way?'

'Then how do you see them? You even saw the sparkle of the pearl in the oyster shell which Ahmad Manzuri retrieved from the sea, did you not?'

For each of my querulous objections, Solomon had an answer which was logical and relentless.

Seeing three missed calls from Samad, I bid farewell to Solomon. Sandra and Varun dropped me home. I was still wearing the hospital uniform. When I opened the door with my key, to my astonishment, I found Samad inside the house.

He was walking about the hall, displaying much impatience and anxiety.

'How come you are so late? Do you come home every day at this time? Why are you unsteady? Your face looks so...?'

When Samad aimed a barrage of questions at me, I sat down exhausted in a chair.

'What is this stink?" Samad grabbed my arm and started sniffing.

'Nazia, you smell of alcohol! Where the hell are you coming from?'

My eyes drooped. I clutched the wall and slowly made my way to the bathroom. Even after a shower and change of clothes, the headache and drowsiness did not let go of me. Samad was banging on the bathroom door without any respite. He was yelling some gibberish.

'What a horrid stench! I feel so repelled! Instead of going to the hospital, where were you gallivanting about every day?'

I did not have the courage to open the door. After a while, when I heard the sound of a door being shut with a resounding bang, I slipped outside. I lay down on the bed and applied some Tiger balm on my forehead. There was thunder and lightning along with a mild drizzle. I felt very cold. Due to the sting of the Tiger balm, my eyes welled up with tears.

After a while, Samad appeared at the door. The expression was accusatory and the questions were excoriating.

'All of this stuff happened because I brought you to the Gulf! Like all typical Gulf employees, I should have insisted that you stay back at home in the village taking care of the kitchen and safeguarding the money! You would have looked after my umma, given birth to my children, and lived a proper domesticated life. You would have received my monthly money orders and lived like ordinary women! I was the one who made a mistake. I helped you don a suit and coat, sit in a grand office chair and speak a few words in English! I have ended up stabbing myself in the back, right?'

Samad was hitting his head desperately and pulling at his hair.

'And just see how coolly she lays on her back as if she is so innocent!' Rasping thus, he grabbed a bottle of talc and threw it at me. Even though I tried to evade, it hit my neck and bruised me.

'Get out right now! I don't need a wife who comes home stinking of liquor. I have never touched alcohol or cigarette ever in my life. And look at my wife... Can't believe it!'

The normal time for Samad's return from his shop was yet to arrive. Usually, he closed his shop at eleven at night. That particular night, he had to drop someone at the airport and had come home to change his dress. In fact, he had mentioned it in the morning to me but it slipped from my mind.

The events which transpired in the flat afterwards led to my walking on the road, in a nightdress, in the pouring rain. While I was walking to Sandra's flat in the freezing temperature, the flight carrying Solomon took off. As I shivered in the bitter cold, I glanced up at the sky. Solomon had long moved away, after carving a path in the clouds.

∞

Soraiyya sat with her face downcast, amidst the women. Jadda and Khadeeja were sitting on the handwoven mattress, their legs stretched out. The *tasbih* prayer beads were rolling at more than normal speed through Jadda's fingers, while her lips were murmuring prayers unceasingly. Mariam was gently applying myrrh unguent on Soraiyya's bruises. As Mariam wept, Soraiyya was consoling her.

'Why are you weeping? I hate it when anyone cries in this home,' Soraiyya's voice took on a hard edge.

'There are two types of tears: happy and sad. Both are produced by the same set of eyes,' Shamsa spoke.

'These tears are sorrowful and I refuse to watch.' Soraiyya turned her face away.

'Mariam, have you heard of Shamma's legendary tears?' Shamsa raised a whimsical question.

'Which Shamma?'

'A girl who lived in our Deira once upon a time...a pearl diver's daughter.'

'No.'

And Shamsa started her tale.

Every year when Falah, the pearl diver, went off to sea, his daughter Shamma used to accompany him till the shores. When he returned after every trip, Falah would bring a unique gift for her. Beautiful gemstones, rubies, seashells...many were the curiosities in Shamma's treasure chest. During his last trip, Falah had brought a violet-coloured sparkling stone for Shamma. While handing it over to his daughter, Falah had warned: 'This stone is a key to unlock another world.'

Four months passed. The ships started returning home and Shamma would eagerly visit the shore every day. Despite waiting for many days, her father's group did not return. One night, Shamma had a strange dream. A shimmer of light which had the colour of the sea... and slowly the face of a woman glowing inside it. Soon, the face turned into the shape of a ship. It was the sambuka *ship of Falah! Shamma saw her father and his henchmen pleading for help inside the ship.*

The woman with the glow of the blue sea spoke to Shamma: 'Come to the beach tomorrow at dawn.'

When Shamma woke up the next morning, she was clutching the violet stone close. She was utterly surprised because she had left it locked inside the box, the previous night. She reached the beach early morning. Then, the woman from her dreams emerged from the sea.

In a sharp tone, the woman said: 'I am the Queen of the Sea. Your father and his men have caused me much agony. They killed the magic fish which used to craft precious and powerful gemstones of the sea. Who shall make those powerful ornaments for me now?'

'Dear Queen! It must have happened inadvertently. Kindly tell me if they are safe.' Shamma gathered her courage and asked.

'Nothing will happen to them. But you should make ornaments for me.'

'But I have never made any!' Shamma replied.

'I shall teach you. Mix your tears with the sea waters. Dip your violet stone in it. When you raise the stone, the drops which drip down shall turn into precious stones. Make seven such ornaments for me by working every evening. If you reveal this secret to anybody, you shall never see your father again.'

Every evening, Shamma started visiting the shore and made precious gemstones. On the third day, a young man approached her.

'Why are you weeping, sitting all by yourself?'

'I am waiting for my baba, Falah.'

'I know your father. Once he saved my life when I was drowning in the sea,' the youth replied. His name was Muhammad and he lived in the neighbourhood.

The next evening, Muhammad observed Shamma's doings surreptitiously. Shamma had created six ornaments by then and the Queen of the Sea appeared before her. She was pleased with Shamma's work. Using her magical powers, the Queen noticed the hidden Muhammad.

'You revealed my secret to someone else. You shall never see your baba again!' Saying thus, she vanished into the waves.

Shamma was heartbroken with grief. Muhammad dived into the waves after the Queen. He did not return from the sea either.

Shamma wondered whether she could get both Muhammad and her baba back by making fourteen precious stones. When she finished her task, the Queen of the Sea, albeit disgruntled, was forced to appear.

'Fourteen lovely gemstones! You have worked hard, indeed! Your baba and his ship shall return tomorrow,' the Queen of the Sea proclaimed graciously.

'What about Muhammad?'

'He shall remain my slave. He encroached upon my palace, following me, did he not?'

'Muhammad came after you to testify about my innocence,' Shamma pleaded.

'I shall free him. But you shall have to pay a steep price for it. From now on, I need pure tears. Those are more valuable than diamonds.'

Shamma replied sadly, 'I shall weep every morning.'

The Queen of the Sea was pleased. 'Your father shall return tomorrow and Muhammad, the day after.'

The next day, the sambuka returned from the sea and anchored at the coast. The news spread like wild fire. The crowd thronged around the sailors and everybody thanked Shamma. The very next day, an exhausted Muhammad floated back to the shore. He recovered fast.

One day, he came to a weeping Shamma and said, 'You saved my life, and I am deeply grateful to you.' Thinking of her new pact with the Queen of the Sea, Shamma could not help sobbing wretchedly. She collected her tears in a clay pot.

Muhammad said, 'Shamma, these are sad tears. That strengthens the Queen. Now start shedding tears of joy.'

'How?'

'Remember how your father returned safely, how everybody thanked you... The sailors' wives, their children were all delighted, were they not? Recollect those memories and cry with joy! Now your father and mother are together, are they not?' Listening to Muhammad's wise words, tears of happiness sprang from Shamma's eyes.

Every morning, Muhammad would sit alongside her on the sand and make her shed happy tears.

One day, an incensed Queen of the Sea appeared before Shamma. 'You are cheating me. Throw away your happy tears. Let them dry up on the sand!'

Muhammad, who had hidden himself, suddenly appeared, carrying the pot of happy tears. He hurled the contents at the enraged Queen. A blue smoke rose and the Queen turned into vapour.

'Oh yes, I know the rest of the tale! From then on, every year, Shamma bid farewell to two men who went pearl diving—Falah and Muhammad. Am I right?' Soraiyya asked wryly.

'Yes,' Shamsa replied.

'I know that all your stories inevitably end in a wedding.'

'Well, I just narrated what happened when Shamma shed happy tears, that's all!' Shamsa sounded peeved.

'Don't argue. Nobody should tell anyone about what Soraiyya suffered. Let it stay as a secret within this house,' Jadda said in a heartbroken voice.

Mariam continued to sob. Zaleekha's death and Soraiyya's tragedy had shaken her up terribly. It was like a tidal wave of anguish.

After the night prayers, as they readied for sleep, Mariam turned to Shamsa.

'Poor Soraiyya, she is handling the situation bravely. Had it been me, I would have most probably died.'

'Mariam, calm down. Soraiyya's body and mind shall soon heal. You just stop weeping copiously in her presence,' Shamsa said tersely.

'No, none of us will shed any more tears.'

Mariam turned her face to the wall, which was exuding heat waves. Her tears having dried up, she slipped into slumber. Shamsa was staring at the sky, which showed up through the one eye of the window. She was busy spreading the magic carpet of a new story on the white clouds. Grumbling about the sun which had been roasting them throughout the day, Jadda and Khadeeja tried to catch some sleep inside the barasti.

Soraiyya tried to sniff at her hands. 'Has the stink of Machboos left her body as yet?' During her disturbed sleep, waking up intermittently, she continued to smell her hands.

Museum

AFTER READING ABOUT MARIAM'S TEARS, I could not suppress the urge to visit Bait Al Banat once more. I applied for leave. Without informing Sandra, I set out all alone. Since it was a working day, the souk was deserted. Small shops were abutting each other on either side of the narrow gully. Most ancient structures were being preserved carefully.

I noticed many passersby carrying heavy loads on their backs, hurrying along the road. Shopkeepers were trying to inveigle passersby with many gimmicks. One noticed me and heckled in English, 'Madam, nice kurti, good colour, only 30 dirhams!' When I ignored him, he effortlessly changed the language of persuasion to Hindi. Before the qualities of the kurti were eulogized in Arabic and Tamil, I scurried away.

Everybody is super busy in the souk at all times. Both the sellers and buyers were in a hurry. I tried to make my way without scraping against anyone's body. The houses where Mariam sold her silk dresses must have transformed into shops. Soraiyya would fearlessly sit in her perfume shop in the souk even at night. Where in the souk was her shop? Children must have raced through the same street to listen to Shamsa's tales. Didn't she wrap up the sweet kunafa and hurry to meet Yakub through this same gully? What was I musing about? Well, I had tricked Sandra and arrived here to wander through the seas, hills and forests of my imagination, did I not?

When I reached Bait Al Banat, it was closed. The working time of the museum was inscribed on the door: Morning six to evening six.

The time was 9.30 a.m. Usually, I was the first customer at

the beauty salon too. Somehow, I liked the morning ambience of the salon run by Sati Chechi. She would play the 'Gayatri Mantra' on the speaker. 'Om Bhur Bhuva Swaha...' Sandra would tease that all I needed was to listen to Anuradha Paudwal on YouTube to enjoy the same music. But I yearned for the fragrance of the incense sticks, and the fresh feeling of the sparkling-clean room in all its fullness. It was a surreal experience.

I leaned against the neem tree in front of the Women's Museum. Could the tree have been a permanent fixture since the time of the girls? No way; it was only ten years old. Caressing the tree trunk, I gazed at the direction where once Nafisa Jadda's barasti was located. It was chock-a-block with concrete buildings. The barasti must have been around fifteen feet away, to the east of Bait Al Banat. Until she died, Jadda's eyes must have watched over the girls like the light from a watchtower.

At ten, a Filipino girl came to open the museum. She was the receptionist. I was welcomed warmly. As soon as I entered, a cloud of familiar smells came wafting close to me. The fragrance of Soraiyya's ittar bottles! I thought I saw someone standing behind the counter displaying the traditional dresses of Emirati women. But when I looked again, nobody was there. It must have been Shamsa for sure! I could see different faces in each corner of the room. Sandra would have concluded that I was loony. But I swear I am speaking the truth, I did see them. I saw all of them, including Nafisa Jadda and Khadeeja...the residents of Bait Al Banat. If I could not recognize them, who on earth could?

Mariam's Butterfly sewing machine, in a glass enclosure, started rotating slowly. Its needles were rising and falling. I stared closely—yes, it was stitching a dress. A blue silk dress slipped from the machine and floated towards me, touching my feet. I stepped back in shock. I moved about the carpet with my naked feet. I experienced the same cold which seeped inside one's soles while walking through the desert at night! My toes froze and I had no sensation beneath my knees. I was either floating in air or I was sinking into the desert sand...

I left the room and started climbing the stairs. Even on the first step, I found my limbs not obeying my command. My body felt fatigued suddenly. Grasping the handrail, I turned to hail the Filipino girl. I do not know what happened afterwards except that I hit my head somewhere.

When I opened my eyes, Sandra was sitting by my side. I was in hospital.

'What was the need to wander about that museum all alone? Couldn't you have called me?' Sandra looked furious.

Varun was in the room too.

'Varun, please book a ticket for Nazia,' Sandra spoke.

'Why?' I protested weakly.

'Not now. You have to attend the book release. The ticket is for that.'

'I can't possibly! See, I collapsed in Bait Al Banat. Imagine a stage, that too with Solomon... I cannot do it.'

'We will cross the bridge when we come to it. Your book is getting released. And you are attending it. No second thoughts.'

Once Sandra took a decision, she would implement it, come hell or high water. I would have to go. The only thing needed was amassing the energy for that effort. I contemplated calling Rukhiyami.

Dr Peace Amin came to do some preliminary check-up. He checked my eyes and commented, 'Seems this girl here has seen something forbidden! Everything is stored inside her eyes. Here, I can see very well!'

'Nowadays, she is seeing only what should not be seen, doctor,' Sandra grumbled.

'Nothing to worry. Once she sees those who should be seen, all will be fine!' Dr Peace Amin winked playfully.

After the doctor left, Sandra started goading me again.

'Shall I tell you what you are brooding over now? *Once this brattish Sandra leaves, I shall call up Rukhiyami*. Am I right? Tell me!'

I felt miffed that she was entering my mind and digging up

unnecessary details. She could even deduce the dreams I had at night! Solomon used to warn that one should be wary in front of those who could read one's mind. They would even analyze your life-blood!

However, Solomon himself could read minds. He must have predicted with precision every thought of mine after receiving the book. My facial expression on seeing the book release announcement... Undoubtedly, he would have visualized my surprise, with portrait-like clarity, in his mind.

∞

Soraiyya would feel like throwing up on smelling sandalwood and frankincense. She stopped going to her perfume shop in the souk. Ali was looking after it now. Whenever she stepped out, Jadda would push an iron dagger in her abaya. The belief was that it protected the pregnant woman from bad spirits. She had also tied amulets carrying verses from the Holy Quran around Soraiyya's arms and neck. Jadda forbade Soraiyya from stepping into the yard after twilight.

Once, an owl hooted from the neem tree in front of Bait Al Banat. Jadda shut the window for four days in a row! Apparently, it was inauspicious for the unborn child if the mother sighted an owl! Khadeeja's peeve was that Soraiyya never asked for favourite snacks. She threatened that if Soraiyya did not eat what she wished for, the child would be born with birthmarks—with shapes and colours resembling the desired food! Whenever Khadeeja spoke about the baby's dresses and cradle, Soraiyya responded as if they were discussing a stranger's child.

Jadda sold off her old gold ornaments in Harilal's shop in the souk and purchased a new taxi for Soraiyya. She also hired a new Omani driver. Soraiyya's main interests became checking the accounts of both the taxi and her perfume shop.

It was Soraiyya's third month of pregnancy. Mariam often wept recalling the incident. While stitching *sabiha* frocks from cotton for the newborn, her eyes streamed over. Everybody would pretend not to notice; even Jadda seemed to have shrugged it off. 'There is no point in pleading for help after the judgement has been passed,' was her brusque take on the events. When a disaster occurred, what was the point of screaming and shouting. One should face it boldly, what else? As far as Jadda was concerned, it was irrelevant whose child Soraiyya was bearing. What mattered was that she was going to give birth to a new life. Once the child was born, he or she would live in their midst as one of them. That was all.

Jadda wished for a girl while Mariam preferred a boy. She could not bear the thought of another life pining away in the house.

'Mothers who do not have daughters die of mysterious reasons,' Jadda quipped in reply. The implicit meaning was that if one did not have a daughter who would take care of one during old age, it was like being childless and barren!

After seeing Soraiyya on the day of her assault, Shamsa had wished to get in touch with the British Agent or at least the police. But it was Soraiyya who had refused to go ahead. Jadda knew that it was against her character. However, Soraiyya had stuck to her stand. When signs of her pregnancy showed up, everybody's attitude changed. No one asked Soraiyya about Manichand or that tragic event.

All the women were determined that Manichand should never know about Soraiyya being pregnant with his child. Soraiyya stopped stepping out when her stomach bulged prominently. Once, helpless in finding excuses, Shamsa ended up sharing the news with Zaleekha's sister without revealing any details. Soon, the neighbourhood women started trickling into Bait Al Banat and tried their best to extract the facts and figures from the residents. There were many who mocked the 'immaculate conception'. Most of them cast their doubts on the Omani driver, Mubarak. Khadeeja thought it best to let them believe so.

One day, a woman came with dried powder made of camel

manure. It was supposed to be spread on the floor, just below the cloth cradle. The urine would be absorbed by the manure and the stench would not permeate the house. She would not go away and narrated many tales of other pregnant women. The woman cross-checked the circumference of Soraiyya's stomach and continued to gossip for long. Shamsa asked sharply whether she did not have any work at home. The brazen woman was indifferent to the blatant sarcasm and sat determinedly in the room. She was apprehensive if it was actually a human child in Soraiyya's tummy! She started on a tale of an old woman and a young girl who died recently due to protuberances. Soraiyya continued unperturbed and the woman felt disappointed at not being able to provoke her. Then Shamsa pitched in cattily, 'Don't you know? Inside Soraiyya's tummy is a huge sparrow fledgling!'

'What?' The woman gawked at her.

'Yes, a female sparrow! Haven't you heard the Egyptian folk tale about the female sparrow which stood guard over a cumin field?'

Expecting to unearth the secret of Soraiyya's pregnancy from the story, the woman pulled her mattress near Shamsa and leaned in to listen.

Once upon a time, there was a childless woman in Egypt. She prayed to God, 'Dear God, give me at least a sparrow fledgling as a child!' God answered her sincere prayer. Soon, the woman gave birth to a little female fledgling.

The woman's husband had a cumin field of his own. One day, he called the sparrow fledgling to him and said, 'Go and stand guard over my cumin field.' She promptly followed her father's orders. Just then, a loafer sneaked in to steal the cumin seeds. The fledgling chirped warningly, 'You better not steal! Or your hands shall be chopped off. May everything turn topsy-turvy.' In moments, the man became suspended upside down. Frantically, he made his escape from the field.

After some time, another man encroached upon the field and met with the same fate. The news spread all over the land. Finally, it reached the ruler's ears. The Pasha reached the place with his horseman. 'Go and pluck some cumin seeds,' the Pasha ordered. When the henchman tried to grab some cumin seeds, the little sparrow tweeted, 'Let go at once! Or your hands shall be chopped off. May everything turn topsy-turvy!' The man dangled, upside down! Panicking, he managed to get away.

The Pasha himself reached the cumin field. The sparrow squeaked its curse but the Pasha quickly grabbed the little creature. In a flash, the sparrow chirped in sweet tones, 'Mother, don't think that I am guarding the cumin field. I am in the Pasha's hands and I am travelling to Constantinople.' Hearing the enchanting voice of the bird, the Pasha melted. He said, 'I would like to hear you yet again.' Then the sparrow retorted, 'Until you put me in your big pocket, I shall not utter a word.' When the Pasha did so, the sparrow twittered, 'Dear Mother, do not be mistaken that I am standing guard over the cumin field. I am in the Pasha's big pocket and I am travelling to Constantinople.' She started gobbling down all the gold coins in the pocket.

After a while, the Pasha tried to persuade her again. 'Come on, little sparrow. Let me hear you talk.' 'Until you put me in the pocket of your royal robe, I shall not utter a word.' The amused Pasha tucked her into his robe's pocket. The sparrow cheeped, 'Dear Mother, don't think that I am watching over the cumin field. I am in the Pasha's robe pocket and am on my way to Constantinople.' She swallowed the golden watch in the Pasha's pocket.

The Pasha entreated after some time, 'Talk to me, little sparrow.' The sparrow fledgling said, 'Not until you put me on the tassels of your grand Turkish cap.' As soon as the Pasha put her atop his cap, the wily fledgling flew away. Then she cursed, 'May everything turn topsy-turvy!' The Pasha found himself hanging upside down.

The little sparrow flew back to her mother. She knocked on the door with her beak. 'Mother dear, please open the door. It is your sparrow daughter.' Immediately came her mother's incensed retort: 'I am not your mother and neither are you my child. Where did you take off without seeking my permission?' 'Mother dear, I was on my way to Constantinople. Just open the door and see what precious gifts I have brought for you.' Her mother opened the door and the little sparrow spat out the gold coins and golden watch. Her mother's peeves melted away.

By the time Shamsa narrated half the tale, the woman started fidgeting. She put down her coffee cup and adjusted her shayla. Then she scratched at her arms and legs and before the tale ended, she had walked away after bidding 'Ma'a Salama'!

'Shamsa, you have the gift of the gab. You can push away invaders and entice others at will! You are truly blessed,' Mariam was all praise for her younger sister.

Mariam was especially gifted in praising others. She was also adept at bundling up her own sorrows. That was why she remained mournful and in love with darkness. Whenever she confessed that she still dreamt of Farhad, Soraiyya would laugh at her. 'Does he have a thick beard or a thin one? Is he flabby or healthy? Without knowing whether he is bald, whether he has turned into a hunchback or grown blind, in which form are you dreaming of him?' Mariam could never get her wits around Soraiyya's practical nature. She still dreamt of Farhad as the erstwhile handsome young man, full of vitality. Mariam was a ship who was anchored forever in an unknown shore!

Shamsa scolded, 'Don't you see Soraiyya boldly handling her predicament? Am I not living with the pain of Yakub's unexpected disappearance? Soraiyya does her daily chores and I take refuge in my stories. Why can't you overcome Farhad's loss, using your beautiful embroidery skills? Dear Mariam, do not get depressed; it will destroy you inch by inch.'

Mariam just sighed in reply.

The women in the neighbourhood were busy casting aspersions on Nafisa Jadda. When Khadeeja went to draw water from the well, the women avoided her and continued to gossip salaciously in a distant group. 'The head of the family herself is busy purchasing clothes for the illegitimate baby and preparing the cradle! What strange times!' When Khadeeja was walking with the water pot on her head, two women who lived south of the creek, Haleema and Sabeera, accompanied her. The clayey water droplets from the almost dried-up well traced rivulets of brown on their cheeks. On reaching the chin, the droplets sparkled and then evaporated before moving down the neck.

'Khadeeja, you are the slave of the household. Shouldn't you have intervened? Do you bring up the girls to turn wanton?' Sabeera jeered.

Haleema interjected immediately, 'What can she advise? The younger girl is having an affair with her son, isn't she? What a shame!'

'It would not have happened if their baba was around. There is no man to restrain them. Children of Iblis, I say!'

Khadeeja put down her pot and stood with arms akimbo, staring at the vicious duo.

'You both have been brought up by decent fathers, right? Did they teach you to speak rot about other human beings? Daughters of fathers who never taught them to love one's neighbours, bah!'

Khadeeja spat with derision and moved away fast. Since Jadda did not step out often, she did not have to face such circumstances. Khadeeja poured the water into the long-necked jug. The same medley of anxiety and apprehensions, displayed on the face of a young child as she tried to walk for the first time, clinging to the finger of her mother, was visible yet again on her aged face.

Seated on the ground, her hand on her head, Khadeeja rued bitterly: 'I do not understand why this house is so messed up! The eldest has no life at all. The youngest fell in love with a slave and caused a ruckus. The middle one suffered a sexual assault and has conceived an illegitimate child! Their mother died an untimely death too! This house is surely accursed, Ya Rab!'

'No Khadeeja, we are not accursed at all. Your son Yakub will return and marry Shamsa. Soraiyya's child is ours too. It is a life which has sprung inside Bait Al Banat. It is better that there is nobody claiming rights over the newborn. Mariam is still young and her days for blooming are yet to arrive. It shall all turn out fine. Let us be patient.' Jadda's words silenced Khadeeja.

Nazia Hassan

LIZZY CHECHI RETURNED HOME AFTER her delivery. I wished to visit her. It was her third baby. She had wanted a daughter but again, had been blessed with a son. When the gender of the baby was revealed in the fourth month, she had spoken emotionally.

'Naz, I believe that my yet unborn daughter shall always look after these three boys like a guardian angel.'

Lizzy Chechi, who could visualize a guardian angel in her unseen daughter, would have been happy with the sparrow fledgling of Shamsa's story!

It was Friday and I was busy chatting with Rukhiyami for over an hour. We hadn't spoken about Solomon for ages. A book and its release became the topic of our discussion. Without any preface, Rukhiyami commented, 'I don't think that Samad will ever re-enter your life. But another man had been there, someone who played a prominent role. *Aap jaisa koyi mere zindagi mein aaye…*' As she hummed, I wished to cut short the video call. Then abruptly, I started enquiring about the monsoon and sunshine back home.

'Naz, you really miss him, don't you?'

'Of course, but…'

'Solomon has no idea that you have separated from Samad. Neither does he know that he is the reason behind it,' Rukhiyami said.

'Rukhiyami, Solomon is not the reason for my separation. Samad has no clue that such a person exists in my life. He asked me to move out of his house because I carried a different smell that day, not alike the normal one. He decided in a few hours that he didn't need a differently smelling wife. And I did not feel the need to live forever with the smell, colour and shape which he decided to allow me. I did not plead with him or offer an apology. Neither did I endeavour to explain my position. I never felt that my decision to leave that house was a mistake,' I replied firmly.

'Sure, sure. See, the relationship with Samad has now become an old story. Let us speak about the future. Solomon is the only one who matters here. You should meet him definitely. I don't think your life should be wasted in this manner.'

'Rukhiyami, if you are hinting at marriage, Solomon is not cut out for it. My Sol will never become my husband. In my mind, he stays as a figure who transcends all such descriptions.'

'Have I ever spoken about marriage with you? I just say that you should meet him. Can't human beings meet without a reason, my child?'

'Hmm, maybe. I am enjoying the presence of Solomon who came searching for me in the form of a book. That's my current mood.'

'Your stupid mood! Once you see him, all your moodiness will vanish!'

'Rukhiyami, when I read this book, I am not seeing the Solomon who walked with me, with his fingers clasped around mine, through the streets of Deira. Instead, I see the Solomon who has taken over my thoughts, my imagination… Someone who turned my fantasies into words…who is quintessentially me, perhaps?'

'If so, what preparation do you need to see someone who is essentially a part of you? It is like looking at your own image in the mirror. Right from childhood, you would weave a tale around even your evening tea! Even before putting the kettle to boil, you would visualize the scene of sipping the tea, the tea flowing down your throat, and staring afar while holding the hot cup of tea… But not everything can be planned ahead, Naz. Think of the moment when you first met Solomon. With the same light-heartedness, handle this situation too. You just go… Let your mind and body behave the way they wish to! You just let things be. Events will unfold by themselves.'

I felt that Rukhiyami's long, grey tresses too would be laughing at me. Jadda and Shamsa hadn't been devastated by the tragedy in Soraiyya's life, had they? They had been determined to handle it with equanimity. What disaster had befallen me? The universe had given me an opportunity to meet someone very dear to me. As Rukhiyami said, I just needed to stand still and let things be!

My parting with Samad too had happened that way. I did not bother to argue with him. I just walked away. I recollected the mayhem unleashed when a teacher had discovered my love letter inside Samad's notebook. The teacher had ordered me to fetch my mother. Rukhiyami had always played that role in my life—now as well as then. I had stood tightly holding onto Rukhiyami's hand.

'What's the proof that Nazia has written this letter with no name or address?' Rukhiyami had asked. When the teacher revealed that Samad had revealed my identity to her, I was shell-shocked. Since the teacher had not known about my handwriting, since she taught a different class, the conclusion had been factual. When the teacher had called Samad, he confessed that I was the culprit. I bore the brunt of the moniker 'the girl who waylays young boys' for the rest of my school days. But I had continued to love the same Samad.

I still remember the penetrating look which Rukhiyami had given me in front of Samad and the teacher, warning me about his character. I had never asked Samad about that betrayal ever. I am sure he would have found a convenient explanation. Even after our marriage, I never asked him about the incident. In life, I never could twist things out of proportion to justify my stance.

When I eloped with Samad, my father had shouted, 'He is a total pauper. That I would have forgiven. At least my daughter should have chosen someone personable…who was tall or good-looking! Now this damned fellow…!'

Samad is short by stature but I have never seen it as his shortcoming. Besides, I don't consider colour or complexion as relevant yardsticks for measuring beauty. In fact, when Rukhiyami had told me about my Baba's reaction, I had sniped how a native could never take after any European! What if the whole world had one language and one colour? No way! Matilda looks pretty in her Filipino style. Dr Peace Amin looked perfect in his rosy hue. How would Rukhiyami be beautiful without her honey-coloured cheeks? Every human being has been born with the most perfect design and form, suitable to his or her self. Just let them be!

⌒⌒

Soraiyya's body burgeoned beyond the confines of her abaya. The men who smoked sheesha in the shops of the souk indulged in lascivious witticisms that the women of Bait Al Banat did not need a man, even for conceiving a child.

Soraiyya shrunk into the darkness of her home. Lying on the cot abutting the wall, she gazed at the single window, and listened keenly for the sounds from the souk. Slivers of light slipped in through the square window. The sounds of a jostling crowd could be overheard, as also the harsh breathings of those staggering onwards with heavy loads on their heads. Some leaned against the wall and shared small talk. The details of the money to be given and received, coagulated like phlegm in some men's chests.

Soraiyya lay still with her eyes closed. It was then that she heard an unfamiliar footstep at the door, along with the braying of a donkey. When Mariam opened the door, she saw Jadda's sister Ayesha from Ras Al-Khaimah, accompanied by her grandson. Once in a blue moon, Ayesha would descend the mountains to visit the souk and Deira, and drop in to meet Jadda. During winter, the people of Ras Al-Khaimah lived in tents made of wool. And in summer, they dwelled in hovels made of reeds and leaves of date palm trees.

Ayesha hugged Shamsa and Mariam, kissing them soundly on both cheeks. Mariam fetched Nafisa Jadda and Khadeeja from the barasti. Soraiyya did not move from her cot. Ayesha sat next to Soraiyya and checked her pulse. For Nafisa Jadda, her sister's visit was as precious as receiving a Cat's Eye crystal unexpectedly from the seas! They sat chatting amicably, and occasionally stroking each other's arms affectionately. Mariam prepared coffee for the old women while Shamsa busied herself making fish and rice for lunch.

Ayesha's grandson, who was a goatherd in the mountains of Ras Al-Khaimah, was extremely restless and slipped away to explore the souk. Ayesha was all praise for him; apparently, he could graze goats and camels better than his father! He could discern who it was from a man's footsteps. Leave that aside, from the hoof marks of the camel, he could easily predict whose camel it was! He could even prophecy whether it was carrying merchandise on its back. He aided people who got lost in the desert and the owners whose camels had strayed away. Ayesha was endlessly boasting about Amir's multiple skills and capabilities.

Jadda tried to tactfully change the topic. 'Why can't you stay here with me until Soraiyya's delivery? She shall benefit from your care.'

Ayesha's husband had been a famous Sayyid. There was no disease which he had not healed with a touch of his hand. His brother-in-law was always sickly. The lad, who suffered from epileptic fits, was subjected to treatment by Ayesha's husband on a full moon night. He ordered a vessel of boiling water and dropped a dry lemon in it. Holding the sick lad's head, Ayesha's husband recited many sacred verses from the Quran. Then he sat with his eyes shut for a long time. Soon, Sayyid became drenched in sweat. The lemon in the vessel started moving. It gathered speed as if possessing life. Next, it bubbled up due to intense heat. Suddenly, a horrendous voice could be heard in the vicinity. As if subjected to a great force, the lemon was hurled upwards. It vanished from sight. The lad was completely cured and never suffered from epilepsy again. He was living a healthy life now.

Jadda had narrated all these tales to her granddaughters in their childhood. Ayesha had learned a few remedies from her healer husband. She offered herbal concoctions to the village women. She used a burning hot iron rod to cure sores in the mouth.

Jadda vouched that as soon as Ayesha's iron rod was placed on a particular spot on the neck, many a sickly woman suffering from horrible mouth sores were healed! If it was a case of jaundice, the rod would be applied on the small finger. To heal a fungal infection, the burning rod would be placed on the head. It was a matter of absolute skill; the piping-hot iron rod would firmly press against the selected spot only for a second.

Ayesha examined Soraiyya's eyes and tongue. She pressed her stomach at different places and searched for something among her toes. From the bundle tied to the donkey's back, the old woman retrieved two small poultices tightly packed with herbal medicines. She made a liquid concoction using those and dripped the medicine into Soraiyya's mouth.

'You have knee pain, don't you, binti?'

Soraiyya nodded.

'No need to worry. If you drink this medicine early morning, it shall become alright.'

Jadda edged closer, complaining about her own multiple aches and pains. Ayesha gave her some green cures. For Khadeeja's toothache, Ayesha advised her to smoke the roots of water hyssop, which was from Africa. She should also expose her chin to the fumes. Ayesha entrusted Jadda with the 'Al Habba Al Hamra' medicine for Soraiyya. The ingredients were garden cress, pepper, cinnamon and ghee.

'Ayesha, why don't you take Soraiyya with you? Look after her until she has a safe delivery.'

When Ayesha looked askance at Soraiyya, she lay with utter indifference on her cot.

'Nafisa, will she be able to travel on a donkey at this stage of pregnancy? I have no objections to taking her home.'

Shamsa and Mariam stood stunned at the unforeseen turn of events. Sending Soraiyya away?

'Jadda, are you banishing her? Everybody knows about the baby by now. What are you scared of?' Shamsa could not contain herself.

'Binti, Soraiyya needs someone like Ayesha near her now. Let her go. She will come back healthy and well. See, how drained she looks!' Nafisa Jadda justified her request.

On hearing those words, Mariam was convinced. She started packing Soraiyya's clothes in a bundle and filled a water bottle made of goat hide with drinking water. Promising to return with Soraiyya and the newborn on the forty-first day after delivery, Ayesha took leave. She embraced her sister warmly. Amir helped Soraiyya onto the donkey's back and tied up the cloth-bundle behind her. Four women stood agape in front of Bait Al Banat, bringing to mind the 'Alif'—the first of the Arabic alphabet.

'Farewell, my child. May Allah bless you with good health and a long life. Jadda shall wait for your newborn with sweets,' Nafisa sobbed.

That wintry night, one leg of Mariam's cot broke. She managed to escape unhurt. Later, she shared Shamsa's mattress. They covered themselves with the woollen blanket brought to the coast by Iranian traders.

'It will take another week for Soraiyya to reach the house, I guess,' Shamsa observed soberly.

'Yes, how will she ascend those formidable mountains? I am feeling terrified at that thought!' Mariam voiced her apprehensions.

'The cot has now only three legs left. Does it remind you of something, Mariam?'

'Well, four legs imply stability. The cot is useless now.'

'And tell me, what is the stability of Bait Al Banat?' Shamsa queried.

'We three girls.'

'Yes, and one has left. The very foundation of this house has started shaking.'

'It has never happened before. It feels as if one of the limbs has become diseased.'

'Do you know that the Bedouins of Ras Al-Khaimah still practise female genital mutilation?' Shamsa asked.

Mariam shut her ears with her hands. 'I don't want to hear about it. If Soraiyya had protested, I would not have let her go! It seemed it was her wish to go with Ayesha Jadda.'

'Haven't you heard that during pregnancy everything gets upended? Neither her body nor her mind is under Soraiyya's control now. Poor girl!' Shamsa sighed.

In the night breeze, plumes of dust were rising in the yard. There were only few scatterings of stars in the clear sky. Could the bright moon have suppressed their starry presence?

Mariam stared at the splinter of sky outside, visible through the small open window. A small star! She got up gently without disturbing Shamsa, and stood beneath the window. It was nearly two feet below the roof and too high for her to access. Mariam raised her hand and tried to hide the star. Then she created space between her thumb and forefinger and peeped through it. Where had the little star gone? As she stood bewildered, staring in different directions, she heard the sound of knocking. Mariam woke up Shamsa. When they opened the door, there stood a fatigued Soraiyya! And above her head shimmered the little star! Mariam beamed at the sight. Soraiyya looked up and she too noticed that glimmering star. She hugged her sisters. Her abaya was covered with dust and sand.

Soraiyya sobbed wretchedly. 'I couldn't go with them. I insisted on returning. Amir requested the traders coming to Deira from Ras Al-Khaimah to accompany me home. They trade in the souk, you know.'

'Why did you go with Ayesha Jadda? You see, we were dumbstruck at that turn of events and could not protest,' Shamsa said.

'I thought a change would do us all good. Our house has become the cynosure of all eyes, of the neighbourhood, of the traders in the souks, our relatives... I thought Jadda was shrinking in front of them all. I even wondered whether she had sent word to Ayesha Jadda to come over,' Soraiyya explained.

'Why did you brood so much? We know that you could not spend a single night away from us. Please come inside...'

Shamsa gave her water to drink. By this time, Nafisa Jadda had come to check on the commotion. In the darkness, her hunched form edged closer to the girls.

'Binti, how did you travel alone in the night? Did something happen to you, my child?' Jadda was utterly flustered.

'I am fine, Jadda. Do not worry. I just followed the path of my mind, that's all.'

Jadda embraced Soraiyya smilingly.

'You should not go anywhere, my dear! When I saw Ayesha, suddenly I thought Allah had sent her over. I wished that what happened to your mother should not happen to you. I thought you would be safe with Ayesha. That was why…'

Mariam interjected, 'Enough of talk. Ayesha Jadda and her bragging about her accomplished grandson! I'd had enough.'

Shamsa agreed wholeheartedly. 'Oh yes, Amir grazes donkeys and goats and jumps around with the camels! Shaheen falcons and Amir are like siblings. What bluster and swagger!'

Soraiyya stopped their sardonic outpouring.

'Please don't! Amir is smart, I dare say. He is very familiar with the mountains and the desert. He told me in detail about flying the Shaheen falcons. He is as gifted as the Bedouins in that matter…'

When Ayesha's husband and henchmen went hunting for birds, they took Amir along. 'How excitedly he jabbered about the Shaheen falcons which hunt down the Houbara bustards and feast on their brains! As the Shaheen falcon pounces, the Houbara bustard spits out an oily liquid on its face. If it falls into the eyes, the predator is blinded; or if it falls on its wings, it forces the wings shut with its stickiness and prevents it from flying… Then the Houbara bustard…' Soraiyya was prattling on and on.

Jadda closed Soraiyya's mouth shut forcibly with her hand. 'I am going to have clever grandchildren too. You just watch! The one going to come out of your tummy is going to be smarter than Amir!'

There was a sudden movement inside Soraiyya's stomach. She pulled her sisters closer to her dusty abaya.

Shamsa listened and smiled, 'A lovely little pearl is growing inside the oyster shell.'

'Yes, when it emerges from the shell, its light shall set aglow all of Bait Al Banat!'

Khadeeja's hair stood on end.

'Light on this cot, that sewing machine, this mattress, the kitchen utensils... Hay, hay! Masha Allah, I can't wait!'

■

During all the distance which Soraiyya had travelled on the donkey, seated sideways, she was gasping like a fish thrown out of the water. The flat lands filled with sand, without the souk, the Khor or the sea terrified her. She had heard that the lives in the mountains of Ras Al-Khaimah were very primitive. The family had wept as if someone had died when Ayesha Jadda was married off to a man from the area.

Though it was just a hundred-odd kilometres away, for the residents of Deira, Ras Al-Khaimah was like another country. Soraiyya started worrying that her baby and she would be forced to live a backward, primitive life among the mountains, like Ayesha Jadda. She would suffocate in the folds of the mountains. No sound reached there except the whistling of the wind and the hubbub of the goats. How could Soraiyya tolerate such solitude, used as she was to the thronging crowds of the souk and its varied smells? Her heart started beating fast. The newborn should wake up to the sea water; the baby's pulse should be attuned to the siren of the ships and the energetic cries of the traders. The child should sense the liveliness of the merchants in the souk.

The sea came flowing through the creek, twisting and turning, seemingly carrying the spirit of the whole world with it. There were ships which anchored at the port, hailing from diverse countries. The differently coloured men who stepped out of those ships, the variegated fragrances of the fruits the traders brought in, and the spread of spices wafting different odours...what a wide world they opened up! A few footsteps from one's home, the whole world was flowing in front of the eyes! Soraiyya was determined that her child should grow up seeing that sight. She had insisted on returning home then. When she disembarked from the donkey and sat down resolvedly on the sand, Ayesha Jadda had no recourse other than to send her back.

■

'When I was walking homeward, near the creek where the boats are built, I saw that lad…Ibrahim,' Soraiyya commented.
'You should have asked him to go to hell!' Shamsa raged.
At first, Ibrahim had not recognized Soraiyya. Nobody had ever seen her dressed in soiled clothes, looking exhausted and moving with stumbling footsteps. She was struggling to hold on to the fluttering abaya and shayla. Ibrahim and his pals had been smoking narilla and chatting lazily. Through the fumes of the smoke which he puffed, Ibrahim had seen the blurred figure of Soraiyya. When she came nearer, the roundness of her tummy and the weariness of her limbs provoked him. Ibrahim got up and started following her. It was after a while that Soraiyya became aware of someone following her.
'Zahran's camel used to waddle about with its monstrous tummy too…let me show you how!' Ibrahim did a coarse mimicry by spreading his legs and supporting his tummy in his hands. Soraiyya ignored all his crude overtures to garner her attention. When they reached Bait Al Banat, he called out, 'Is it a ghost in your stomach? The one which has arrived to ensure that Ahmad Manzuri is sent to his grave?'
Soraiyya's pace slackened at those words.
'As your tummy grows bigger, Ahmad Manzuri grows thinner! When he shrieks around, writhing in insufferable agony, the ghost inside you must be hollering in happiness! Am I not right, woman?' Ibrahim mocked.
Nafisa Jadda, who heard Soraiyya narrating the incident to Shamsa, blanched in shock.

'What did that lad say Ahmad was suffering from? Allah!'

'He was just trying to goad Soraiyya, of course!' Khadeeja interrupted.

Jadda recollected the remnants of a recent nightmare. For a few nights, her son's childhood days had been flashing through her dreams. Those days, Ahmad was a scrawny young boy who cuddled next to his mother. His father Shihab Manzuri had been off to the sea in search of pearls.

When the dates ripened, Nafisa and her four children would venture out to harvest them. The youngest, Ahmad, was the most skilful when it came to clambering up the date trees. His mother would count the ribs which became visible as he scaled the tall date palms. Despite seeming to be the frailest, Ahmad Manzuri was the most enthusiastic among Nafisa's children. Though the women in the neighbourhood would climb the trees when the men went to sea, Ahmad never allowed his mother to trouble herself.

Date palms were like human beings. If you hacked off some part, it would never grow again. Nafisa, consequently, took great care of her trees. She would often narrate to Khadeeja the anecdote of what happened one burning summer when they went to harvest the ripe dates.

After gathering the dates, Ahmad was playing with his siblings and friends. The women were sorting out the dates into Jafir baskets. Suddenly, Ahmad had rushed towards his mother from a remote corner of the orchard. Hugging her tightly, he had started screaming in terror. None of the children were tagging along. He hid his face on Nafisa's shoulder and simply pointed afar.

When the women gazed in the direction of where he had pointed, they saw a desolate date tree, standing unobtrusively in a corner. It was an ancient date tree and from the apex, four shrivelled palm leaves thrusted out like spears in the skies. It was an ungainly sight. It looked as if the head had been scorched in fire, and some loathsome, blackened excrescences jutted out from the peak. Two women who stood nearby covered their mouths while whispering in dread, *'Ummu karbah va leefah!'* (The date palm is infested with a djinn!) Their eyes widened in fear. If anybody went near such a tree, moving its crooked, sharp nail-like roots and spear-like trunk, it would grasp the intruder!

In seconds, the women had gathered their bundles and fled from the place. They began discussing how Ahmad had noticed the possessed tree and how he had ventured near it. Many were saying that the child could discern the presence of evil spirits very quickly. That night, little Ahmad had woken up screaming many times.

Nafisa's heart would still palpitate remembering the wild heartbeats of her son as he came running to hug her. His face had been a sheath of horror. After that episode, Ahmad Manzuri had never ever accompanied his mother to harvest ripe dates.

■

Nafisa Jadda, who observed that Shamsa and Mariam were not paying much attention to Ibrahim's cryptic words, held her tongue. The girl who had set out for a secret delivery in the mountains had come home within hours of departure. Jadda realized that her sudden wave of inspiration, trusting Ayesha's therapeutic knowledge and wisdom, might have been misplaced.

Her granddaughters would never be able to live away from Bait Al Banat. They would be unable to sleep a wink without the light and sounds of the souk. The ships and the sea with which they had grown up would not leave them alone even in their dreams.

How could Soraiyya give birth without the wafting fragrances of the perfumes? Her lips would have dried up in the mountain breeze. She would have jolted awake at the sound of rocks crashing down the mountain paths. Listening to the hoots and grunts of corpse-eating vultures and owls, her ears would have been devastated. Without hearing the murmurs emanating from the Khor, Soraiyya would have lost her soul. What a cruel deed she had nearly committed! Nafisa Jadda sat clutching her hair in despair.

Novel

*T*HIS NOVEL IS NOT MINE. But I am responsible for the characters and their experiences. Ever since they entered my mind, they had days and nights, and reasons for both waking up and sleeping. I laid down the paths for them to walk and the steps to climb up and down.

Since it was Friday and a holiday, I woke up late. It was time for lunch. Varun had ordered mutton biriyani in remembrance of his father who had passed away eight years ago on the same day, while eating the dish. Every year, Varun ensured that this ritual was scrupulously followed. What a fortunate man his father was! To draw the last breath while eating one's favourite food is not trivial.

Inhaling the delectable smell of mutton biriyani, Varun quipped, 'Maybe it appears to be a stupid story, but I have saved the last bone which my father was relishing when he passed away. That hollow bone, bereft of any flesh, is the metaphor for the intensity of the emptiness which he left behind.'

Probably because Sandra guessed Varun's glumness was looming around, she started besieging me with her conversation.

'Naz, why are you pecking around the mutton like a pigeon playing with seeds? After you eat to your fill, we should visit the Women's Museum again.'

'God, no! Why do you plan to scare people?' Varun said, relishing the spices of the mutton curry.

'You chill, my dear! We should go with Naz again and explore what made her head spin! The head which stayed on its course at the Burj Khalifa had no business to spin inside the museum,' Sandra laughed.

'There is nothing new to be seen there. For me, it is almost a personal space. You might not feel like that,' I tried to explain.

'Oh, personal space!' Sandra wiped her plate clean, licked her fingers and spread them for me to see. 'Even if you were to sniff at my fingers, you won't be able to decipher what I have just gobbled down.'

'And even if you sniff around for ages, you will never gauge what I saw in the Women's Museum either! New-age detectives, indeed!' Scoffing, I went to wash my hands.

'Fine, it is your museum. We are not entering it or trying to detect anything. Hopefully you will not mind going out for dinner this evening?' Varun gently teased me. I smiled in reply.

I slipped into a half-sleep after lunch. The sedative effect of the medicine was obvious. The novel was tucked beneath my pillow. Sandra gripes that I hide it there because of her. The truth is that when the book is close by, I feel an inexplicable sense of security. As if many dear ones were constantly with me! Those who accompanied me in sleeping and waking were inscribed in it as letters and I loved to spent time in their world.

My mother had told me to disbelieve anything I couldn't see with my naked eyes. But Rukhiyami had taught me the opposite lesson: 'What you see is not the reality. The little lamp's wick blazing brightly inside you, that is the ultimate truth.' I have been travelling until now guided only by the light of that tiny lamp wick.

Mariam and Shamsa appeared intermittently in my sleep. I also saw Soraiyya lying with her head on Nafisa Jadda's lap. I overheard what they spoke. On waking up, I became befuddled about whether I had read all those in the book. When I flipped through the pages, I could not find any similar descriptions.

Sandra shook me awake by evening. We went for dinner to a Lebanese restaurant with a beautiful ambience. Varun had got us a seat in the open. The sea gleamed a fluorescent green. There was a pleasant, cool breeze, heralding the onset of winter. White winged birds were whizzing past the sky. I felt envious of the beautiful patterns they created as they took flight. Who had taught them to make such gorgeous patterns? It was an original work of art, where the sky was their canvas.

As I looked at the birds, Shamsa's face flashed in my mind. Could she have ruminated over these migratory birds too? The three girls would have seen the same sight all those years back, wouldn't they have? The birds have been flying past since aeons. They were enroute Africa from Siberia or Alaska. Another gaggle of birds, with long yellow beaks and black crown-like head-feathers, were wailing on the shore. After moistening their brown-coloured wings in the sea, they were hopping atop their eggs to hatch them. They knew perfectly well that the black speckled eggs would rot due to too much heat. These birds knew absolutely everything! They reached their destination, criss-crossing continents without Google Maps or a compass. The birds knew where to mate and when to lay eggs. Their calculations never failed.

There were petunia flowers next to our table. The flowers had a white-and-red mixed hue. There were other varieties of violet and white too in the vicinity. At the entrance of the restaurant, marigolds were aplenty. But no fragrance had wafted from those. Perhaps the breeze carried it away, who knows? Like Solomon said, 'Give it up. The breeze shall look after it like a child.'

The spring must have blossomed not only on the shore but also in the sea. It was the time for sea turtles to mate. These were the days when the typically solitary turtles came together to reproduce. If only one could catch that unique sight of the mating turtles coming up to the surface to inhale air!

As I gazed to my heart's fill at the sea and birds, Sandra approached me with a sheesha. She made a 'gulu gulu' sound and blew fragrant smoke on my face. It smelled of fresh apples! From the pipe of the Iranian girl sitting at the next table came the odour of some other fruit. She sat there like an oil painting, with a book in one hand and the pipe of the sheesha in the other. The tea has probably grown cold on her table. But she seemed to be oblivious to such facts. I wondered whether she would melt like a candle as the smoke columns covered her face. Did I look as entranced while reading *Bait Al Banat*? How did I look in another's eyes when my mind was beyond my control?

I had never read that book in front of Sandra or anyone else. To hide the discomfort of reading a book published under one's own authorship, I was forced to hide myself while reading it.

Sandra took a pinch of the cotton wisp-like grilled flesh of the Hamour fish, and started relishing it. She proceeded to lick her finger after dipping it in garlic sauce. The Hamour was lying along with a mélange of veggies on an oval-shaped silver plate. Its edges were red due to baking. The combined smell of pepper and lemon juice penetrated my nostrils. I remembered Soraiyya. Manichand had told her of a dish, hadn't he? What was that? Ah, Machboos!

It was in Dubai Heritage Village that I had eaten it for the first time. Solomon was with me. I had felt like puking on seeing the Hamour's head. Solomon had broken off a piece of its cooked flesh and inserted it in my mouth. Then he had followed it by offering me a ball of rice. I felt as if the fish had gone straight to my head and not my tummy! My body felt as if it were disintegrating into pieces.

'Naz, for the fishes, all the seas are the same. Hamour is the fish belonging to the Gulf Sea, while sardines and mackerel belong to the Arabian Sea. There is not much difference. Your aversion to the taste is due to the discrepancy in your thoughts,' Solomon said.

That day, he too had dipped a finger in garlic sauce and touched it against my tongue. The sting of the garlic had pulled down the Hamour from my head to the tummy.

'Inside the sea, the sardine and mackerel dine on the same stuff which the Hamour dines on, dear! While swimming around the sea without a care in the world, when a predator fish suddenly appears, the scream of panic shall be the same for both mackerel and Hamour,' Solomon had pointed out.

■

'Varun, he has not arrived as yet,' Sandra said, at the end of the dinner.

'He is on his way...stuck in traffic. I got a message,' Varun replied.

'Who are you speaking about?' I asked.

Both Sandra and Varun took hold of my hands.

'Listen, Varun went out of the way to trace Mahesh. When he went to the flat where Solomon stayed, Mahesh was not to be found. It was after quite an arduous search that he could find his location. You should speak with Mahesh when he comes.'

'Me? I have nothing to speak about.'

'Mahesh is the only person who knows Solomon's whereabouts. I am sure he will have some information about him,' Varun said.

'What new information do we need? You have even booked a ticket for me to travel home, Varun,' I protested.

'Just because a courier delivered a book, we cannot stay lazy and do nothing! See, there are wily ways of fooling others nowadays.'

'I was planning to go home only due to your insistence. And now...' I was angry and confused.

Sandra intervened, 'Varun's line of argument is sensible. Solomon sort of vanished into the blue. Though the book arrived, we are clueless about his whereabouts. There is a notice for the book release. But how can you attend it all by yourself? We should try to extract the maximum information from Mahesh.'

I felt that the Hamour fish was re-entering my head. I tried to recollect Solomon's words and even tried licking up some garlic in vain.

Mahesh seemed to be fully bald. He looked frailer than before. The fluorescent green of the sea glistened in the hotel lights. Mahesh sat opposite me. Seeing us after a pretty long time, he grinned like a fool for some time. He just sipped some coffee, making excuses of a diet plan. Solomon became the topic of our discussion much later.

'The last I saw of him was with you all. No messages or calls after that,' Mahesh pulled a face. 'These cinema guys and writers are all eccentric... Who knows if he is wandering around Dubai with another set of friends?'

A white bird could be seen flying overhead before landing on the nearby handrail. I saw that one of its legs was broken. When I exclaimed about it, Sandra went near the creature. Suddenly the bird flew away.

'Mahesh, we need to see Solomon to discuss a project,' Varun said.

'Sorry, I cannot help you in this regard. I have absolutely no idea where he is. See, I can give you his home address at best,' Mahesh opined.

Varun noted down the address in his phone. I knew that except his aged mother, there would be nobody in Solomon's house. I had no wish to re-enact a clichéd scene from old Malayalam movies—the role of a sweetheart meeting the hero's mother in her house.

'An old friend of Solomon lives in Fujairah. He had slipped and broken his leg at his place. That's how he had landed in the hospital,' Mahesh looked at me meaningfully and grinned.

Varun called up the number of the friend in Fujairah and asked Mahesh to speak with him. After chatting for a bit, Mahesh informed us, 'He apparently saw Solomon back in Kerala. A few days after he left Dubai.

'Where did he meet Solomon?'

'At a common friend's place. You guys won't be knowing him. Anyway, Solomon got real drunk that day and created a ruckus. Nobody has seen him after that.'

I glared at Varun, hoping that he had received all the necessary information by now.

'It seems Solomon confessed that he had fallen deeply in love and there was no way out!' Mahesh added.

'Fallen in love with whom?' Varun furrowed his forehead like a detective.

'Who the heck knows? He was frazzled and upset, that's all we know,' Mahesh said and got up to leave. The vexation of having wasted his time was clearly obvious on his face.

Sandra picked up Varun's phone and re-dialled the number. I sat like the serene, aquamarine sea, observing everything unfolding in front of me. When the phone got connected, Sandra walked to the handrail where the bird with the broken leg had perched. In the dim light, her waxed legs seemed to smile at me from beneath her skirt. She often expresses her envy at my legs which are hairless. Her peeve is that I haven't experienced the agony of the skin being peeled off during waxing sessions. I tease her by consoling that the coefficient of pain during natural child birth was far higher!

Solomon used to grasp my legs together and recite an English poem.

'I do not need legs anymore
Let them turn into a fishtail;
I am swimming, how delightful the coolness;
Far away, a bridge vanishes from sight...'

I just recollect the first few lines. I should ask Solomon the poet's name when we meet next time.

Next time? My mind was busy weaving so many plans. Let things happen as they are supposed to! I refused to wish for anything, since wishing for anything was terrifying.

Sandra returned and sat down again. 'He told me what Mahesh had said. Solomon parted after admitting about being in love.'

'With who, I ask?' Varun wondered aloud once more.

'Who else? This brat, of course!' Sandra poked at my cheek. 'Solomon left the place after jabbering that he wished to free himself of it!'

'Sandra, a man like him must have been caught unawares by love! There are men like that. Love must have baffled him utterly. He is running away from his own feelings now.'

'From Naz? She is madly in love with Solomon. Why do they play hide-and-seek like this, eh? Totally loony!' Sandra twisted her loose hair into a knot. Seeing my agitation, she sipped some water and cooled herself down. 'Naz, this is not to fluster you at all. Just an uncleared doubt of mine!'

'What doubt, Sandra? This book is an offering of love from Solomon. What superior commitment can any lover give to his sweetheart?' I asked.

I wondered at the number of misgivings they all had about Solomon. It seemed as if I was the only one who was untouched by qualms. Am I someone who trusted others blindly? I have no idea.

'So much mystery surrounding a man? He is showcasing shades of light and dark at the same time,' Sandra's forehead creased increasingly.

Everyone wished to know basic information about a human being. His address, job, parents, family, education… Having received these tidbits, the biodata form seemed to have been deemed complete. Then the data was tucked away in some corner of the brain! Wasn't there anything else worth knowing about a man? The only knowledge I lack is Solomon's biodata. I have absolutely no doubt about what goes on inside him.

The waiter arrived with the bill. The rest of the diners had arrived along with us, but were just starting their dinner. The multiple fare of vegetable salad and fruits were spread around them. They were smoking the sheesha pipes and chatting unhurriedly while sipping beverages in between.

It seemed we Keralites were yet to learn how to relish food at a beautiful place, with a twilight ambience and surrounded by friends. Once the food arrived, the single motive was to chomp through it quickly!

The waiter was a Lebanese national. I was surprised to see his shy grin. Such shyness in someone who dealt with strangers on a daily basis? Indeed, I wished to smile shyly like him. When was the last time I had smiled like that? I could not recall the moment.

Soraiyya's bloated fingers kept drawing circles around her engorged navel. Usually, she woke up listening to Mariam crushing the coffee beans, seated in the majlis. Today, there was no sound at all. There was silence in the kitchen where Shamsa, according to routine, should have been busy. Soraiyya concluded both girls must have gone to visit Nafisa Jadda at the barasti. She felt an ache in her limbs and reminded herself to start taking the herbal medicines which Ayesha Jadda had left for her.

As the months went by, Soraiyya had started brooding over the little life growing inside her. When the child moved, it brought to mind a few shocking memories too. Soraiyya felt terrified to watch her slender body growing flabby. Even the ever-lasting hollows of her cheeks had filled out. Was pregnancy a process of elevating all the depressions of a woman's body? Perhaps such an elevation might occur to the mind too. Rather, 'the sunrise of the mind' would be the ideal description!

In the strong breeze blowing outside were rustling sounds of the palm leaves, which were used in the construction of the barastis. Ever since the girls had shifted to Bait Al Banat made of cement, they had stopped fearing sandstorms and extreme winters. Soraiyya realized the huge relief of not having to fear either rain or sun. Indeed, nowadays she ruminated often on those who slept inside hovels made of palm leaves and reed stalks.

As the baby moved inside her, a tremor seized hold of Soraiyya's body. She thought that this phenomenon of a body giving life to another was among the most wondrous miracles of the universe. Did every child born into the world assume that he or she was the first human ever? Soraiyya felt dizzy.

Nobody in the house bothered about the gender of the child. But the baby would have a face: the eyes, lips…who would it resemble? Would the smile be similar to that of any person she knew? Soraiyya recollected the faces of her Ummi, sisters and Jadda. She tried to imagine her child's face by fusing the vignettes of the features of her dear ones. She could draw up the innocence of

Shamsa's smile on her child's face but the sound of the laughter pushed her into doldrums. That mocking roar of laughter was Manichand's! Soraiyya covered her ears. She felt like puking. What was the speciality Manichand gave to her child? If only nothing of him showed up in the baby's form and sound!

Wishing to drink some SulaImani, Soraiyya hailed Shamsa.

Khadeeja replied from the yard, 'Your Jadda is unwell and all are with her. She failed to catch even a wink at night. When she woke up for the subhi prayers, she collapsed. I forced her to lie down, but she hasn't eaten anything nor sipped a drop of water,' Khadeeja wept.

'Don't cry. Once she awakens from sleep, she will be better. You please recite the Quran,' Mariam consoled her.

'Binti, she was going on and on about only one person all through the night,' Khadeeja whimpered again.

'Which person?'

'Your Baba.'

'What's so special now? This uncalled-for concern, all of a sudden?'

'She is his Ummi, after all. When she heard that her son was not keeping well…' Mariam gestured to Khadeeja to not speak further.

'Just offer *dua*, prayers, Khadeeja. All will be well.'

Khadeeja believed that people remembered the past when they were nearing death. Nafisa Jadda had been chattering about her husband Shihab Manzuri and her four children all through the night.

Ahmad had been born after three daughters. He had been her favourite child. The Khor in those days was akin to a half-dried reservoir, with stagnant water. The ships and merchandise and boats were not to be sighted in those days. A few folks could be seen waiting with nets cast into the Khor waters. Except for the fishermen, wearing knee-length clothes and head gear, sitting on their haunches, awaiting the fish to be caught in their nets, Nafisa had not seen much else in those parts. The crowds would swell only two times of the year—during the pearl-diving seasons of Ghous Al-Kabir and Ghous Al-Saif. The women would visit the seashore as thousands, including Shihab Manzuri, ventured into the sea. They would bid farewell to their husbands, sons and brothers as they set out to the depths without any guarantee of a return, accepting the invitation of many unknown sea creatures which lay in wait for them with their jaws open.

As the sacks filled with rice, sugar, dates and tea were carried into the Jalbut, the women and children would silently watch with tear-filled eyes. Though the nukhadh would distribute money to the families of the sailors, it wouldn't last very long. Rice worth a few rupaiyya and another three hundred as cash was all the women received. When it got over, they would be forced to step into the souk to sell whatever little valuables they possessed.

Nafisa had to bid goodbye not only to her husband but also to her son in the course of her life. After the ships departed, the days belonged to the women and little children. The womenfolk would be busy stitching clothes and creating handicrafts. Nafisa Jadda often narrated about the insecurity and solitude she faced in such times.

Once, Shihab Manzuri had gifted Ahmad a football obtained from a British ship. The boy had been gobsmacked, and wondered what to do with it! Nobody had ever seen such an object in the Khor before. Football was an unknown game altogether! It was Shihab who taught his son to play football, having seen British sailors play in their spare time.

When the boy tried to kick around the half-deflated ball on the muddy sands of the Khor, it had not obliged. The other lads had teased him calling the ball a *gubbat shaitan*—globe of the devil! With one vicious kick, the brats had sent it to the waters of the Khor which were gleaming in the sunshine. That day, Ahmad had come home crying and Nafisa had prepared his favourite snack, *luqaimat*. Ahmad adored the taste of the little round balls of luqaimat which were soaked in either date syrup or honey. Nafisa had laughed recollecting his greed when it glistened with the overtones of honey.

When Jadda had slipped into deep sleep, Khadeeja coughed discreetly. 'Binti, your Jadda has grown in years now. How many more days are left, nobody knows. She really yearns to see her son.'

'Khadeeja, Jadda has four children. What extra happiness is she going to derive by seeing her son, which cannot be obtained from her three daughters?' Soraiyya lashed out.

'I can ask all of them to come over. Let their children and grandchildren come along. But why should we usher in someone who is awaiting the destruction of this house?' Shamsa asked bitterly.

'Ssshh...speak softly,' Mariam cautioned. She called Shamsa to the side and advised, 'Stop discussing this topic. Let Khadeeja go on with her lamentations. We are called many names including "worthless children who abandoned their father on his death bed!" There are more on the list...debauched, vain, proud, living according to their whims and fancies...no point in bothering much.'

After the second marriage, Ahmad Manzuri had kept his distance from his sisters. Consequently, there were no siblings waiting to rush to his side on hearing about his sickness. Only his Ummi had wept on hearing about his illness.

Shamsa followed Soraiyya as she made her way back to Bait Al Banat. Seeing her once energetic sister labouring over her steps, Shamsa felt sad. Soraiyya would not step out when the driver of the taxi came to submit the daily accounts. Shamsa had taken over the duty. The girl, who once hated to sit still, now spent her time staring at the sky through the solitary window, all the while stroking her stomach.

'You brood a lot over your child, don't you, Soraiyya?' Shamsa asked gently.

'Yes, but I do not know what I am thinking about.'

'Are you wondering about Manichand? Someone said he has gone to Bombay.'

'Huh? I feel like retching whenever I remember him. I wished for a Sulaimani and was searching for you,' Soraiyya replied.

Shamsa laughed and embraced her sister.

That night, all three sisters heard the flapping of the migrating birds as the flocks moved towards the shore.

'They shall be around for a while now.' Mariam and Soraiyya could understand that Shamsa was referring to the birds.

'Why don't they stay here forever?' Mariam pondered aloud.

'Why should they? If we had wings, we would have escaped from this place quite a long while ago. Am I not right, Soraiyya?' Shamsa retorted.

'Most definitely. I always wonder why we were born in these parts. The world is so big, isn't it? Mariam's Farhad left because he thought on those lines himself,' Soraiyya replied.

'If there are so many places to stay, why do the Engleesis, Khojas and Bombayites crowd over these shores?' Mariam persisted peevishly.

'They are like these migratory birds, Mariam. Their families are in their native countries. They trade in our country and finally return to theirs.'

'Is there so much money here? Then why are we struggling? How many houses in this Deira are assured of a regular meal, tell me?'

'The ones who mint money from a land where the sea and sand are merged inextricably, should be hailed as heroes indeed! We are the useless ones, I say! Our people only know how to burden donkeys, preen atop camels and dive for unseen pearls.'

'Listen, everybody is speaking about the black liquid nowadays. Even yesterday, the gossip in the souk was about it. Someone has dug out the black liquid from some interior village in Abu Dhabi, apparently!'

'No, I heard differently. It seems the seabed is chock-full of that black liquid. If we can extract it, we shall turn into the richest countries in the world, they said!'

'Jadda says that the discovery of the black liquid is inauspicious. It shall harm the land!"

'Aha! If so, this land should have been burnt to cinders seeing us women who are perpetually clad in black!' The three women burst into laughter. Hearing the commotion, a little life started leaping inside Soraiyya's stomach.

■

The maternal home of the girls' Ummi was in Bur Dubai. There were almost twenty-five members in the joint family, including their grandfather and uncles. When Soraiyya had visited the home some months ago, her uncle's younger daughter Ameera, all of eighteen years, was present. She was heavily pregnant. Ameera was stunningly pretty, with doe eyes and a perfect smile. Soraiyya had seen younger girls, pregnant, moving around the souk. Yet, she had been inexplicably upset at the sight of Ameera that day.

Never had Soraiyya expected to be pregnant herself one day! She had been ruminating over Ameera during the return trip in the abra. The women around her often had their first child at sixteen or eighteen. Would it be tough to have a child at her age? Soraiyya found herself flustered. Ameera would never be able to assess life or people with the maturity of the middle-aged Soraiyya. Neither did she have any definite plans for her future. It was either her husband or her baba who handled all her concerns. Ameera must have enjoyed the period of her pregnancy with colourful dreams. She must have dreamed of breastfeeding her infant, dressing the baby, singing lullabies... As Soraiyya ruminated over all this, suddenly she wondered about breastfeeding.

'Would she remember the loathsome Manichand when the infant suckled at her breasts?' Soraiyya shuddered at the thought. It became evident why she was not having colourful, hopeful whims like other pregnant women. Age had nothing to do with that fact. But Soraiyya was aware of the truth that she had faced situations which other women in those shores never encountered. Hadn't she handled businesses which no female did? She had been earning her own livelihood unlike other women. And nobody had faced the tribulations which she had run into. In her life, which had been filled with unexpected events, many more such challenges were to be expected. She told herself firmly that Allah thought her capable of facing her destiny. 'I am not an ordinary woman. Let life bring on more inexplicable occurrences!'

Soraiyya jolted awake at the sound of someone pounding loudly on the door. Shamsa and Mariam were deep in sleep. Shamsa was very prone to sleep during the onset of winter. They would joke that when the cold breeze started from the Hajar Mountains, Shamsa would start searching for a warm woollen blanket! When Soraiyya decided to go back to sleep, the knocking started again. By this time, her sisters awoke.

Shamsa lit the hurricane lamp and went near the door. They presumed that Jadda must have fallen ill again. But Khadeeja would never knock so frantically.

Shamsa called out, 'Who is it?' A moment's silence reigned. Then the flurry of knocking continued.

'Go on, open up. Let us see who it is,' Soraiyya said.

Shamsa opened the door slightly. She adjusted her shayla and placed the lamp on the ground. She could see a dark shape ahead. It was a man! He was clutching at something and had no hair. The man was dressed in white. Mariam picked up the lamp and stepped out. It was Yakub! His face was bloodied and dirty, and his eyes were streaming! Shamsa was shell-shocked. Staggering, she leaned against the door for support.

'Yakub, you?' Mariam stopped him as he moved forward. 'What happened to you? Why is your body full of blood? Where were you all this time?'

Khadeeja had arrived by then. She embraced the dirty and bloodied body of her son and sobbed. They took him to the barasti and made him sit. The women stared dumbly at the wounds and bruises on Yakub's body. It was Soraiyya who poured water for him to drink.

'Yesterday I reached Ras Al Khor... There was nobody to help me,' Yakub wept. Nafisa Jadda went near him and embraced him.

'I escaped from Saudi in a ship. There was no food or water for days on end. I was determined to endure any calamity to return to my shore. The householders at Saudi were kind. They never physically hurt me though there was no pay for the work. They gave me food. But how long could I live like that? I wished to return to the Khor and meet my Ummi, my Shamsa... I can never leave this shore,' Yakub cried.

'Child, what happened to you? All these wounds?' Khadeeja wiped Yakub's face with her shayla.

'Yesterday, I hid in a godown behind the customs building. When I could not bear the thirst, I stepped out. I knew that if anyone saw me, I would be handed over to the British or sent back in the ship. Suddenly, someone caught me by the neck. A few men started beating me up mercilessly. Though I pleaded that I was not a thief, they kept assaulting me. When it was over, except one, others went away. I recognized his voice though not his face. The brute dragged me to a room in the godown and there he undressed me...' Without saying anything more, Yakub tightly pressed his lips close.

Soraiyya turned her face away after noticing the bite marks on Yakub's neck and shoulders. She remembered a Hamour fish with its jaws wide open! Yakub tried to hide his bruises.

A slave boy who had run away from some country. Someone who was driven away from the shores of the Khor. Wherever he went, he was doomed. Even if someone were to eat him alive, nobody would question the atrocity. It was with full knowledge of Yakub's utter helplessness that the cruel man had taken his pleasure and satiated his lust. When he slapped him while spouting filthy abuses, in the glint of a passing ship's mast light, Yakub had recognized Manichand! Soraiyya understood that Shamsa had been merely trying to pacify her by telling her about the evil man being away in Bombay.

As Manichand brutalized Yakub's body, a thousand venomous Buthidar scorpions had twitched their tails inside him. The deadly yellow poison oozing from those creatures had permeated every cell of Yakub's body.

After sexually abusing Yakub, the damned man had pantingly withdrawn and spat on the ground, cursing profusely. As he swayed on his way out, something felled him. Yakub had hurled a stone at him which toppled Manichand. These were heavy stones usually tied to the divers' legs. The Hajar stones weighed four or five kilograms. These were tied to a rope called *zubail* and used to weigh down the diver as he penetrated the depths of the sea. It was the same Hajar stone which resurrected Yakub. He sat on top of the unconscious Manichand and pounded at his head with the Hajar stone. Despite the spurting blood, Yakub had continued to hammer at Manichand's head relentlessly. He pounded at Bait Al Banat's door with the same, seething intensity.

Manichand's eyes were staring lifelessly at the iron roof. Yakub's hands were still shaking with the horror of knowing the man's last, shuddering life breath.

'Has anybody seen you?' Mariam asked fearfully.

'I don't know,' he replied listlessly.

When they asked how he had disappeared from Deira, Yakub started sobbing again.

'That night, when I was asleep, Ibrahim and his gang kidnapped me and took me to Ahmad Manzuri. He asked me whether I was unaware that slaves were no longer welcome in Deira. I knew that the Engleesis had brought in the law banning slavery. But in Deira, there are blacks like me in every home. My Ummi had given birth to me here and I had grown up in this land. I know no work other than what I had learned to do in the Khor. I pleaded with Ahmad Manzuri, "*Arbab* Master, you better kill me than banish me from this land!" He ignored my pleas and got me brutally beaten up by Ibrahim and his other flunkeys.'

'Did Ahmad Manzuri tell you why he was sending you away?'

'No, he did not. But Ibrahim was abusing the girls and Bait Al Banat endlessly. For two days, I lay tied up. The brutes denied me even a drink of water. On the third day, they forced me to walk to the Khor and made me board a ship. I have no idea how long I lay unconscious in it. I was drenched in blood and urine when I woke up. My bones seemed to be broken as I inched my way on the shore when the ship anchored. I fainted again. I, who was discarded like filth on the road, did have some value. Someone sold me off to an Arab and I lived there till now.'

Shamsa covered her mouth with her hand as she cried. She did not dare to look at Yakub's face.

'You can stay here, my son,' Khadeeja consoled him.

Soraiyya felt the baby moving inside her. Swaddling her stomach with her hands, she traced her steps back to Bait Al Banat. She whispered to her child, 'Did you hear anything? The news of someone's death. He was someone important to you, my dearest.'

Soraiyya did not feel like sleeping. In the barasti, the others were busy taking care of Yakub. It was the night of endings for Soraiyya too. Now, when she thought of her child, the roar of mocking laughter would never arise again. She would no longer have to hear about Manichand being sighted anywhere. The sharp teeth of the Hamour fish would never haunt her again.

Journey

I TOLD EVERYONE IN THE HOSPITAL that I was planning to go home to Kerala because the Martyr's Day and National Day were conveniently close to the weekend. I did not dare to confess that I was going to attend my book release function. Would I end up introducing myself as an author soon?

I told the truth only to Dr Peace Amin. When I asked him for a few tips, to handle the moments when I faced Solomon, he quipped, 'Thinking of me, hold back your breath and close your eyes for a few seconds!'

'What will happen then?'

'Absolutely nothing!' He chortled in glee.

I acted disgruntled.

'My dear Naz, you should simply run to him and give him a warm hug! What sort of a sweetheart are you?'

How effortlessly the good doctor soothed my nerves! I bid farewell to my colleagues happily.

As I dusted my suitcase, I realized it had been a long time since I visited home. I planned to reach Rukhiyami's house straight from the airport. I did not have any house to call my own. Whether it was Dubai or Kerala, that was the truth.

Solomon would wax eloquent about people without homes.

'A place of one's own is a rather boring idea! The concept that there is only one place to call one's own in this vast world, is rather ridiculous. Are we not limiting ourselves by thinking in that manner?'

When I argued that one needed a roof over one's head, Solomon countered, 'Such a roof has too heavy a price to pay, my dear! Just think that every place belongs to you... You shall transform as a person.'

Unwittingly, my life seemed to unfold along Solomon's ideas of living.

I stood staring at the dress cupboard, unsure of the clothes to choose. I had never attended a book release function in my life. I had watched such events only on TV. One person handed the book to another, who officially declared it released. The writer stood timorously to one side, smiling equivocally. Which was the dress which helped one to stand indifferently during such an event? I had no saris. Rukhiyami could lend me one, if I needed. No, Solomon would not like me dressed in a sari!

Maybe I shall feel the same panic on seeing Solomon after such a long time, like Shamsa felt at the sight of Yakub. I had no clue on handling the moment of our expected union. Nobody other than Rukhiyami could throw light on that dilemma. Anyway, I was not planning to follow Dr Peace Amin's advice. After all, we were speaking of an event in Kerala!

Whenever I had gone home with Samad for a vacation, the suitcases would be packed with common household stuff. To gift his innumerable relatives, he would pack the bags with sundry items including sweets, milk powder, spices, soaps... When he would fill the shopping trolley, I would ask without enthusiasm, 'Who are all these meant for, Samad?'

'For my Umma.'

'Does she need so much?'

'Anyway, everything will get used.'

Since every house regularly purchased grocery items, I could never fathom the need to buy such objects as gifts to a mother. Usually I never interfered with Samad's decisions.

Now, the journey home seemed lighter, compared to the earlier ones. It was a trip without being overwhelmed with unnecessary shopping items. I wished to get another copy of *Bait Al Banat* for Rukhiyami but did not know where to procure one from. Would these be available in bookstores? I packed a pair of *jhumka*s, earrings, considering the possibility of Rukhiyami asking me to dress in a sari.

Perhaps I had never readied myself for such a significant journey ever in my life. When I eloped with Samad at the tender age of eighteen, I had never comprehended the enormity of my journey. It was like Soraiyya's mulling: was a mother in her forties similar to a mother in her teenage? The naïve girl who had run off with her lover was not the one readying the suitcase now.

Sandra and Varun dropped me at the airport. Sandra waved and Varun offered a flying kiss as I walked away, pushing the trolley. I was sure Sandra would be worrying about me now. Rukhiyami would be sending a vehicle to the airport to pick me up. My father must have got to know about my journey. But I felt sure that he would not want to meet me. Neither did I wish to meet him.

○○○

They woke up to see two unfamiliar faces the next morning. Two kids who used to come over to listen to Shamsa's stories were yelling *'Shurta, Shurta'* (Police! Police!), as they raced their way to Bait Al Banat. When the police were sniffing around the souk, someone had asked them the reason. They spoke about the murder in the godown at the Khor. The boys had eavesdropped—the police suspected that the murderer was a slave who lived in Bait Al Banat. They had come running with that hot news.

When the police arrived, dressed in red-and-white keffiyeh, with a red sash across the chest, Khadeeja had desperately implored her son to hide. But Yakub stepped up before the police men without any hesitation. As he trooped after them, as obedient as a dog, Khadeeja raised both hands skyward and offered a prayer. For Yakub, the house and jail were the same—both kept him imprisoned.

Shamsa withdrew into the darkness inside her house. Mariam and Soraiyya became silent. There was an uproar as Yakub walked away with the police. A jostling crowd of young boys and men followed them in a procession till the police headquarters at Naif. Some were remarking that such slaves would commit more murders and thievery. All slaves should be banished from these shores. The old men were vouching that the slaves were behind every atrocity in the land.

Yakub walked with drooping shoulders, his face downcast. He was utterly silent. Another prison was awaiting him! The same incarceration he had endured inside Khadeeja's tummy had been his fate every single day after birth too.

Shamsa stared at the roof as if all stories had long abandoned her. From the wooden rafts, the princesses and princes of all the stories she had narrated till now seemed to mock at her. They called out, 'Shamsa, *Taal Ila*... Come here.' With her head on her knees, she kept glaring at the roof ahead. Her eyes slowly moved from one face to another. She tried to recollect the listeners to whom she had told the tales featuring all those characters.

The three sisters who fought over a pot of meat curry accused her to her face. They were hanging upside down and spoke in the same voice: 'Did you not say that the youngest of us ran away with the pot of meat, unable to control her greed? But the real culprit was our pet dog. But you said that our father punished the youngest sister and pushed her out of the house. Did you not? How many allegations you raised against us, Shamsa!'

Shamsa sat miserably, admitting that she, the storyteller, was responsible for the ill-fate of the characters. From the corner of the kitchen, another girl cursed Shamsa harshly. 'Cruel wench! You destroyed my life! I was born a princess but you married me off to an old, doddering fool. I was doomed to carry him in a basket. He would not even give me a piece of the bread which we got by begging.' She started weeping. A few tears fell on Shamsa. She protested vociferously, 'Stop saying that, dear princess. Wasn't it a louse which caused all this mess?'

'Oh, is that so? True that a louse fell down while combing my hair. But it was you, the storyteller, who made me show the excrescence to my father and hide it in a well! When it grew as big as a cow, he killed it and ripped off its hide. Then he challenged that anyone who could identify the species of the creature would marry me. That was how the wretched old man became my groom. Ahhh…' She started weeping inconsolably.

Shamsa turned her head away, unable to witness that scene.

When she got up and walked away from the kitchen, a stunning Egyptian beauty could be seen near the kitchen door's latch. Her eyes and colour were enchanting. Her body was utterly gorgeous! The woman said, 'Nobody could resist me because of my beauty. Men, however, feared my loveliness and did not dare marry me. While I was enjoying tantalizing everybody, you married me off to that coward, didn't you?'

Shamsa retorted, 'Not at all. He was deeply in love with you. Didn't he take good care of you when you fell ill?'

'When I was sure of my death, I asked him to chop off his manhood. I was determined that he should not marry another woman. It was your punishment by forcing me into an unsuitable marriage, Shamsa!' The woman mocked.

The ghosts of the stories hung over Shamsa's head. She sat down in a corner, covering her face and head with a dark cloth. Every nook and corner of the house seemed to be threatening her. Khadeeja came near her, gently removed the black cloth, and forced her to lay on her lap. She kindly wiped away Shamsa's tears.

'I know what you are thinking, dear. That is what Allah has destined for Yakub,' she said.

'You are not to blame. Shamsa, do not berate yourself that he has been punished for loving you. That is not so, habibti… This house of yours is like my own. I have no other place to call a home. From the day I arrived here as a young slave girl, you have been my family,' Khadeeja said, struggling to console the girl lamenting over her son.

Soraiyya knelt down with great effort, despite her burgeoning stomach, and kissed Shamsa's cheek.

■

In Jumeirah, Ahmad Manzuri's two young children were standing near his cot. Nearby, their mother was grinding herbs. Intermittently, Ahmad groaned in agony. The children would massage his feet then. He opened his eyes and gazed affectionately at both.

The sea urchin, with spikes all over the body, seemed to be rolling inside his head. Its needles seemed to be poking out through his ears! He tried to wriggle free and often caressed his finger tips as if testing the sharp blade of the knife used to open an oyster shell. Would there be sparkling pearls inside the shells? When shall such a day arise when he got a huge pearl? As he wondered feverishly, Ahmad Manzuri recollected the days when he wandered with his father in the sea, facing the hot winds. When the pain intensified, Ahmad opened his eyes; the rest of the time, he was watching the sights beneath the sea. When the sting of saline water irritated his eyes, he called out to his Ummi. Ahmad Manzuri's wife gently applied a black-coloured ointment on his eyelids.

Jellyfish blooms, with long, reddish sensors, expanded and contracted their umbrella-like forms and neared Ahmad Manzuri. One or two lashed at him viciously. 'Ahhh,' he couldn't bear the venomous impaling!

Ahmad Manzuri's wife asked her children to recite the Quran loudly. Her husband started screaming. The children did not understand that he was shrieking at the sights he saw beneath the sea. Or else they would have soothed him, 'Baba, the sea creatures will attack the intruders who encroach upon their home.'

Ahmad Manzuri tied up the heavy Hajar stones to his legs and wound the zubail rope around his waist. The diyyin bag was also tied to the rope. His nostrils were closed with a clip called *fettam*, made of animal bones. As he dived into the water, he felt acute pressure crushing his limbs. The *khabt* covering over the fingers was in place. But was the *fettam* loosening its grip?

When the children saw their father thrashing about, they tried to catch his hands and contain his movements. 'Don't remove my *khabt*,' Ahmad Manzuri screamed.

Ahmad Manzuri, who was wearing a white cotton overcoat and ear covers, swam around a huge oyster shell. Its edges blossomed forth like petals. The middle was swollen and was shimmering in a bluish hue. There was a green tint on the outer folds. Never had Ahmad Manzuri seen such a magnificent shell. He scooped it up and deposited it inside the diyyin bag. Then he tugged at the rope. Within moments, he was hauled up to the surface.

After removing the fettam, he took a few deep breaths before enthusiastically jumping into the boat. Then he took out a knife and tried to prise open the oyster shell. Determined not to lose the beautiful shell, he cleaved it apart with his knife. There were three pearls inside! He shrieked in joy, *'Lulu, lulu, talata lulu!'* (Pearls, pearls…three pearls!)

Ahmad Manzuri's wife asked the children to leave the room. She sat on the bed and tried to muffle his screams. Ahmad slapped away her restricting hand and cried again, *'Lulu…lulu…talata lulu…'* He gazed carefully inside the shell. The three pearls turned into three faces! The middle one was of Soraiyya and the others were Shamsa and Mariam. Ahmad Manzuri stopped making any more sounds.

His wife removed her hand from his mouth. The pearls started swelling up inside the shell. As they engorged and emerged outside, his eyes popped out in equal proportion. Ibrahim and the others were waiting outside the room. As the men stepped inside, Ahmad Manzuri's wife got up from the cot and stood politely to a side.

Native Land

I LANDED IN KERALA. DURING THE trip to Rukhiyami's house, I intended to finish the final chapter of *Bait Al Banat*. I retrieved the book from the inner recesses of the handbag. I disliked reading in the flight; it was far more interesting to read while being close to the earth. It was then that one understood the bliss of 'walking on air'. It was then that the eyes saw visions far beyond the obvious. It was then that the alphabet took possession of one's senses.

I lowered the glass pane of the car. My face, depicted on the back cover, became reddened due to the heat. I panicked momentarily, thinking that the driver might have noticed it. Shutting the book, I placed it by my side on the seat. The breeze started playing with the pages. Before my eyes, Mariam, Shamsa and Soraiyya slowly moved forward. Like the oyster shells which float to the sea surface in search of raindrops, three women bobbed up and down rhythmically, at tandem with the undulations evoked by the wind.

I took up the book again and cast a surreptitious glance at the driver. He was busy chatting with someone. I covered my photograph on the back cover with my fingers and read quietly. In the whole world, there wouldn't be another writer more mortified about themselves than me!

Rukhiyami kept calling at frequent intervals. I might have to hand over the copy to her, though I would feel very empty afterwards.

Rukhiyami was waiting for me at the gate. I was visiting this house of hers for the first time. It was built by her daughter Nadira, who lived with her family in Qatar. Rukhiyami lived by herself in the house.

'Only one bag?'

'Yes, I did not come to supply washing powder or banana concentrates, did I?'

Rukhiyami laughed delightedly. The same smile, sparkling cheeks and attractive teeth! She hugged me and gently bit my cheek. I usually don't wipe my face after her affectionate overtures. She herself would do so with the end of her sari.

'Can't you stop wiping clean my face as if washing up after eating? Am I still a small kid?' I pretended to be aggrieved.

'Yes, a small novelist!'

We relished appam and egg curry together. I noticed a small girl, peeping at us from the kitchen as we had our food.

'Small girl…she came to steal the rose apples. I asked her to stay with me. She likes it here…,' Rukhiyami explained.

'What? You know this unknown girl came to steal and you asked her to stay? A small-time thief? Not a good idea…might create a new headache someday,' I demurred.

'Is there anyone who is not a small-time thief? If you can catch anyone red-handed, you call her a thief. But there are those who steal quietly. What do you call such people?' Rukhiyami asked slyly.

'I know you are hinting at me…me alone!'

'Not you, my girl! Your Solomon! Did he not steal all your stories?'

'But he returned them to me,' I said.

'Oh yes! Using some raw material, you created a handicraft. Solomon took it away, burnished it as a final product in his factory, gave it a trade name and handed it back to you!' Rukhiyami laughed.

'Ah, you are worse than Sandra! Of course, when viewed from a different perspective, it will seem like that. Very natural indeed.'

'What is natural in your eyes?'

I hugged Rukhiyami as she stood washing the dishes.

'Sol desired that I write. If I did not do that, he would. That's what happened.'

'You mean it is insignificant who actually wrote the novel—you or him,' Rukhiyami persevered.

'I have no idea. Let it go.'

I sat down with the little girl and asked her a few questions.

'Don't pester her with many queries. She has no home or whereabouts. In case someone comes asking, she is free to go with them. I don't mind,' Rukhiyami said.

Suddenly, I thought of Sandra and Varun, and the night when I had stood shivering at their doorstep, like an orphan.

'I saw your book. It was lying on the table,' Rukhiyami said as she sautéed the mustard seeds to make sambar.

I was shocked. Oh, I had forgotten to hide the book when I went to take a shower.

'I loved that photograph of yours, Naz! Your eyes are full of love…'

I had opened up the darkest corners of my mind before this woman. Why should I be wary if she took a look at the novel?

'I wanted to give you a copy, Rukhiyami. But I don't have another to spare.'

'Don't worry about it. You will get a few copies during the book release function, of course.'

Attending the book release function was slowly turning into a reality.

We did not step out anywhere during the day. As I went in for a short nap after lunch, I saw Rukhiyami take up *Bait Al Banat* to read. When I woke up, I saw that she was immersed in the book. But we did not discuss anything about the novel. I took out the dress for the function and started ironing it.

'When will your Solomon reach the place?'

'No idea.'

'Shall I call up the publisher? There has to be someone there familiar with the itinerary of the event.'

When Rukhiyami went to the hall, I folded my white dress perfectly. I had worn this dress while visiting the Women's Museum with Solomon for the first time. There were lace edges on the shawl and an embroidery of ivory-toned flowers on the white kurti. It was nothing spectacular, but I felt instinctively that I should wear this particular dress.

'I called them. Are you sure it is Solomon who will be doing the book release?' Rukhiyami queried.

'That was what the invitation said.'

'There is definitely such an event. They told me the location and time correctly,' Rukhiyami said.

'Then what's the problem? Won't you come with me?'

'No, my dearest. I will try and finish reading the book by that time.'

I had known the answer even before she uttered it.

That night, we sat on the terrace for a very long time. The girl was wandering in the vicinity all the while. She offered us some roasted groundnuts and ran away.

'The novel is interesting...' Rukhiyami said.

'Hmm.'

'I can see bits of you in those three women.'

'Not women, Rukhiyami, girls! They were unmarried and did not even wear burqas. The society viewed them as girls.'

I could hear the tinkling of anklets on the staircase again. Rukhiyami had purchased those for the little girl. I too once had tinkling anklets. The girl had curly, brownish tinted hair. The oil applied on her hair had dripped on her face, making it gleam. Her limbs were thin but firm. Though she had told me her name was Malarmagal, Rukhiyami called her Thankam. I too called her Thankam. The child responded to any name, ate anything given to her, and slept anywhere she was asked to sleep. If I were to call her Matilda tomorrow, she would still answer with the same eagerness!

Now, she was making a jingle with her anklets and peeping from behind the door to the terrace and smiling at us. What made her so happy? When I called her to me, she came gambolling by and curled up near my chair obediently.

'She is from a Sri Lankan refugee family, Naz. Her father died. She has three sisters. They were in some refugee camp near the

Tamil Nadu border. This girl told me the name of some estate… I could guess that it was some rehabilitation centre. She escaped from that place. The girl does not wish to return and I don't think the mother bothers about her either! Let her stay with me as long as she likes.'

I gently touched the hair of the girl, who was cuddling against my feet. She gazed up and smiled at me.

'Naz, do you wish like kissing Solomon?'

'I don't know, Rukhiyami…'

'Then who will know?'

'Sometimes, I feel as if I can't live for a moment without seeing him. Then I feel that my love is about living like this…heavy like a rain-filled cloud.'

'You are sure that your love exists even if you cannot see him, right? I am sure that Solomon feels the same,' Rukhiyami said.

'I was not too sure about attending the function when I boarded the flight. I am here only because of Varun and Sandra. He booked the tickets and she pushed me relentlessly.'

'Our journeys often do not end at the destination we aimed for, my dear. Do not be stubborn about it. When you start a story, never decide the ending… Let it flow… The story shall find its own ending,' Rukhiyami said.

'My aim right now is to attend the book release function. The rest is not in my hands.'

'Tomorrow you should have a detailed discussion with the publisher. Check the terms of the contract.'

'I haven't planned to do anything, Rukhiyami. Maybe I will change my mind after meeting Solomon?'

'Solomon is seeing you at all times. And you see him too. Can you deny that?'

I did not answer. We chatted till eleven at night. The little girl had gone to sleep on the terrace floor. When I patted her awake, she screamed in panic. On seeing my face, she started smiling again.

Even as I slipped under the bedcovers, I could see the dim

glow of the reading lamp streaming in from Rukhiyami's room. She had gone inside with *Bait Al Banat*. The previous day's travel started taking its toll on me. I am not accustomed to sleeping while travelling. Solomon used to say that the time one is forced to sit still is not meant for sleeping. 'Travel while travelling, sleep while sleeping.' The umpteen things Solomon used to say!

⌘

Soraiyya was still overwhelmed by the sparkle in those tiny eyes. Though the tiny being had been born seven days ago in Bait Al Banat, she had not gazed at the baby to her heart's contentment yet. A baby girl, like an alluring magic box full of secrets! Everybody was getting ready for the rituals of the seventh day. Today, the baby would be given a name.

After giving a bath to Soraiyya, Mariam was helping her wear a gorgeous thawb she had stitched in Bombay silk that was purchased from the souk. It was embroidered with exquisite needlework. Probably it was the best of Mariam's handiwork yet. Jadda had appointed an experienced midwife to avoid any of the contingencies that were faced during their Ummi's time. The woman buried the sundered umbilical cord—the secret thread connecting the mother and child—behind the madrasa after tying three knots on it. Even after birth, it held within itself the spiritual connection between the mother and baby. It was not to be discarded aimlessly lest the future generations suffered the consequences. The woman had handled the cord as if it were alive. Had the newborn been a boy, she would have buried it in the premises of the mosque. The child would then grow up to be a true and disciplined believer. Since it was a girl, it was intended that she should learn the Quran well, and hence the cord was buried near the madrasa.

The slight fever which Soraiyya had, left her when a cloth dipped in curd and turmeric was placed on her forehead. After sprinkling Ya's powder on the baby's navel, she was wiped clean using a cotton cloth dipped in warm water, before wrapping her up warmly. A round ball of salt, as big as an egg, was inserted into Soraiyya's body, to heal the wounds of birthing. When Soraiyya complained that it was stinging badly, the midwife muttered that it was necessary for healing her insides, and pushed it further inside. To deflate Soraiyya's tummy, the midwife tied a black stone tightly around her stomach.

The little boys and girls who scampered around the streets could not help peeking inside Bait Al Banat, which was full of the baby's cries and gurgles. Shamsa would beckon them inside and ask them to tenderly touch the baby's tiny limbs. When asked to bestow a kiss, the children would shyly run away.

The women in the neighbourhood started trailing in, eager to catch sight of the infant. On the seventh day, they trooped into Bait Al Banat carrying many gifts. Nobody enquired about the child's father nor about her name. Zaleekha's brother gave the goat which was cooked for making the delicious dish *khuzi*. Khadeeja purchased two camel-loads of Ghaf wood from the souk for the purposes of cooking rice and roasting the meat.

The woman who came first laid down her vessel to draw water, and recited verses from the Quran so that the baby was protected from any evil eye. After mentioning that she would be back for the child's hair-removal ceremony on the fortieth day, she left. Relinquishing all her pregnancy-related exhaustion, and donning Mariam's beautiful thawb, Soraiyya applied kohl on her baby's eyes and started humming songs.

'*Ya Ummi, Ya Ummi Yamma Yah...*' It was a folk song about a young girl informing her mother about a sailor's proposal.

Suddenly a strange form entered the room. It was none other than Rosa, who cleaved her way through the thronging kids near the doorway. The hat and the camera were in their place! She looked exactly the same as before. With the same warmth, as if she had left them just a night before, Rosa embraced each resident lovingly. When she had to return for yet another project to the Trucial States, which other house was there for confidently waking into, other than her favourite Bait Al Banat? When Rosa lifted the baby carefully, she felt a thrill running through her body.

As she gently cradled the infant in her arms, Rosa asked, *'Ma Ismak? Ma Ismak?'* What's your name?

'We have not given her a name yet, Ummu William,' Shamsa said.

'Why? Are you waiting for someone who has the right to do so?'

'No, we were just wondering what to call this starry-eyed beauty?'

'See, we thought of all names for children in the Khor and Deira...nothing strikes us yet as suitable!'

'Why? Your typical names don't match this beautiful baby, is it so? Maybe she deserves some other name?'

Rosa gazed at the three women.

'Ummu William, the baby has no father. But she has three mothers. She has been born into a house flourishing with stories. There is no shortage even of tales relating to the house itself! The little one has stars in her eyes and the red of the coral reef on her lips! Which name shall suit her?' Jadda was anxious to find a perfect name for the representative of the third generation.

'A name uncommon in Deira and Al Ras...' Khadeeja put forth her demand.

'Many a Scheherazade, many princesses from my stories, are seated on the roof. They are hanging upside down and smiling at me. But none of their names would be proper for this little one. Ummu William, why don't you suggest one?' Shamsa said.

'Maya! Let us name her Maya. In every language, she will have a meaning. In Sanskrit it means 'illusion', 'magical illusion'. The mother of the great Gautam Buddha was known as Maya. For the Greeks, the mother goddess of Hermes was Maya. In Persian, Maya means 'benevolent'. In Biblical terms, it means 'nectar of life', that is water! The Roman goddess Maya is the mistress of everything green, the flowers and nature! For the little girl born with a light in her eyes, let the name be Maya.'

Jadda murmured into the baby's ears thrice, 'Maya, Maya, Maya.'

Mariam, Shamsa and Soraiyya followed Rosa who carried little Maya out of the house. Jadda and Khadeeja followed them. Soraiyya's driver was given the task of capturing the picture of the seven, standing shoulder to shoulder outside Bait Al Banat. Rosa wished to paste a picture of those seven smiles on the wall, next to the photograph of her son, back in her house at England.

The women walked through the souk and approached the Khor. In the warm breeze, Maya's cheeks flushed. Rosa climbed into an abra which would take her to the hotel in Bur Dubai. Standing inside the boat, Rosa handed the infant back to her mother. As the abra moved away, Rosa's face gleamed like an enchanting oasis. Rosa's face was like the reflection of the sparkling waters of the Khor!

When Rosa disappeared from sight, the five women returned to Bait Al Banat with Maya. In the evening sun, five shadows moved on the sand along with them. They were dressed in black, and the shadows were shaded in the same hue too.

When Maya furrowed her little eyebrows as the sunlight fell on her face, Soraiyya whispered to her ears, 'Don't be afraid, my darling. Shadows are always dark.'

Book Release

AFTER A GREAT SLEEP, I awoke afresh, at four sharp in the morning. My whole body was full of energy. I opened the window. Dawn was a long way off. There was a gentle, cool breeze in the air. When I returned after my ablutions, there was a hot cup of tea on the table. The one who had made it was folding back her mattress. Her eyes were still dazed with sleep.

I caressed my white kurti lovingly. The light in Rukhiyami's bedroom was still shining. Wondering if she had not slept through the night or woke up early to read, I knocked at the door. Rukhiyami was also in great spirits. I turned to call out the little girl. 'Thankam, we are going somewhere. Go brush your teeth and change your frock.'

Thankam raced to the kitchen. Rukhiyami had bought her a new frock splattered with red flowers. When Rukhiyami stepped into the bathroom for a shower, I moved eagerly to the book lying open on the bed. I wished to know at what page she had stopped reading. But the sound of the door being unlatched stopped me short.

'So, are you not getting ready?' Rukhiyami asked smilingly.

Her smile was full of meaning. I dressed in my white kurti. Slowly, I combed my hair, applied kohl in my eyes… We chose not to awaken the driver who was fast asleep in the outhouse. I drove the car to the beach. Malarmagal was breathing the fresh morning air through the open car window. As she laughed in delight, the flowers in her frock seemed to laugh along.

Even the crows were not around when we reached the seashore. We sat on a cement bench, facing the sea. The streets, hitherto dimly lit with street lamps, soon woke up to the red sunlight and chirping of birds. Malarmagal's mane was tossed about in the breeze. She gazed at the rising red of the sun, with her head on my shoulder. Seeing the yellow light in her pupils, I was deeply touched. Seeing the sunlight burst through the clouds, Rukhiyami pressed my hand. In our lives, probably this was the most beautiful sunrise ever.

I felt as if I was the lone listener of the murmurs of the sea. With the movement of the sun, the sea waters gathered pace too. Each wave trying to ascend the rocks failed miserably and withdrew. Rukhiyami blinked while gazing at the milky, frothy waves. The ivory flowers of my kurti and the red ones on Thankam's frock, all acquired the colour of the rising sun. When the serenity of the sea started fading away with the morning, we rose to leave.

As we drove back to the house, Rukhiyami asked, 'When is your flight?'

'At 1.30 a.m. But I have to report at the airport by 9.30 p.m.'

Until I was ready to leave for the airport, Malarmagal kept traipsing into my room with different trinkets to fill my bag. All were her favourite knick-knacks: rose apples and guavas, and seashells woven in a golden thread which her mother had bought for her. Probably it had been her lone ornament. Somehow, I did not wish to give it back to her. I tucked it into my handbag.

'I have nothing to give to you, Thankam,' I murmured.

'Next time, you can bring me something,' she chirped. I hugged her and planted an affectionate kiss on her cheek. When I locked the suitcase and moved out, Rukhiyami entrusted me with the copy of *Bait Al Banat*.

'I haven't finished reading it...a few pages are still left,' she said.

'Let a few pages always remain to be finished, Rukhiyami... that's the beauty of it...' I replied.

I stayed wide awake until the plane landed at Dubai. My eyes sparkled with the same liveliness I had experienced in the morning. Without any ado associated with a long travel, I landed in Dubai airport at morning four o'clock. When I got into Sandra's car with my luggage, she cast an accusatory glance at me. When Varun enquired about my journey, she was the one who responded.

'Of course! She went straight home, hugged Rukhiyami and went off to sleep. Then she picked up her bag and boarded the flight to Dubai!'

We whizzed past the streets as Sandra sped on at 120 kilometres per hour. Varun tried to smile at me but I could discern the lack of joy on his face. We stopped near a café and bought three cups of tea. I got out of the vehicle and sipped my tea, gazing at the lights reflected from the city. I remembered the sunrise of the previous day. Sandra leaned against the car and sipped her tea while Varun approached me slowly. When I looked questioningly at him, Varun showed me a photograph saved in his mobile phone. There were three men standing in front of a banner which read, 'Book release of *Bait Al Banat*'. One was handing over the book to another, while the third person was applauding politely. My Solomon was not among the trio!

'Fathom the reason why Sandra is peeved?' Varun asked me.

'I understand, Varun. She will be alright. Can you drive me to the Deira creek, please?'

'Right now? We can go home first and freshen up, Naz!'

'No, I wish to see the sunrise.'

Varun drove the car to the creek.

The Deira region was still asleep. The abras were tied up at different spots. The traders in the souk were yet to open their shops. Varun and Sandra went off to park the car after letting me disembark at the creek. I walked towards a bench facing the creek waters. A few Pakistanis could be seen having tea, seated on the neighbouring benches. A few birds took flight, almost scraping their white wings against the sea waters. One landed on a handrail next to me. It was balancing on a single claw! Could it be the same bird which I had seen in the Lebanese restaurant? Some vignettes never disappear from one's mind. The sea-bird with its broken claw is one such image which has been indelibly imprinted in my mind.

The call for subhi prayers rose from the mosque across the creek. The abras started moving. I could see five shapes in the vague darkness. Two were aged women wearing abayas and clad in burqas. The other three women were donning colourful long dresses, flowing in the breeze. One woman carried a newborn in her arms. Soraiyya! I got up from the bench and watched as they climbed into an abra. Soraiyya's abaya was coloured in circles of orange and black. The end of it stuck to her shins, dampened by the waters of the creek. I leaned forward to catch a glimpse of Maya's tender face. A flock of birds whizzed past me from the sea. By the time I could look again, the abra had started moving. Five women were smiling at me from the abra. The sun's yellow gleamed on the shayla covering their heads. I stared at that light and its reflection in the creek waters and felt tears springing up in my eyes.

They were gazing unremittingly at me from the abra. Wasn't that an open invitation to me? I wiped my tears and waved at them. The women waved back at me. Before the boat reached the other shore, a mist surrounded it and the women disappeared from my view. In the background of Bur Dubai, I could make out only the sharp jutting bow of the abra and its roof, before that sight too vanished into a haze.

I returned to my seat and took out the novel from my bag. I stared at the emptiness of the page in front of my eyes. A simple white paper, where many pictures were taking shape. Swaying to the rhythm of the wind, many faces and events were being displayed on it. Whenever Solomon's face showed up, my heart started beating faster. Placing a hand against my chest, I soothed myself before caressing his face. Faces...more faces...of Rukhiyami and Malarmagal...orange hues as the sunlight glistened on them.

'She is Thankam...a joyous little girl, gleaming with a dusky, oily shimmer, comes jingling her anklets! A golden girl who was begging around the street with her mother and siblings, coated with dust and muck. That night she had narrated her ordeal at the Kulathupuzha rehabilitation centre for Sri Lankan refugees. As she curled up like a puppy beneath my chair, I tried to caress her forehead and then...'

I jolted awake when Sandra put her hand on my shoulder.

'What are you busy scribbling? Sunrise is over now...let's go. Aren't you happy?' She hugged me close.

'Yes, the happiest woman in the world!'

'Wow! That's all I wish to hear,' Sandra laughed in delight.

I reached the flat and took a shower. As I retrieved my passport and other documents from the handbag, I saw *Bait Al Banat* inside, with a pen sticking out from it. I took it out and opened the last page. Those were my words, weren't they? Biting into a rose-apple which Malarmagal had gifted me, I picked up the pen and added a few more lines to the last sentence.

The little girl reappeared in my memories and dreams. A journey to her rehabilitation centre and then to the country of her birth... that would be my next destination.

Whenever I got onto a video call with Rukhiyami, I caught an occasional lightning glimpse of Thankam, her face lit up with a smile, as she peeked from the kitchen, the doorsteps or from behind doors. If I invited her to talk, she would shyly demur. Let her keep hiding, that would render more strength to my words!

Glossary

Abaya	A black cloak
Abra	Wooden boat
Abu Dhabi	Land of the gazelle
Alhamdulillah	Praise be to god/Thank god
Al Maktoum hospital	First hospital in Dubai
Astaghfirullah	I seek forgiveness in god
Bait al shaar	Bedouin's tent woven from the hair of domesticated goats and sheep
Bakhour	A kind of incense that contains various smells put on a piece of coal to aromatize a room or the clothes
Barasti	Hut made using palm fronds, mangrove poles and palm trunks
Bastakiya	Historical neighbourhood in Dubai. The locality was capable of 60 housing units, most of which were separated by narrow, winding lanes. The town of Al Bastakiya was primarily built by immigrants from the city of Bastak, Persia, who left their native homeland due to ongoing religious persecution, and lured by tax breaks and incentives offered by the Emirati government
Bedu/Bedouin	Nomadic Arabs

Boom/Boum	Known as dhangi in india. it is a medium-sized deep-sea dhow, a traditional Arabic sailing vessel. This type of dhow has two masts with lateen sails, a stern that is tapering in shape and a more symmetrical overall structure than other dhow types. The Arab boum has a very high prow, which is trimmed in the Indian version
Burqa	Handcrafted of delicate fabric and worn over the face, this accessory is traditionally worn by married women. The fabrics used to make it were imported from India and known for their ability to absorb sweat. Not to be confused with the head-to-toe cover used in Afghanistan, the Gulf burqa is a traditional metallic-coloured embroidered cloth used to cover part of the face. Upon first seeing it, most people mistakenly think that it is made of gold or some other metal. The cloth is dyed blue or purple and then rubbed down with a ball of glass until it gets that shiny metallic finish. The design of the burqa is meant to mimic the features of the falcon, a symbol of grace, pride and strength
Dallah	A coffee pot to preserve Arabic coffee
Dana pearl	The most expensive pearl that can be found in the ocean. It's the largest, is darker in colour, and is worth lots of cash. Back in those days, it used to be a treasure for any pearl-diving boat captain who managed to find one
Deira, Bur Dubai, Shindagha	Three major provinces in old Dubai. Deira and Bur Dubai lie on opposite sides of the creek. Bur Dubai literally means mainland of Dubai. Shindagha is a neighbourhood where most of the sheikhs in Dubai lived. Deira: the commercial centre Bur Dubai: the governing centre Shindagha: residential area

Dhow	One- or two-masted Arab sailing vessel, usually with lateen rigging (slanting, triangular sails), common in Indian Ocean and the Gulf
Emirati	Natives of UAE
Gargour trap	Dome-shaped trap used to capture fish unharmed. It is weighed to the seabed with rocks. Fresh or rotting fish are placed inside to bait larger fish into a one-way tunnel
Halol	Laxative plant used in the treatment of digestive disorders
Harami	Bastard
Hares	A dish of boiled, cracked, or coarsely ground wheat, mixed with meat and seasoned. Its consistency varies between a porridge and a dumpling
Jadda	Grandma
Jafir	A container used to gather dates and carry goods, made out of tree fronds
Jahannam	Hell
Jalbut	Widely used in the Gulf as pearling boats, and 20 to 100 feet long, with the largest capable of carrying up to 200 tons of cargo. Normally has one sail, but larger vessels would use two for long journeys
Kaftan	Long, lightweight dresses that hang loose on the body. They're like long-sleeved tunics but tend to have wider sleeves and are made from lighter fabrics
Kahwa	Arabic coffee. Made from roasted coffee beans. usually spiced with cardamom and served without sugar. It tastes bitter
Khajoojah	Round cushion used as an embroidery tool. Craftswomen use it as a surface to spread the cloth

Khalas	Finished/That's it!
Khaleegy	Folkloric dance performed by girls during weddings and festive occasions. The hands make figures with different meanings: representing sea creatures like fish or turtles, or they can also represent feelings. The hair is the main element in performing Khaleegy: women let their long hair 'dance', moving it from side to side, back and forth, in circle, and making other figures
Khor Dubai	Dubai creek
Khanjar	Traditional dagger
Khubz or Kubus	Arabic bread
Kohl	Kajal made from crushed and softened ithmid stones. Although it is often associated with the pharaohs or Cleopatra, kohl has also had a starring role in the beauty rituals of Emirati women for thousands of years. She might apply it in the morning, and again before going to bed. Three things were buried with an ancient Emirati woman: jewellery, pottery and seashells containing kohl. Those were considered the essentials a woman would take with her to life after death
Kufiya	Arabian headdress worn by men
Kunafa	Sweet made using cheese, seviyyan and honey
Laban	Buttermilk
Luqaimat	Sweet dumpling
Ma'a salama	Goodbye
Madrasa	Religious school
Mahr	Pre-nuptial marriage gift given to the bride. The purpose of the mahr is to provide the wife with independent financial security, whereby this amount becomes her exclusive property

Glossary

Mandoos	Handmade traditional wooden box used as a gift box or for storage
Masha Allah	Phrase used to show joy and praise, and is evoked upon hearing good news
Mikab	A cover made out of fronds, used to protect food
Mirwa	A small Arabic drum
Mutawa	Religious teacher
Myrrh	Natural gum or resin extracted from a number of small, thorny tree species of the genus *Commiphora*. Myrrh resin has been used throughout history as a perfume, incense and medicine
Ruba'al khali	The Arabic name Rub al Khali means 'empty quarter'. The name was given to it because it's a huge stretch of unbroken sand desert that has bested kings, adventurers and nomads for thousands of years. It encompasses most of the southern third of the Arabian Peninsula. The desert covers some 650,000 km² including parts of Saudi Arabia, Oman, the United Arab Emirates, and Yemen. It is part of the larger Arabian Desert
Sabkha	Salt flats
Saluki Dog	Speedy and savvy, the Saluki has been a hunting and guard dog for the desert people of the Arabian Peninsula for 5,000 years. Indigenous to the region, this dog's fast pace, intelligence and loyalty make it a breed much beloved by the UAE people
Sandouk	Wooden box
Sayed	Spiritual healer
Serwal	Pyjamas worn under the abaya
Shamal wind	Sandstorm
Shayla	Head scarf worn by women; it can be of any colour
Shurta	Police

Sikham	Type of coal which has bleaching properties. It was ground with salt and thyme to give a good taste
Sikkat al khail	Street in Deira
Souq	Bazar/Street market
Subhanallah	Glory to god
Tawash	Pearl merchant; they had a prominent position in society. At a time when most of the population merely scratched a living, these men were extremely wealthy. They were able to finance diving trips and at the end of the season, captains would visit their homes to sell their haul of pearls to them
Thawb	The traditional women's dress of the UAE, refers to a loosely comfortable garment with graceful needlework. Elaborately decorated and vibrantly coloured thawbs are used for ceremonial occasions like weddings. A thawb is generally worn over a qamis, but it can be worn on its own in private, especially during hot weather. The garment is free-flowing and does not cling to the body. When the wide sleeves catch the breeze, it keeps the wearer cool.
Thawmina	A festival to celebrate children completing their Quran lessons
Wadi	The bed or valley of a stream that is usually dry except during the rainy season and that often forms an oasis
Ya ibn al sharmoota	Son of a bitch
Ya sharmoota	You bitch!
Yazra	Container made of rubber and wood used to carry water, and was possibly transported by animals
Yehla	An earthenware pot that keeps water cool
Zaatar	Refers to both a herb spice mixture and also a distinct herb in mint family